D0050717

COLD SPELL

JACKSON PEARCE

LITTLE, BROWN AND COMPANY
New York Boston

Little, Brown and Company

Hachette Book Group
237 Park Avenue, New York, NY 10017
Visit our website at www.lb-teens.com

Little, Brown and Company is a division of Hachette Book Group, Inc.
The Little, Brown name and logo are trademarks of Hachette Book Group, Inc.

The publisher is not responsible for websites (or their content) that are not owned by the publisher.

First Edition: November 2013

Library of Congress Cataloging-in-Publication Data

Pearce, Jackson.
    Cold spell / by Jackson Pearce.—First edition.
        pages cm
    Summary: "When her boyfriend disappears with a mysterious girl, seventeen-year-old Ginny leaves her hometown of Atlanta and fights wolves, escapes thieves, and braves the cold to rescue him"—Provided by publisher.
    ISBN 978-0-316-24359-9
    [1. Love—Fiction. 2. Rescues—Fiction. 3. Supernatural—Fiction.] I. Title.
    PZ7.P31482Co 2013
    [Fic]—dc23
                                                                              2012046186

10 9 8 7 6 5 4 3 2 1

RRD-C

Printed in the United States of America

For John, because he always
laughs and sometimes cries

PROLOGUE

❧

(1947)

There were plenty of reasons to love winter.

Warm fireplaces. Stews. Christmastime. In her head she listed everything pleasant about the season, yet she still pulled a handmade quilt closer around her body, like a shield that could protect her.

It rarely snowed here—Atlanta usually settled for a motionless, quiet winter, with the sort of cold that crept into her bones and was hard to shake. Before Christmas the cold seemed a necessary price for the holiday, the presents, the celebration. Now, in January, still months to go till spring, the weather was hateful. It felt like an enemy bearing down on her, something not to be trusted. Something she should fight.

There were plenty of reasons to love winter, but Dalia did not.

She shivered, let one hand slink out from under the quilt to the end table—it was beaten and dented, one leg steadied with the X volume of an otherwise-missing encyclopedia set. Her fingers fumbled to pick up a penny, which she held over the closest candle for a moment, till it got just hot enough to burn her fingers. She leaned toward the frostbitten window and pressed the penny against it for a moment, then pulled it away. It left a perfect, watery circle, like a ship's porthole. She peered out. Was he there?

Wait.

Wait.

There he is—at the window on the other side of their apartment building's courtyard, only a dozen or so feet away but separated by air and cold. A penny pressed to the glass, and then an eye with long lashes looked out. A green, bright, warm eye, the sort of color that made her think of grass and the sweet-scented Southern heat of August. She smiled, and through the frost she could see his face break into the same expression. He pulled back from the glass for a moment, and then the penny returned. He dragged it along the frost, creating a shape—an arrow, pointing up, an unspoken question: *Can I come over?*

She traced a *y* for *yes* with her penny, then leaned away from the window, buried her arms back underneath her quilt. It wouldn't take him long to arrive—the building was shaped like a squared-off U, the bottom of the letter composed of overflowing storage lockers for each floor. It was difficult to cut through those and no fun to walk downstairs, through the courtyard, and back up six flights of stairs, so they usually took a shortcut across the roof, through the garden their parents had planted together ages ago.

He didn't understand why, exactly, she was so reluctant to go outside this time of year, but it didn't matter. He was willing to come to her. They played board games and he made up stories by the fire until her parents began to look between him and the clock sternly. Then he'd go home, and she'd hold her breath until she saw his face in the window, confirming he'd made it through the cold.

Or at least, that's how it used to be.

Now they sat by the fire, a largely untouched board game between them, watching each other, smiling at each other, and recently—very recently—leaning in to kiss each other when Dalia's mother wasn't looking. It was terrifying and wonderful, kissing your best friend. Dalia cast a wary eye at her mother folding laundry in the kitchen. They'd have a moment, a few moments, maybe, when her mother went to put the clothes away....

Dalia smiled and shivered, and this time it wasn't from the cold. She dropped the penny back in its place on the end table and stared at the fire, waiting for him to knock.

A moment passed.

Another.

Another.

She frowned and leaned back toward the window to see if there was another message, if he was trying to get her attention—maybe his mother wouldn't let him come, or maybe he couldn't find his coat...though those things rarely held him up for long. But no, he wasn't there, and the arrow was slowly being devoured by new frost.

Another moment.

Dalia rose, pulled the quilt closer to her body. She walked to the door anxiously and looked out the peephole. The hallway was freshly painted, with shiny new gold knobs on all the doors. No movement, no sign of him...

"What're you doing?" her mother asked, raising her voice to be heard over her favorite radio show.

"He said he was coming over..." Dalia started, trying to sound bored, like it was nothing.

"Of course," her mother sighed. She liked him well enough, but he made her nervous—*all* boys around Dalia made her nervous, especially poor boys like him. Dalia walked into the kitchen and slumped down at the table, watching her mother's hands grab and fold sweaters, quick and precise. Take away the fabric and her hands would be whirling about, as if she were dancing or casting spells.

The radio sputtered, and static filled the air. Dalia's mother groaned and walked to it, popping it on the side a few times. It behaved itself for a moment, but then the static continued, growing louder, till it sounded like wind through the speaker.

It wasn't until her mother looked up and gasped that Dalia realized the wind sound wasn't coming from the radio—it was coming from outside. Wind streaked through the building's courtyard, throwing trash and dead leaves into the air. The windowpanes rattled as if they might shatter, and fingers of cold inched their way across the apartment and into the kitchen, wrapping themselves around Dalia's cheeks, neck, and ears.

"Look at that," her mother said, walking to the window. Snow. It was snowing.

Not the thick, fat flakes that were perhaps the only friendly-looking thing winter had to offer. Tiny flakes that whirled around like bits of ash. More and more of them, until Dalia could barely see his window across the courtyard. It felt as if they were being buried, even on the sixth floor.

"Your poor father. I hope it lets up before he has to walk home," her mother said absently, then returned to the kitchen as if this were nothing. Dalia, however, was certain her heart was stopping.

He could be on the roof, trapped in the storm. There was nowhere to hide up there, nothing but rosebushes and a rickety trellis. *It's just snow, it's just snow, there's no reason to be scared. Just snow, frozen rain, nothing more.*

But even as she tried to calm herself, she grabbed her shoes and yanked them on. She ran for the door, tangling herself in her coat. Her mother called to her to stop, but Dalia was already in the hall, feet pounding up the steps. Two floors till the roof, and he'd be up there, he'd be right by the door. He'd laugh at her for her worry and step inside, and then they'd let their fingers link together as they walked back downstairs. The wind howled; was it growing stronger? It sounded like an animal, like a wild thing that would dash inside and devour her as soon as she opened the roof access door.

She grabbed the knob, winced in preparation, then forced the door open. Snow poured in, knocking her a few steps backward. Dalia gritted her teeth and found her footing, leaning into the wind to step onto the roof. She looked up, ignoring the stinging pain of the air whipping her hair into her eyes. There was the trellis, bits of it breaking free and flying off the building's edge into the street below. All the empty pots were tipped over, leaving only the rosebushes; the gusts tugged at their empty vines and thorns but couldn't sweep them away. Where was he? She yelled his name, but it was lost in the snow.

He must have turned around and gone back home. She took a few more steps, all the way to the trellis. *Yes. He's gone back home; he's fine. If I can walk through this, however slowly, so can he. He turned around and went home and—*

A shape, a figure. *It's him*, wearing a tattered coat, standing close to the edge of the building. The wind tossed his bright red hair around, and though she could see only the back of his head, she could tell he was staring at something. She shuffled toward him, but the wind changed direction and pushed her back—the harder she tried, the more ground she lost until, slipping and sliding on the ever-increasing ice, she found herself back at the door. Dalia looked down, baffled, then back to his shadowy form.

He turned, but she couldn't see his eyes through the snow and shadow. She stared back anyway, hoping he could see hers, that he would understand the plea, the desperation, the want for him to come to her, how hard she was trying to get to him. *Please, please, come inside, come out of the cold, come out before something terrible happens.*

Her eyes watered; the tears were raw and sharp on her cheeks. The wind pressed against her, like hands pushing her back down the stairs, back inside, away from him. She fought against it, but it was strong, so much stronger than she was.

He turned his back to her. Reached a hand out to his side. Dalia's eyes narrowed against the wind and stinging snow, trying to see what he was reaching for. No, not what—*who*. A woman all in white with hair so blond it almost matched the snow. Was she real? She looked too perfect to be real. The snow increased; the world was becoming whiter and whiter as it piled up. Dalia grabbed the door frame to keep from being blown down the stairs. She gasped in the icy air, tried to call for him again, to scream. The woman—no, the *girl*, as she wasn't much older than Dalia—glanced back toward the door, her eyes the same blue-gray as the snow-filled sky. Her lips curved ever so slightly into a gentle, elegant smile.

The girl reached out and wrapped her fingers around his hand. He jolted, as if she had shocked him, but then he stood up straight and stiff.

Dalia stopped screaming. She stopped everything, frozen by temperature, fear, and confusion. She opened her mouth to call the boy's name once more—but just as her lips formed the word, the door slammed shut.

She never saw him again.

CHAPTER ONE

∾

(Present Day)

The best thing about going to public school is the testing.

It's also the worst thing, sometimes, but testing means that every week or so, we have a strange schedule. More often than not, it's last period that gets affected—it gets extended, making it twice as long, three times as long, once four times as long as normal. I have Intro to Theater last period, which basically means I paint sets for the Advanced Theater class's productions. That, and I watch the teacher struggle to keep an eye on the plethora of "bad" kids who got signed up for the class because they hate school too much to choose their own electives.

Which, incidentally, is the second-best thing about public school: If you're not a genius or a future crackhead, teachers pretty much don't notice you. That's why it's so easy for me to skip the end of the school day every round of standardized testing. I'm not really sure how Kai manages it, since he *is* a genius, but he figures it out. We don't even have to plan it anymore—if sixth period is extended, we duck out right after the fifth-period bell rings. Today is one such day. I slink around the back of the school, where he's already waiting for me, anxious to hurry off into the early afternoon like the city is ours.

"What takes you so long?" Kai mutters, leaning against a trailer classroom's wall. The annoyance in his voice is betrayed by the way his eyes shine at me.

"I had to go to my locker," I answer. "Otherwise I have to walk all the way home with my chem book."

"Excuses, Ginny, excuses," he says, knocking the backs of my legs with his violin case, grinning as he does so. That's where Kai's supposed to be in last period—orchestra—but he and the orchestra teacher are more friends than student and teacher, largely due to the fact that the teacher could probably learn more from Kai than vice versa.

It's cold, especially for October. Usually Georgia is in between summer and fall this time of year. The chill makes my nose run and my eyes water, but it also makes me feel more alive than the lazy summer heat from last month. Kai and I trudge across a bridge that's been painted with our school colors and leads from the school's property to a public park. The park is largely empty, save a few overweight cops on Segways and some sketchy-looking guys hanging out by the entrance. They're the reason that Kai's expensive violin is in a crappy-looking case: to keep anyone from knowing just how much it's worth. Even I'm not supposed to know, really, but of course he told me.

We ignore the sidewalks and cut straight through the park, heading up a few blocks toward our building. It's one of the few brick structures in a cityscape of steel, neon, and concrete. I turn to say something to Kai, but he suddenly grabs my hand and tugs me around a corner. He puts his arms on either side of me, palms against the concrete I'm pressed up against, as he peers past the building's granite edge. I raise my eyebrows at him, fighting the blush that's creeping onto my cheeks over how close we are.

"Is there a problem?" I ask.

Kai turns back to me and smiles. "Sorry," he says. "Grandma was at the window." He's whispering, as if she might be able to hear us from half a block away.

"I'd be willing to place a bet that if she catches us, it'll somehow be my fault," I say, and Kai laughs, his chest rising and falling against mine as he does so.

"It's always your fault with Grandma," he agrees. As far as Grandma Dalia is concerned, I'm the ultimate distraction in her Kai-is-a-prodigy plan. Kai says she's always been like this—she keeps her things close, and Kai is her most valuable thing. Our apartment building itself is probably a close second—she persuaded her husband to buy it ages ago, then got it in the divorce. It can't be torn down, since it houses Atlanta's oldest (if broken) elevator, but I don't think she'd let a wrecking ball touch it anyhow. She loves it—though I can't, for the life of me, figure out why. If I had the money Grandma Dalia has, I'd live somewhere—anywhere—else.

Kai hesitates, then drops his arms so I'm freed—though he doesn't take a step back. I keep my back firmly planted against the stone wall, unwilling to disrupt the feeling rippling between us, the pull to be closer still. We watch each other, waiting for it....

The first time I kissed Kai was when we were in the vacant lot by our building. He was holding an acceptance letter to a music intensive in New York, and I was holding nothing but his hand, and then his arms, and then his cheek as we pulled in to each other and kissed for what was only moments but felt like hours. We were high on the idea of living in New York together, of the tiny coffee shops we would visit and the museums we would sneak into. We dreamed of late-night stops at street-food vendors and a handful of artistic, clever friends, the philosophical sort we'd never find in our school. It was *his* acceptance letter, of course, but it was our dream, our shared fantasy, and it boiled over in our minds until the only thing left to do was to kiss, to kiss as if we'd done it a million times before.

Now I wait, not letting my eyes waver from Kai's, and watch the rhythm of his breath. His skin is olive, his hair dark, and it's falling across his forehead the way it always does. I reach up to brush it aside, but Kai leans in before I can do so, letting his breath dance across my skin for a moment. I let him pull me up onto my tiptoes and press in until our lips touch. His hand is on my back, my fingers drifting down the front of his chest, and in my head a thousand fires spring up all at once.

It's several quickened heartbeats before we release each other; Kai's hand immediately trails along my forearm before he laces his fingers with mine. I lean close to him; he grins at me, looks around the corner. . . .

"Coast is clear," he says, and we come out of hiding. For a moment, I wonder if we shouldn't hold hands, just in case his grandmother sees us—cutting class *plus* holding my hand? Grandma Dalia would be furious. Kai seems less concerned, though, which quietly pleases me—his desire to touch me is stronger than his loyalty to Grandma Dalia, which I know is no small thing itself. Kai drums his fingertips on my knuckles and moves so that our lower arms are curved around each other as we get closer to our building.

It was a pretty place at one time—I've seen photos of it when it was brand-new, back when Kai's grandmother lived here as a little girl and this was still a decent neighborhood. The stonework above the door is still kind of pretty, actually— marble carved into a lion's face with a cloth banner around it. But the lion aside, 333 Andern is mostly a pile of bricks with an ever-changing sea of graffiti on the outside walls.

Kai hands me his key chain and I select a small silver key, then use it to open the door leading into the basement. We creep past the washing machines, all of which have OUT OF ORDER signs on them, and around bottles of cleaner so old that the logos look all wrong. Up the back stairs, one flight, two flights, three—eight altogether, each with its own litter and grime and collection of rattraps, until we reach the rooftop access door. I select another key from Kai's key chain, a key he isn't supposed to have, and insert it in the lock. Slowly, carefully, I open the door—it usually squeaks, but over the years I've perfected opening it silently. I slip through, Kai close behind me, then turn back to shut it.

I exhale when I turn around. This is the only thing about the building that's not only still pretty, but *beautiful*. Kai and I found it when we were little, prompting his grandmother to declare the rooftop strictly off-limits and install a new lock. It was only a matter of time before he stole the key and I had it copied before she missed it. His grandmother would kill us—well, me, anyway—if she found us here. *But how could we stay away?* I think, gazing across the rooftop.

Roses, roses everywhere. What was once a large rooftop garden is now a mess of rosebushes, wild and resistant to the constant breeze. The roses have devoured an old trellis, long fallen and decaying, and were on their way to eating an iron bench before Kai and I cut the thorns away and rescued it. They're still in bloom—they're almost always in bloom, save around Christmas. Bright reds and fuchsias and shades in between, blooms so big that when Kai moves down the path we forged through the briars they almost hide him completely. I follow him to the bench, then pull out my math book and sit on it so I don't get rust all over my clothes. We're silent for a few moments, the comfortable sort of quiet that exists only with someone you've known forever.

"Two hundred seventy-three days until we're in New York," Kai finally says, sighing as he gazes across the rooftop. Looking backward, all you can see are roses, but forward, over the building's edge, past the courtyard and the bars and the parks, is the Atlanta skyline. It looks massive yet cage-like. The buildings aren't places to go but enormous walls, keeping us in.

"I'll have to get a job," I say. "I guess I could...waitress or something."

"You can do a lot more than waitress," Kai says a little tensely, and I feel the ghosts of old arguments rising between us. It's not that I *want* to be a waitress or cashier or parking lot attendant. It's that when your best friend is a prodigy, it feels a little dumb, auditioning for choir or joining the science team or the newspaper—you wrote an article on the student council election? Great; Kai went to San Francisco to play with an international youth symphony. The symphony flew him first-class.

It's not Kai's fault. I know it and he knows it, but I think he's stuck at an intersection of responsibility and pity for me. He's always trying to make up for it and feels the need to push me into doing something, anything, when the truth is all I want is for him to *pull* me closer.

I lean into him as a particularly cold breeze whips across the rooftop. "Anyway. I can be a waitress even though I'm under twenty-one, right? I was thinking about this. Even if we pull off me sleeping in your dorm room—"

14

"You're not sleeping in my dorm room; you're just an accomplished vocalist helping me practice in the evenings," he reminds me, repeating the lie we constructed together. He's better at lying than I am, but I'm the one who researched vocal classes on the Internet, who learned a bunch of music terms, who practiced the confident, tall way that singers sit in chairs. Kai can invent the lie, but I've always been better at the details, I suspect because while he's always been busy *doing*, I've been busy *watching*.

"Yeah, yeah," I answer. "But even if we pull that story off, I don't want to be broke in New York, living off your dorm food. So I need a job, but I bet they'll cross-reference or something and figure out I ran away."

"You won't be a runaway, though, since you'll be eighteen. And I mean...I don't think your parents will..." Kai drifts off. The end of the sentence, I know, is "be looking for you." Dad lives a few hours away, and Mom works two jobs—maybe three now, I'm not sure. It hurt when I was younger, but now I can't help but think of their indifference as a good thing—it'll be easier for me to break ties. To leave with Kai and...

I pause, exhale, and say the thing I *really* want. "What if we just never came back when the intensive ends?"

Kai looks at me, then down, playing with a briar that's pressing against the bench. "I can't leave my grandmother forever. Five months away from her will be bad enough. You know how she is."

15

Crazy is how she is. All right, maybe not crazy, but neurotic at least—she sprinkles salt around the entire building on Halloween. She once refused to allow a couple to rent an apartment because they owned a black cat. She spends most of the winter locked up inside, wary to go out among "the beasts." Winter and the beasts it supposedly brings are what she fears most of all.

Neurotic at the *very* least.

"I know. I was just wondering," I say, which isn't entirely true—I wasn't wondering. I was hoping. For me, it'll be easy to leave and horrible to come back. But I can't stay in New York without Kai, and I'm certainly not going someplace new without him, so . . .

Kai slides his hand across mine, and I move closer to him in response. One inch at a time, testing the water until I'm leaning against him, relaxing against his side. He exhales and rests his cheek against my forehead.

"Anyway," he says against my skin, "you never know. Maybe New York will end up sucking."

I frown. "It could really go either way. TV shows have taught me I'll become a fashion magazine intern *or* be murdered in Central Park."

Kai laughs and pulls me toward him, kissing my cheek briskly, easily. It's a gesture that's evolved—he used to shove me playfully whenever I said something funny, or weird, or particularly *me*. Then the shove became gentler, then it became him wrapping his arm around me, and now finally, he kisses me. Silently says he loves me without me even trying.

"I guess it doesn't matter," he says as he pulls away, squinting as the sun creeps lower, its bright light rebounding off a condo building. "In the end, it's always just us. Together." It's not a question, not something he doubts or wonders about. "Unless that Central Park murder thing happens."

Now it's my turn to laugh, and as I do I lift up, feel his breath warm my still-freezing nose. We pause for a moment, just a tiny moment, and then our lips meet. This time, it feels like the kissing in movies looks, long and powerful and sweet and as if it's melting me. He smells like cinnamon and soap, same as he always has—

"Whoa," he says, pulling back.

I freeze. "What?" I ask, wondering if I should be embarrassed. *What happened?*

"Look," he says, pulling one hand away to motion at the world around us. "It's starting to snow."

CHAPTER TWO

❧

It's tiny snow, sharp and icy, the sort that you don't want to play in. I see people running to the windows of the glass-and-steel buildings to stare at it whirling around the city. It's gotten colder almost instantly, a fact I don't notice so much as I notice how hard I'm pressing against Kai to combat the new chill. His arms are still around my waist, the unzipped army jacket he always wears open on either side of me.

"It's early for snow," I say, mumbling the words into his shirt.

"Way early," he agrees. "The roses aren't going to last if we're already getting snow in October."

He's right—I look around at the tiny specks of snow that cling to the flowers. They make the roses look sick with something akin to chicken pox, tiny spots covering bright red flesh. The wind rattles them around a bit. Is it snowing harder?

"Let's go inside," he suggests.

"We aren't technically out of school yet," I remind him. "We could build a fire?"

"Yeah..." Kai says, glancing to the metal barrel on a corner of the roof. We hauled it up here ages ago. Probably not the safest thing in the world, but it's pretty glorious for roasting marshmallows over.

"We could go to my apartment," I say, "if we're quiet. Mom's still sleeping, I think." Truthfully, I'm not sure she knows what time school gets out anyway, though I've never told Kai this. The magic of us sneaking around would be lost if my mother made it easy by way of apathy.

"Nah, I don't want to risk it," Kai says as the snowfall undeniably intensifies. "We can just wait by the roof door till we're out of school. I don't want to be out in this."

"All right," I agree, and he steps away from me; the icy air sweeps around my body. I hug my own coat closer, but it's nothing compared with Kai's chest against me. He lets his fingers pause on mine for a moment, but then releases them, too—the path out of the roses is too narrow to walk side by side. We weave through the flowers, listening to the traffic below slow down to a crawl, drivers inching through the snow as if it's feet thick instead of barely coating the ground. As we reach the access door, the wind picks up, blowing so hard that Kai struggles to open it. He yanks and tugs, and the wind grows stronger.

Are we trapped up here? Kai finds my eyes, and his are full of matching worry. He turns back to the door, leaving room on the handle for me to grab hold, too. Together we wrest the door open, sliding into the stairwell. We're barely on the top step when the door slams shut. The wind howls behind it, as if it's angry.

"I wonder if Grandma has noticed the weather yet," he says, sitting down on the top step. He checks his watch—thirty minutes until we'd be out of school. Is she ranting about the Snow Queen already? Winter's royalty, the ruler of the beasts Grandma Dalia fears. We've heard about the other beasts in somewhat disgusting detail—how they turn from men into monsters with fur and fangs, that they rip you limb from limb, eat you from the inside out. But the Snow Queen…we know little of her, other than that the thought of her makes Grandma Dalia's face go white.

There are no windows in the stairwell, but we can still hear the storm outside. How much is on the ground now? Is it sticking, or just melting away like most Southern snow? It's only October; surely it isn't accumulating.…The wind howls again. Kai grows quiet—though he'd never admit it, sometimes I think he's inherited Grandma Dalia's fear of snow and the cold. Only fifteen more minutes till we can go downstairs, pretend as if we ran home. Seconds tick by slowly, then minutes, ten more to go—

There's a crash downstairs, a bang. Voices shouting, someone running. We're on Kai's side of the building; he rises and walks down a few steps. The noise continues, muffled voices…Kai glances back at me and in a split second, we've decided to ignore the fact that we're ten minutes early. We bolt down the stairs together, drowning the sound of the wind with our heavy footsteps. Down to the eighth floor: nothing but closed doors and piled-up newspapers. The seventh, all's quiet. I swallow. The sixth. The floor Kai and I live on. Is someone being robbed? Arrested? We round the corner.

The hall is packed with people.

Doors are open, neighbors in graying robes and boxer shorts leaning out to see what's happening. Kai speeds up, we run, which one is it—*oh.*

Paramedics are running in and out of Kai's apartment; the floor is wet with snow, making their boots squeak on the dirty tile. Kai skids to a stop at his door, eyes wide; we reach for each other's hands automatically.

Inside the apartment, it is dark. Stained-glass shades on lamps, blinds on windows, clouds outside. It smells like baking and scented candles, things that have always contributed to it feeling more like home to me than my own apartment. Perhaps that's why it stabs at me to see the paramedics inside, bunching up rugs and knocking around furniture. They're using flashlights, moving them so quickly that it's almost like watching lightning flicker across the room. The paramedics surround a white thing in a sea of darkness—a gurney, with an old woman in a nightgown on it.

Grandma Dalia probably once had Kai's olive-toned skin, but now it's pale with age and illness. Her eyes are cloudy, her hair wispy, and an oxygen mask is pressed against her face, fogging up the tiniest bit with each exhale. They push her toward us, running over the remains of a broken mirror that's fallen from the wall. Kai steps away from me to meet her at the door frame.

"Grandma?" he says weakly, like a child. She looks at him, stretching her fingers out like she wants to reach for him.

"You must be Kai. She was asking for you," a thick, strong-looking paramedic says, capturing Kai's attention. He stops in the door frame for a beat as the others move the gurney to the stairs.

Kai and the paramedic talk, but I don't hear most of it—I'm too busy watching his grandmother's chest rise and fall, so shaky that it looks like it might shatter on the way down.

"She was stabilizing fine, but then she got scared when the wind cracked a window. Do you have a preference where we take her?"

"A preference?"

"Which hospital?" the paramedic says.

"I..." Kai looks from his grandmother to the paramedic and back again, as if he's being asked something in a foreign language.

"Piedmont," I cut in. "She went to Piedmont last year when she fell, right, Kai?"

"Right," he says, staring as the gurney disappears at the top of the stairs. The paramedic nods and jogs after his fellows.

"I'll go get the station wagon so we can follow," I say quickly, grabbing the keys to his grandmother's car off the counter. Kai looks at me blankly. "Maybe you should bring her medicines, so you can show the doctors what she's on?" I suggest. He half nods and disappears deeper into the apartment.

I'm held up by the paramedics in the hallway—they've made it to the third floor and are negotiating around a corner. Grandma Dalia's eyes are open, and for a moment I don't think she's conscious—but then her gaze finds mine, and she stares at me so long that I feel frozen. Her lips are parting; is she speaking? Then she's jostled, and they move again, down to the second story. The first. The double doors leading to the courtyard are ahead; it's still snowing, with at least an inch or two built up on the ground.

The red light from the ambulance bounces off the fallen snow and off windows that are full of neighbors staring. Grandma Dalia's bony hands form fists, and she closes her eyes. Her chest starts to rise and fall faster, and I see the paramedics glance at one another. They try to hurry, but the snow makes the ground slicker than normal, and they can't rush without risking the gurney's stability. A younger paramedic leaps from the ambulance and rushes to throw another blanket over Grandma Dalia.

I run across the street to the little parking lot attached to our building. The snow hides the uneven concrete underneath; I trip and fall, skin my palms, and finally make it to the station wagon. It's burgundy, both outside and in, and it's shiny and sleek—it was top of the line when it was new, and I don't think Grandma Dalia has driven it much since then. I slide into the front seat and jam the key into the ignition. *Breathe. Just breathe. And don't crash.*

I put the car in reverse, turn around, and look back at the building. They're bringing Grandma Dalia around now, about to load her into the ambulance. Her eyes are still squeezed shut; the paramedics have grown almost silent. I tap the gas, ease the car back—

The tires spin. I turn back to the wheel and press down harder—nothing. The rear begins to fishtail a little, but I can't get enough traction to back up. I curse—this isn't working. I punch at the steering wheel, pull the key from the ignition, and get out. *Solution, think, Ginny, think. We have to get there somehow.*

As I jog back toward the building, Kai bursts through the doors. He holds a plastic bag full of pill bottles, rattling like maracas with each step. I pull my phone out of my pocket to look up a cab company....

"Everything okay?" a female voice calls out. I look up— it's a girl, driving a silver Lexus. She leans across the passenger seat, platinum-blond hair spilling over her petite shoulders.

"Yeah, yeah—" I say, waving her off. I hurry over toward the ambulance, finding Kai's eyes in the fray.

The paramedics begin to make sounds—not really words, just sounds. "Oh, whoa, oh, oh, whoa—" all in unison. I spin to see the cause. Grandma Dalia is grasping for the oxygen mask, trying to sit up. They hold her down, but she struggles, fighting with strength I didn't know she had, yet is still nothing compared with a team of thirtysomethings. She succeeds in getting the mask off, but only for a moment. She gasps for air, inhaling flecks of snow and ice. Her lips move; she's speaking; she's trying to reach out to Kai as he runs to her side. His hands and knees are scraped; he must have fallen on the way—

"Don't go," she whispers. I hear her only because the wind has changed direction, blowing against her, carrying her voice to me. She sounds like a ghost, as if she isn't really here. I slide up beside Kai just as she speaks again; her eyes find me and narrow accusingly. She points at me. "Don't go with the girl."

"Ginny and I aren't going anywhere, Grandma, not right now," Kai says immediately. He allows the waiting paramedic to replace the mask; Grandma Dalia inhales fully, her chest arching up against the blankets. "We'll meet you there, at the hospital."

He steps back as the ambulance doors slam shut. I grab his hand. I have to do something. I have to figure out a solution—Kai can't, not right now. *Think, Ginny, damn it.*

"Let's go—"

"The car," I say, shaking my head. "It's stuck in the snow. I'm going to call a cab. I'll tell them to hurry." Kai's face falls—cabs are epically slow, especially on this side of town. I can't help but feel I've utterly failed him.

"You sure you're okay?" the girl in the Lexus calls again.

She's parked directly behind us and is standing outside the car now, tall and bright in a sea of whiteness. Kai stares at her, confused.

"Wait—can you give us a ride?" I shout to her. "To the hospital? His grandmother—"

"Sure," she says, nodding. "Come on, get in."

I know I should feel surprised that she said yes—she's a total stranger—but my mind is too preoccupied with worry. I lead Kai across the snow to the Lexus and sit down in the backseat with him. The girl is barely running the heat; the leather seat feels like ice under my legs. Her eyes flicker to mine in the rearview mirror, two bright blue stars.

"Thank you," I say as we pull forward. "I tried our car, but—"

"Don't worry about it," she says smoothly. Kai leans against me, keeping his head down—I worry, for a moment, that he might throw up in a car we can't afford to have cleaned.

"Don't be scared. She's tough," I remind Kai as I look out the window, watching the world growing ever whiter. People are sledding on trash-can lids and flattened boxes, since no one in the South actually owns a sled. They're laughing and playing, while Kai holds back tears.

"She looked awful," Kai says, exhaling. "What if she doesn't make it?"

I want to tell him that she will, but I'm not so sure. I open my mouth to speak, but the girl driving us breaks in.

"Then you'll still be here," she says. Kai lifts his head; she

26

speaks again. "You can't let yourself die when someone else does. When my sister died, I thought my life was over. But it was just beginning."

"But," I say, squeezing Kai's hand, "that's something we can think about at the hospital."

"Your sister died?" Kai asks. The ambulance skids through an intersection; the girl expertly navigates the gearshift, jetting through the red light to keep up.

"Ages ago," the girl says. "My whole world changed."

"I'm sorry," Kai says. "What's your name?"

"Mora," she answers.

"I'm Kai," he says. "And this is Ginny."

"Thank you for driving us," I add. "It's a nightmare, driving in the snow."

"Not a problem," she says, smiling at me in the rearview mirror. Her teeth are as perfect as her skin, and I hate that I can see my reflection next to hers. I turn back to Kai, who is staring at the back of Mora's head.

"Your grandmother plans everything, right?" I say.

"Yeah," Kai says, sniffling. I can't tell if it's the cold or the emotion making his nose red and eyes watery.

"She planned your clothes every day until last year. She planned each and every trip to the grocery store. She even planned arguments she suspected she'd get into. You think she'd really plan for her last words to be about *me*? She hates me."

Kai almost laughs, but not quite. He shakes his head and looks away from Mora's head and at me.

"Then those aren't her last words," I say, a promise I'm afraid will become a lie. "She isn't done yet." Kai lifts my hand and kisses it, then rests his head against the back of the seat, eyes closed.

It was a lie after all. Grandma Dalia died before she even got to the hospital.

CHAPTER THREE

I saw Kai playing in the courtyard the day we moved in. It was December, a few weeks before Christmas. My dad and his brothers handled the furniture, while my mom lugged box after box of lamps and books and silverware up the stairs. I was too small to really help, and eventually my mom got so irritated with me weaving around under her legs that she told me to go play with "that little boy in the courtyard, the one with the ball."

It wasn't a ball—it was a Frisbee, and neither of us actually knew how to throw it. Kai and I pretended it was a weapon, something we flung at our enemies to knock them off their horses. They didn't stand a chance against us, and we'd slain dozens before we got around to sharing our names.

"Kai," he said.

"I've never heard that name before."

"That's because you've never met me before."

He had a point.

Becoming fast friends when you're that small is easy, because the only requirement is that the other person likes to play games. We eventually made our way up to his apartment and were drinking juice boxes when Grandma Dalia found us. She was already old, even then, but she stood a little straighter, and her hawk eyes were a little brighter. She looked at Kai warmly for a split second, but then her eyes moved to me. Everything changed; she darkened and beckoned Kai to come to her. Seeing I wasn't following him, he turned around, blissfully unaware of the look she was giving me.

"I'm Ginny," I said, trying to look polite despite the fact that my hands were grubby and the cowlick on the back of my head was sticking up. I desperately wanted Grandma Dalia to like me—I didn't have grandparents, and my parents were already starting to drift away from me. Even at that age, I knew what I wanted: to have a home. To be loved. To be cared for. To have someone look at me the way Grandma Dalia looked at Kai—

"Ginny," Grandma Dalia said coolly, like she didn't believe me, and I deflated. "Kai has to practice his violin now, and you have to go home. Besides," she said, "he doesn't play with girls."

"I did today, Grandma!" Kai said, proud. "We played all afternoon, and it was great."

"I'm glad you enjoyed yourself," Grandma Dalia said, looking down at him. She wrapped a claw-like hand around his shoulder protectively. "But little boys and little girls don't play together."

"Why not?" Kai asked, disappointed.

She looked back up at me and narrowed her eyes. "Because, sweetheart. It isn't safe."

After a morning of debate, we decide that Grandma Dalia will be buried in a fuchsia suit, one that has a matching hat and looks like something I'd expect to see on the Queen of England. Kai and I sit on the couch, ignoring the television in front of us, the suit laid across the dining room table. The TV is the one modern thing in the room—when Grandma Dalia realized she could watch soap operas and the Home Shopping Network in HD, she bought it and had it same-day delivered. The rest of the place is a strange combination of old lady and...something else.

There are knitted holders on the tissue boxes and bits of John the Conqueror root on the bookshelves. Statues of kittens sit beside house-blessing incense, black hen feathers hang by the windows—thousands of little things that would supposedly keep her, Kai, and the apartment safe. There's an ashtray of dimes at the door; she insisted Kai tuck one into his sock each time he left, so he'd be protected even away from her fortress of charms. More than once, Kai removed it at school to contribute to the cost of a candy bar at the vending machine.

On the couch, Kai frowns—we're trying to work out how to personalize the funeral service. "We could sing that song." He coils his fingers around my hair, which is spread out across the pillow in his lap. I look up at him and raise an

31

eyebrow. "You know," he says. "That old one she sang all the time, the Kelly one—'*Has anybody here seen Kelly? K-E-double-L-Y, has*—'"

"Oh god, now it's stuck in my head," I groan, curling in and covering my face with my hands.

"What? She loved it. We could sing it in rounds at the funeral," he says, laughing a little. The sound seems to throw him; he swallows the happiness down, then speaks. "Maybe I should just play the violin."

I pause. "I think she'd really like that."

Kai looks at me—there are still red spots under his eyes from crying earlier. "Thank you, Ginny," he says quietly. "I know she wasn't your favorite person."

"I wasn't her favorite, either," I remind him.

"No one was her favorite," Kai adds. "Let's be honest. She was mean. And I think a little racist."

"She is going to haunt the hell out of you if you keep talking like this," I say.

"Yeah, well . . . she was. Is it wrong I loved her anyway?"

"No," I say firmly. "Not at all. You're family." I say that like I understand the misery on Kai's face, but to be honest, I think only losing *him* could make me look that way.

We're silent for a long time.

"When is your aunt getting here?" I ask. Kai's aunt is related by marriage and met Grandma Dalia only a handful of times. Still, she was supposed to show up and help Kai with the mountain of paperwork piling up—life insurance forms, credit card debts, estate taxes.

"I'm not sure," Kai answers. "She said today, but it doesn't look like that's going to happen." He glances at the window—it's still snowing heavily, the cold seeping in through the pane that cracked while the paramedics were here. We repaired it as best we could with duct tape, but it felt a little like taping up a leak on a submarine.

Kai shivers and looks back to me. "You don't think my aunt will miss the funeral, do you? I'm worried." Kai was the center of Grandma Dalia's universe; this is his first time being alone among stars. I imagine it's jarring, having your world change so fast, and I'm oddly grateful that my parents distanced themselves from me a little at a time, farther and farther away from the center, until I was barely in their orbit.

"Let's just figure out the music," I suggest, avoiding his question. "Work that out, and then we'll start worrying about your aunt after dinner."

"Right. Dinner. I'm not hungry," Kai says, seeming confused that meals are still a thing.

"Get hungry," I say firmly. "Because every old lady in the building has brought over a casserole. Anyway. Music—we're figuring out music."

"Okay—what if I can't play tomorrow?" Kai says. He swallows. "What if I'm not able? If I'm too . . ."

Sad.

I nod and think for a moment. "Then we should have a backup plan," I say. "And I think I know where to look." I hurry to the kitchen, nearly sliding on the beat-up rug on the linoleum. There it is, on the shelf above the oven, wedged between a statue of a chicken and a dozen editions of the annual *Southern Living* cookbook.

I pause. I shouldn't touch it. It's not mine. It's not Kai's, even. It's Grandma Dalia's, even in death, and she was never crazy about Kai and me looking at it. I inhale, raise a hand, and slowly, gently tug it down. It's a book—her cookbook, she called it—spattered with age. The cloth binding is so worn that it's missing entirely around the top of the spine and the corners, and it's misshapen due to all the clippings, photos, and dried four-leaf clovers I know are inside.

"Good idea," Kai says behind me. We sit on opposite sides of the tiny kitchen table, and it feels every bit as weird as holding the book—there are only two chairs, which was Grandma Dalia's excuse as to why I could never eat dinner with them. Kai offered to give up his seat each time he asked me to stay; she wouldn't allow that. I slide the book across the table into Kai's waiting palms as I remember her words. "You're not giving *your* seat to that neighbor child." It feels strange now, to just *take* a seat at the table when for so long one wasn't offered.

The cookbook flops open easily to a page in the middle, one that's marked by a thick collection of magazine clippings, stuck together with a paper clip. This page is still mostly blank, though I suspect it's the only one of its kind. Most of the book is packed with recipes, quotes, and inspirational sayings. But there are pages, several dozen or so, that are very different. Pages of charms. Of warnings. Descriptions of beasts, of their teeth and claws. Grandma Dalia gathered information on them from all sorts of people—psychics, scholars, hoboes—and wrote it all down, as if she planned on writing a book on her paranoia.

When Kai and I were small we loved this section. We'd sneak into the kitchen, pull the book down, and stare at these pages with delighted fear. Descriptions of creatures that ate children, lured them into the forest, broke into their homes—sometimes men, sometimes wolf-like, but always terrifying. There was a map of the country, faded with time, on which Grandma Dalia had drawn thick lines, defining the territories of the beasts: their world, laid atop ours.

Grandma Dalia would inevitably catch us. Her expression was always the same one she gave me and Kai when she found us mesmerized by the body of a dead cat on Seventh Street—horror and disgust. *This is serious. This isn't for play. You'd best learn to mind the beasts, or they'll come for you.*

Yet we'd always sneak into the kitchen again, stare at the pictures, and reenact the horrors described on the page in our play. We had to take turns playing the beast. Just seeing the images for the first time in a few years rushes memories back to me; Kai looks up at me and smiles a little.

"Maybe we can just tell these at the funeral. The world's worst bedtime stories."

I laugh a little at how inappropriate it would be. "Careful, Kai," I say, trying to sound serious. "Mind the Snow Queen." The Snow Queen doesn't have a page full of scribbles and sketches like the other beasts do; her page is the blank one in the center of the book. I could never tell if Grandma Dalia didn't know much about the beasts' ruler or if she was just too afraid to write it all down.

Kai chuckles, raps his fingers against the book, and flips the page. "I can't tell what she'd be madder about—how wrong it would be to use a scary bedtime story as her eulogy, or the fact that I'm telling everyone about the beasts. Though I guess she doesn't need to worry about anyone thinking she's crazy anymore. So...she's got that going for her, at least." The sadness is still in Kai's voice, underneath the joke, but it feels good to hear him push it aside at least for a moment.

"And she doesn't need to worry about the beasts, period," I add.

"True. Though she was never really worried for herself. She was worried for me. Like the whole world was waiting to eat me up." He rolls his eyes but then gets quiet. "I should have come back down when it was snowing, even if it got us in trouble. You know the snow was the worst for her. She must have been so scared for me. She probably died—"

"Knowing you were fine. She saw you before she died," I cut him off. He swallows, and in the silence our eyes simultaneously wander to the window. How is it still snowing? It's over a foot now, record-breaking, I think. When he looks back at me he smiles a little, though it seems as if the expression's only purpose is to keep him from crying.

"It looks like it's just me and you," he says, and manages a small laugh. "You're the only family I have now."

I trail my hands down to his and smile as he lifts my

palms to kiss them gently. Kai has felt like my only family for ages; I'm relieved that he sees me the same way now.

"You know I'm in love with you, right, Ginny?" He's looking at my knuckles, running his thumb across them. His eyes flicker to mine. It's the first time he's said it aloud, or at least, aloud and meant it like *this*. "I've always been in love with you."

"I know," I whisper, and he smiles, leans forward, and kisses me. I lift out of my chair and move to him; he pulls me down into his lap and wraps his arms around me. My fingertips curl at the nape of his neck, and when we break away he finds my eyes and is silent for a long time. He exhales, reaches up, and tucks my hair behind my ears, letting his palm linger by my cheek.

I smile and say, "I'll always—"

Love you, too. That's the end of the phrase, but I don't get to say it, because someone is knocking at the door. Probably another well-wisher, hopefully bearing some sort of pie. Kai and I laugh at the timing as I hop off of him. He walks to the door and opens it slightly, just enough to see who it is.

"Oh, hi," Kai says, sounding surprised. I lean forward, trying to see who's there, but Kai blocks my view.

"Hi." The voice is soft, gentle. "I was just stopping by— thought I'd see how things are going."

"Wow," Kai says, stuttering a little, as if he can't find the word. "That's so nice of you. Ginny?" He turns around and motions me over. When he does so, the door opens a little more, and I see the guest's face. It's Mora.

"Hey," I say, smiling. "We didn't really get to thank you the other day—sorry, we were in such a rush."

"Of course," she says, shaking her head. Her hair tumbles everywhere, looking metallic and glowy in the dim hall. She hands me an expensive-looking bouquet. "I wanted to come by and offer my condolences. I saw the obituary in the paper."

"You didn't have to," Kai says.

"I wanted to," Mora says, flashing her perfect grin. "Well, I'll be—"

"No!" Kai says, sounding strangely panicked. "Don't go. We were going to have dinner." Mora looks hesitant, but Kai continues. "Join us? It'll be my way of saying thanks for driving us."

"I guess I can do that," Mora says, shrugging. She walks into the kitchen and, without hesitation, drops her coat over the back of Kai's chair, the one I was sitting in. I walk to the living room and pull in an ottoman for myself—there's no way I'm sitting in Grandma Dalia's chair, even now that she's gone.

Grandma Dalia didn't mind me going to the grocery store with her and Kai. It was one of the few places where I felt as if she didn't hate me, I suspect because she liked having an extra pair of hands to stoop and grab things off the bottom shelf. She shuffled along the aisles, shouting out brands, and at the end, she'd get us both sugar cookies from the bakery.

One day in July, while Kai and I loaded the purchases into

the back of the station wagon, I saw a man. Tall, dark hair, a perfectly trimmed haze of a beard. He was handsome, and it struck me that even though he had all the characteristics of a man, there was something strange about him, as if he were really just wearing a man costume. Still, he smiled at me, and I took a step toward him.

"Hi there," he said, voice quiet. He was standing a few cars away from ours, his hands shoved into his pockets. "Want to come look at something I found?"

"What is it?" I asked, rolling back on my heels. Grandma Dalia got in her car and started the engine so it would cool off a little. Kai was on the other side, shoving things onto the backseat floorboards. With him and Grandma Dalia so close, it didn't occur to me to be afraid.

"Come here," the man said, and when he grinned, something flashed in his eyes, something that reminded me of the way a dog's eyes look when the sunlight hits them just right. I took another step toward—

"Back!" Grandma Dalia screeched, startling me by appearing at my side. Her wrinkly hand gripped my biceps like a vise; I squirmed, but she held tight. She yelled again, shouting at the man. People were turning, looking over their cars, craning their necks from the display of begonias by the storefront. I began to turn red.

The man looked at Grandma Dalia, then back at me. I expected some sort of apology, a claim that he wasn't hurting anything, palms held up. But instead, the strange flickery thing happened in his eyes again, and he smiled. Smiled so

39

that the skin around his face stretched, like rubber, and he again looked like something in a costume instead of a man.

"Back!" Grandma Dalia screeched again, shoving me behind her. I peered around her flowery dress and watched the man turn and walk away. Not toward the store, but through the parking lot, to the main road. People returned to their conversations, shrugging, and Grandma Dalia all but shoved me into the car.

"Who was that man?" Kai asked as we buckled our seat belts. Grandma Dalia whirled around to face us, and I realized that her face was white, her hands shaky.

"Don't ever be so stupid," she hissed at me. "You think they wouldn't love to eat you up?"

"Who *was* he?" Kai whined.

"Mind them," Grandma Dalia said, pointing a finger in my face. "Mind the beasts, Ginny."

It was one of the few times she used my name instead of calling me "the neighbor child." It was also one of the few times that she seemed to genuinely care about me. But what I remember most was that I knew she was right. That something dark, darker than a man, had been there, and that she had saved me from it.

Ever since then, underneath my certainty that Grandma Dalia was just a crazy, paranoid old lady was a spinning, hungry fear that she was right about the beasts.

"You've been playing a long time, then?" Mora asks as she picks at her casserole, not really eating it. It doesn't *look* like

40

something a girl like her would eat—too much cheese, perhaps. I stick my fork back into my serving, struggle to lean forward over the ottoman I'm sitting on. Grandma Dalia wasn't kidding about there not being enough chairs, I guess.

"Since I was three," Kai says. "My grandmother was a little obsessive."

"No, that's not obsessive. It's fantastic," Mora says. "My family hated the arts. We weren't allowed to dance, and we listened to this awful droning music. All the money in the world, but it was like being trapped in a place without beauty. I got into singing for a little while, after I moved out, but now...I mostly just appreciate musical talent. Are you any good, then?"

"He's brilliant," I tell her, smiling. "He's going to study in New York this summer."

"New York!" Mora says. "I love New York. Only downside is you can't drive there."

"Not a fan of taxis?" Kai asks.

"Ha," Mora says. "Not a chance. I'm antitaxi, anti-factory radio, and anti–automatic transmission. Tell me you know how to drive a stick shift, Kai, or I'll have to leave right now."

"I don't," he admits.

"What! That's crazy!" Mora exclaims, as if this is deeply offensive.

"I don't, either," I say coolly, shrugging.

"Well," Mora says, "I guess I can forgive you this time. But call me when you're there, Kai—I'll show you around.

There's this little comedy club that does musical improv every Thursday...." She speaks quickly and her words flow; they have a cadence that makes me stare at her lips forming each syllable. Kai is nodding, grinning, smiling, agreeing to New York, to plans she's making, plans that change what he and I—

"I'm going, too," I interrupt. Mora looks over at me, surprised.

"You play something as well?"

"Just cards," I joke. She doesn't react. "Er—no. I don't play anything. I'm going just to go. With Kai."

"Oh," Mora says, looking at Kai. He looks a little awkward, but he nods, then smiles at me; I'm relieved. "I see." She looks back at Kai. "What's the plan after the summer, then?"

"Well..." Kai pauses. "I promised my grandmother I'd come back here and audition for the Atlanta Philharmonic so I could stay close. But now..." He looks at his hands and shrugs, and I can see him struggling with the realization that he's free to make other plans—and doesn't want to be.

"So, Mora," I say quickly, drawing her eyes off Kai so he has a moment to recover. "What're you in town for?"

"How do you know I'm visiting?" Mora asks, amused.

"You drove through the snow yesterday like it was nothing," I say. "No way you could live here. Plus, you don't have freckles."

"Freckles?"

"Everyone from the South has at least a few freckles," I

42

say, shrugging. Mora's face is perfectly smooth, a single, solid color—she looks like a photograph.

"Noted," Mora says, nodding. "You're very observant."

"No kidding," Kai jokes. "Don't play poker with Ginny. She'll figure out your hand based on your eyebrows. We used to bet on games of Go Fish in elementary school."

"Not eyebrows," I say. "I just remember when the good cards are coming up."

"Ah. Clever," Mora says, then pauses before answering my question. "I'm from everywhere. I lived on Cape Cod, a long time ago, then in South Carolina by the beach, and now I live up north."

"How long will you be here?" Kai asks.

"Not long," she says, twirling a strand of hair around her finger. "But I'll swing by your grandmother's funeral tomorrow, if you want."

"Yes," Kai says. "That'd be great."

"It's really nice of you," I say, "but don't feel like you have to. You've already done so much."

"No, no." Mora waves me off. "Besides," she says, eyes flickering to Kai, "I should go pay my respects. After all, she's the reason I got to meet you."

CHAPTER FOUR

☙❧

Not everyone can make it to the funeral.
The snow has stopped falling, mostly, but the roads are still thick with ice; the news keeps playing a clip of a man ice-skating down Juniper Street. Still, the funeral home has a decent-sized crowd—Mora and her two young "work friends" included. When Kai plays his violin, tears fall among the guests, if not for Grandma Dalia then for the eerie, haunting notes coming from the instrument.

The somber melodies make my heart beat slower, my breath catch in my throat—if I didn't know Kai at all, didn't know Grandma Dalia, I would understand him right now. And despite knowing him like I do, I learn something new about him through the melody: The thing I want, the family, the love, the happiness, those are things he's already had. Things that he's lost. I reach down and touch the cover of the cookbook in my purse while he plays—I brought it just in case Kai couldn't get through the song. The cover is uneven under my nails, the material soft and ragged, yet it makes me feel better—as if I'm telling Grandma Dalia not to worry. Kai will be happy again; we'll be happy together. We'll make it.

They start a photo montage on the projector; I see Kai tense, the tears building up in his eyes as piano music punctuates black-and-white photos of Grandma Dalia as a little girl. I have to look away, or I'll cry, too; my eyes land on one of Mora's companions. He has red hair and doesn't look much older than me, and his eyes are locked on the screen, which is flashing a photo of Grandma Dalia on her wedding day. He reaches up and touches his temple as if he has a headache. Mora takes his hand and smiles at him, and I'm ashamed to feel something akin to relief wash over me. She's holding his hand—the strange, jealous feeling that's been brewing in me over the way she looks at Kai must be for nothing.

I hate myself for thinking like this at a funeral. I swallow, close my eyes, and leave them that way until the service is over.

The coffin is white, and when they remove it from the hearse after a short drive to the cemetery, it blends in with the ground. If it weren't for the pink roses on top, I think it'd be invisible. It feels wrong, hiding her under the snow, under the very thing that scared her the most.

Mom stands over my shoulder, a few other neighbors beyond that with a handful of our classmates. For all her eccentricities, Grandma Dalia wasn't disliked—she let people slide a few days on the rent occasionally, and she sent Kai to school with cupcakes every holiday during elementary and middle school. The dry cleaner is here, as is the guy who owns the pizza place that delivers to us. Kai's aunt isn't here—she called ahead to say she couldn't make it through the ice.

Kai climbs out of the car following the hearse alone. He's freshly shaven, and his skin looks pale. He keeps his eyes downward, only lifting them to meet mine as we follow the hearse across the cemetery toward the grave. The headstone is heart-shaped, in a pinkish hue that matches the wallpaper in Grandma Dalia's bedroom.

Kai slides into the row of chairs lined up in the front—I step toward him, prepared to take the spot on his right. Now that the business of keeping the violin in tune is gone, I can see the need to occupy his mind swooping in, the want for someone to be near—

"Stop," my mother whispers in my ear right before I take a second step. "Those seats are for family."

"But he's alone," I answer, astounded. *And besides*, I want to add, *Kai and I are family*.

My mother puts her hand on my shoulder, instructing me to stay put. I try to soften my glare, try to relax, but I want so badly to walk forward, sit down next to him, and link my arm through his. He looks back at me as if he wants the same, but seeing my mother's grip he smiles grimly, then turns to face the coffin. *It'll be over soon*, I think toward him.

It'll be over, and then we can run away to New York and forget all this. Just you and me.

Kai asked me to ride home with him after the funeral, so my mother leaves to go to work. Alone, I wait for him to greet all the mourners, meandering around the back of the cemetery, looking at headstones absently. There's a dime rattling around in my shoe, my own quiet tribute to Grandma Dalia. I run my fingers over the slick marble base of an angel statue, then turn back to see how many people are still here.

I frown when my eyes find her—Mora, talking with Kai and wearing a thick fur coat, mostly white with a few gray streaks down the back. I can tell it's real because it isn't glossy and fluffy like the ones they sell at the cheap end of the mall. Her friends are lingering by her Lexus, looking bored. I exhale and walk toward them, my nose red and runny from the cold.

When I'm a dozen or so yards away, Kai and Mora suddenly turn and begin to walk off together—without me— down the hill, back toward the waiting car. Mora's voice is bright and loud, almost wrongly so given the setting, but I can't quite make out the words. I hurry to catch up, running around headstones, drawing in breath that freezes in my lungs. Suddenly I slide on the wet surface of a plaque in the ground. I hinge forward and tumble down into the snow and dirt.

"Ginny—are you okay?" Kai is at my side quickly, looping his arms under me to help me up. He's warm—hot, even—and I relax against him when I stand. My knee is throbbing—I'm sure it's swelling beneath my dress.

"I'm fine," I say, brushing off my hands and ignoring the pain. "Really."

"That looked like it hurt," Mora says to me. Her eyes are even paler blue out here in the daylight.

"I'll live," I answer, sharper than I intended.

"Of course," Mora says, laughing a little. She looks back to Kai. "Hey, give me a call or something—I'm in town for a while longer."

"Great," Kai says, grinning too widely for his grand-mother's funeral. The snow begins to intensify; icy, pelting drops cling to my eyelashes. Kai looks up at the smoke-colored sky.

"See you later, then," I say brightly, and usher Kai away from her.

"Of course," Mora answers, then turns around and walks away. Kai tugs me closer and supports some of my weight as I hobble to the waiting town car. It's so warm inside that it burns; I peel off my coat as Kai shuts the door.

"That was weird," I say as the driver eases the car forward.

"What?" Kai asks.

"Mora. I don't know. She's just . . . weird. I mean, she gave us a ride to the hospital, but . . . you don't think she's weird?"

"I think she's nice," Kai says, voice hard—so hard my eyes widen in surprise. "She was telling me about her sister. It was her twin sister, she said. I feel bad for her. She says she's lost everything more than once."

"I don't think she feels bad for herself," I mutter, though I'm instantly ashamed—why would I fight with him on a day like this? Kai shrugs off my comment. "You sounded great," I say.

"Thank you," he says, looking out the window. When I don't respond, he turns to me, eyes softening a little. "Sorry. I just...I think I'm finally crashing from all the emotion." He reaches across the seat and takes my hand. "Is your knee okay?"

"Yes," I answer. "It'll be fine. How are *you* doing?"

"Surprisingly fine, right now," he says, and it's true—there's little of the sadness I saw on his face during the service, as if it's been washed away by the warmth of the car. "If I have a meltdown tonight, though, I'll signal you."

The flashlight signal is as old as my friendship with Kai. We always leave the bottom few inches of our blinds drawn up. One flash means *Are you there?* Two means *Good night*—which happens nightly, without fail. Three is *Come over.* Four is *Meet you on the roof.* I'm surprised the neighbors have never complained about it, really, since there are some nights where we argue via flashing over who should come over to whose house.

Our building looks almost pretty in the snow—probably because the white covers all its flaws. The car lets us out a few yards away so the driver can avoid going over an ice patch, and we balance and slide our way to the front stoop. The memory of Grandma Dalia being hauled out of the building is fresh in my mind as we trudge through the snow to avoid the slippery sidewalk. I hug Kai tightly before we split to go to our separate apartments.

Night comes early; by six o'clock it's dark. The roads have frozen over again, and thus are nearly desolate—no one is crazy enough to drive on them. At ten, my mom calls—she's not coming home after work. It's not worth risking the car, especially when she technically doesn't have car insurance. I microwave a cup of noodles and fill time flipping through the cookbook—I forgot to give it back to Kai after the service. The pages of beasts feel more jarring and threatening than usual, making me keenly aware of how alone I am in the apartment. I shiver and close the book. *You're not alone. Kai is just across the courtyard.*

There's a strange feeling in my gut as I go to my bedroom—as if what I just thought isn't true, as if Kai isn't really there. I peer across the courtyard toward Kai's window, lifting the flashlight from the nightstand. I flick the light four times in his direction, then grab my coat and make my way into the hall and up the stairs toward the roof. It's relatively easy to convince myself that I just want to see the city in the darkness and ice, to check on the roses, but I can feel the need to see Kai rising within me, the need to feel his hand in mine. I reach the step by the roof access door and sit down, shivering in the cold—there's no heat in the hallways. The door frame is so cold it burns my back when I lean against it, even through the layers of fabric.

A few moments pass. I could go check on the roses without Kai, but it seems wrong, a violation of an unspoken trust.

I let my hair down, hoping it'll offer some warmth against the weather. Another minute; I think the wind is picking up. *We probably shouldn't go out there. I should just go to Kai's house when he gets here.*

Another minute.

Another.

I look at my phone and realize fifteen minutes have gone by. I send Kai a text, folding my hands into my sleeves while I wait for a reply. Nothing comes. Irritation rises in me, nearly overpowering my sympathy. Were it any other day, I'd stomp downstairs and give him an earful for not answering—he'd do the same to me if the situation were reversed. But today was the funeral, so instead, I go back to my apartment, fuming, alone, and, for some reason that I can't entirely pinpoint, afraid. I want to be with him, next to him, and not being able to makes me feel wildly off balance. I inhale, trying to steady the frustration I feel rising like a thick ball in my throat. I lock the door of my apartment, kick off my shoes, and go to my bedroom.

Maybe he's already asleep.

I'm lying to myself, and I know it. Kai doesn't sleep when he's upset. He stays awake, he worries, he paces. I angle the flashlight out the window and flash the light twice. *Good night.* Wait.

No answer.

I flash the light twice again. Nothing. I groan, lean over, and look out the window.

The blinds are shut.

CHAPTER FIVE

❧❦

The next morning, my heart still stings a little from the sight of Kai's closed blinds. It feels silly and stupid and as if I'm the sort of girl who doodles hearts with Kai's name in them on my notebook. It's embarrassing. I nag myself to get over it, that some closed blinds are no big deal, to stop moping, but the voice in my head saying all that sounds like Kai, which leaves me doubly embarrassed to have those thoughts in the first place.

Movement outside the window catches my eye—snow, more snow. Will it ever end? I wonder how the roses are doing in all this. Surely they've pulled through, even if they're losing their petals. They've made it through hurricanes and ice storms, after all. I firm my jaw, feeling as if it'll be some personal victory if I can go to the roof and check on the roses without Kai.

I rise, pull on my warmest clothes, and head for the roof.

I hear people milling around inside their apartments, cursing at the new snow falling and shouting at one another as several days' worth of cabin fever sets in. As I grow closer to the roof, the temperature drops. I hug my coat tight and shiver as I grab hold of the freezing metal door handle, slide the key into the lock—

It doesn't turn. I frown and pull the key out—it's already unlocked. I push on the door, letting it swing to reveal a thick layer of snow on the rooftop, the gray-and-white skyline beyond that. There are roses, still, but they're nearly buried underneath the white, drops of crimson in a monochrome world. I smile when I see them there, struggling but hanging on. I step out onto the roof, extend a hand to swipe snow off the nearest rose—

Kai's voice is just ahead, through the flowers. It's so quiet out here that it feels as if his voice is the only sound in the world. I freeze, my fingertips resting on the rose.

The quiet, low tones, like he uses when he's on the phone with me late at night and doesn't want Grandma Dalia to know. I swallow, try to ignore something stabbing in my chest, and walk forward. Another step, another. The snow absorbs my footsteps as I weave through the briars along the path, squinting to see him. Every breath feels spiky in my lungs, and my lips are chapping—

It's her hair I see first. Frosted blond and sparkling, tossing around in the wind. She's sitting on his right—where I sit. In my place. She's sitting there, talking, her voice soft and light and sweet. I can't understand her words, but Kai nods, heaving his shoulders as if he's sighing. And then her slender hand rises, and she reaches forward, letting her fingers dance across the side of his face. He turns his head toward her and smiles. Something rises within me; I think I might be sick. It's like I'm in one of those dreams where you can't run, can't scream, can't cry.

"We aren't that different," she says; this time her words make it to me, though only just. She's looking at him intensely, and her fingers caress his cheek as she talks.

"What do you mean?"

"Well, we both understand that life isn't fair," she says, voice slinky and soft. "I lost everything, more than once. But we can use loss, Kai. We can become greater than we ever were before. Come with me. Leave this place before it kills you."

Her words have changed—they're hypnotic now. I can't look away; I feel as if I'm falling into something the color of her eyes. It reminds me of the way I felt a long time ago, but it takes me ages to place the sensation—the man. The man in the grocery store parking lot, the one with the eyes that glimmered, the one Grandma Dalia warned me about. I swallow, trying to shake off the comparison, but it sticks in my stomach.

Kai turns his head, and I can see his thick lashes, snowflakes clinging to them. He leans forward, and then, before I can comprehend what's about to happen, his lips touch hers. She presses back against him hungrily, wantonly, and he buckles under her pressure, his head dropping back against the bench as she sits up, swings one leg over him—

"Kai?"

54

The name doesn't sound right in my throat; it's coming from a little girl's mouth instead of mine. Mora's pale blue eyes lift and find me. They're unapologetic—she looks like an animal, leaned over her prey. My lips remain parted, unable to close again to form a second word.

Kai shifts underneath her, turns around, and looks at me. There's a hardness around his jawbone, around his eyelids, something I don't recognize. He lifts an eyebrow at me.

"Ginny? What are you doing?"

"I...Kai..." I don't know what I'm saying; I can't find words because they're falling into the deep pit that's replaced my stomach. I know what I want to say, though: *We belong together. We've always belonged together.*

And you've known her for less than a week.

"That's creepy," Kai says, and there's no joke, no softness in his voice. He rises, causing Mora to sit back. She looks pleased as he takes two steps toward me, bars of thorns and briars still blocking the space between us. "What do you want? Do you need something?" he asks.

I feel anger rising in me, but it's blocked by the thick ball of confusion and sadness that's inflating inside my chest. I shake my head and finally say, "What are you doing?"

"I was talking to Mora about New York," he says.

"You were kissing her."

Kai presses his tongue to his teeth. He looks as if he's considering lying, but finally nods. "Yes."

I stare. There must be more. There must be more to say than "yes."

Kai exhales. "Ginny...you're...you're crushing me. It's like every time I turn around, you're there. In my house, at the window, on the roof. I need a second to breathe, but you never give me one."

"I didn't know you needed that. You never told me." Finally, my voice has some strength, some protest.

"That's just it. I shouldn't *have* to tell you. I don't want to call you *obsessed* or anything, but..."

Mora snickers a little, but tries to hide it in a cough.

"You've got to get your own life, is what I'm saying," Kai says, glancing at Mora knowingly. "I'm going to New York with Mora, and I think in the meantime, you should figure out something to do besides follow me around. Trust me, you'll be happier if you get a hobby or something."

"A hobby?" I ask, voice breaking. I shake my head, offended. Angry.

Mora reaches forward and slides her hand into Kai's. I want him to jerk away, to shift, to look wary, but he doesn't budge, as if he's used to her hand finding his. "Come on, Ginny. Don't get in his way now that his grandmother has stepped out of it."

"I'm not in his way," I snap at her. "We're together. We always have been. What are you doing to him?"

"Don't talk to her that way," Kai says, and it stuns me to silence. "You're acting like some jealous little kid."

"I'm not jealous," I say. "I'm angry. Think about this, Kai. Think about what you're saying. This is *me* you're talking to."

"I am totally aware of who I'm talking to," he says. "I'm talking to a lonely girl who follows me around like some lost puppy. I thought you'd eventually figure yourself out but... look at you! What would you be without me, Ginny?"

My chest is collapsing in on itself, as if I'm being punched over and over again. Mora looks at me, shakes her head, and answers Kai's question under her breath.

"Nothing."

"Leave," I say, voice shaking. I'm staring at Mora, afraid to blink, afraid to move. "I need to talk to Kai. Leave."

"Seriously?" Kai throws his arms up in frustration. "What is your deal with Mora? You hardly even know her."

"Neither do you!" I yell, and tears slip down my cheeks. "You don't even know her and you brought her up here, to our..."

"Our what? We *found* this. It's not like you and I built this ourselves. It's not a church or a temple; it's just a shittily maintained rose garden," Kai says, gesturing around as if shocked I don't agree. He reaches down, grabs a pair of clippers, and opens the end. He places them at the base of the nearest rosebush and, before I realize he's serious, slams the handles shut. The blade slices through the plant easily, and it hangs there, held up by its brambles but separated from its roots. "There," Kai says. "Now it's not our *place* anymore; it's just a dead plant. Better?"

"Kai, I can't." I stop and inhale raggedly. "I can't do this without you."

"Do *what*?"

"This," I say, motioning to nothing and everything, because both are true.

Kai shakes his head at me, almost pityingly, and thrusts the clippers to another rosebush and kills it instantly, as if it's nothing. Another, and another; he moves around Mora as if he's orbiting her. The sound of the clippers on the plants, the sliding of the metal against itself—they become louder as Kai snaps the blades with more and more intensity. In the fray, I find Mora again. She's still and beautiful, while I am a mess of hair and tears clinging to my face. She looks happy.

I turn and run for the door.

CHAPTER SIX

❧

When we were small, Kai and I didn't know all the tricks of the rose garden.

The thorns snagged our clothes; the uneven floor tripped us. Once we accidentally locked ourselves up there. We were able to signal to Ms. Snyder, who was coming home with her groceries, and she agreed not to tell Grandma Dalia if we'd take out her garbage and change the cat box for six weeks. We made the deal. It was worth it.

We cleaned up the garden as best we could, though, not knowing anything about gardening. Mostly that meant we hid Capri Suns in an old toolbox, swept off the bench, and cleared a path through the overgrown bushes. It took the better part of three weeks, but we treated it like a job, going up there immediately after school and not coming down until Kai had to go to dinner. There was an unspoken rule that neither of us ever went up there alone.

We didn't know the trick to the door. It's big, heavy, and metal, and it has one of those mechanisms that makes it automatically shut. One day, I opened the door on the way to get my beanbag chair from downstairs so we had something new to sit on. My fingers were curved around the door frame when I saw it—a bird's nest, wedged under an awning. Inside were three tiny, perfect blue eggs; I stared. There was something so beautiful about them, nestled together, safe from the wind. I turned my head to Kai, who was just walking up behind me, and opened my mouth to tell him about the nest. I didn't see the door swinging back. I didn't realize my fingers were still in the jamb.

Kai shoved me, hard—I almost fell down the stairs, and he tumbled after me. I looked up just in time to see the door slam against his ankle with a resounding *crunch*.

He tried to pretend it didn't hurt, but eventually, he gave in and cried. It swelled up as if there were a golf ball lodged under his skin, and the spot turned dark purple and green. I helped him limp downstairs to my apartment, where we sat in my room with a bag of frozen peas pressed against his ankle for an hour.

I asked him why he didn't just yell at me, or pull me toward him, or let me smash my own stupid fingers. He said it was because he didn't think about it. He just did it.

"And besides," he said, wincing as I removed the peas to inspect the damage, "it would have broken your fingers."

"I think it broke your ankle," I pointed out.

"One ankle. Four fingers. It was the better choice," he joked, though his face was tense from pain.

He didn't go to the hospital, and he forced himself to walk on the foot rather than limp in front of his grandmother. If she had found out what happened, she'd take the garden away. She'd put a new lock on the door. She might even tear down our rosebushes. The break eventually healed, though his left foot is still turned a little funny, if you look at it closely.

He said it was worth it.

I feel as if someone has pulled out an organ. One of those that doesn't seem essential, to the layman—not my heart or my lungs, but rather my pancreas, or my spleen, or my gall-bladder. Something that doesn't seem as if it should matter so much, until it's gone and your body can't figure out how to operate and your heart won't stop beating and just give up already. I sit on my bed, trying to figure out what's just happened. Trying to figure out how he went from loving me to killing the roses.

I don't turn on the lights as the sun begins to set. I want to be asleep, because surely, surely when I wake up Kai will be the Kai I love again. And we'll be together, the way we're supposed to be, and I won't be so confused and lost.

"Is this yours?" my mom's voice calls from the living room. I jump and realize I'm shivering from the cold—how long have I been sitting here? I rise, open my bedroom door, and see her peering down at Grandma Dalia's cookbook.

"No," I say. "It's Kai's."

My mom looks up at me and her eyes widen, as if she's seen something frightening. "God, Ginny, what's going on?"

"I'm fine," I say swiftly. I walk over and collect Grandma Dalia's book. My mom is staring, unsure how to proceed. I head back to my room, eager to get back into the dark cold—

"Are you all right?" my mom asks. I turn in my door frame, a little startled that we're still talking. "You don't look all right."

"Kai and I got into a fight," I say, shrugging. "It's fine." I'm lying.

"Oh," Mom says. "Well... maybe it's not the worst thing for the two of you to spend a little time apart—oh, don't look at me that way, Ginny; I don't mean it like that. I'm just saying, I married my first boyfriend, and look where it got me—"

"That's not it," I say, glowering. I don't mean to slam my door, but I'm not sorry when I do.

My mouth is in a firm line and my hands are stiff as I open Grandma Dalia's cookbook on my bed so roughly that I tear the first page a little. I picture her disapproving glare as I begin to flip through the middle section, through her spells, her charms, her beasts. *Was that your final plan, Grandma Dalia? Die just as Mora arrives, so Kai ends up with her instead of me?* I want to scream at her, even though I know it's mostly because I can't scream at Kai.

I pull the stack of recipes bookmarking the Snow Queen page out and toss them aside, far more careless than I've ever been with the cookbook. When I do, the end of the paper clip sticks under my nail, far enough to sting. I yank my hand back, wincing, and watch as a drop of blood swells, spreading out in a perfect crescent shape just beneath the white part of my nail.

I cuss loud enough that I hear my mom make a disapproving noise from the next room, but I don't care. The paper clip is rusted, old—I should probably get a tetanus shot. I tear the clip off the recipes and toss it onto my desk angrily, as if I'm banishing it. When I do, the clippings slip from my fingers and slide apart as they fall onto the open snow beast page. A recipe for cherries jubilee is on top, but underneath it is something strange—something skin colored. I brush the recipe aside to reveal a picture of a cheekbone, glossy and torn from a magazine. Beside it, a ripped-out picture of a nose.

It's when I see two ice-blue eyes that I understand.

My fingers race across the book, assembling pieces. There are several noses, several eyes, and it takes me a dozen tries before I finally, finally assemble the clippings in the right order. In the right face. Mora's.

The clippings weren't a bookmark. They were the Snow Queen page. No text, no details, just Mora's face.

I rise and back up. No, no, this is crazy. Crazy—Mora is just a girl. Just a girl who stopped to give us a ride. She may be beautiful, but she's not the queen of the beasts. It's a stupid idea, you're just emotional, you're just angry with Kai. She's just a girl.

Don't go with the girl.

Grandma Dalia's last words are screaming in my brain, the magazine-clipping eyes staring at me. I shut my own eyes, try to ignore the rising panic. *You're looking too far into it*, I tell myself. Besides—she pointed at me. Right at me. I remember the way her eyes narrowed, the crook of her finger, the way her hand shook—

I swallow.

I remember where Mora was standing, outside her parked car. Directly behind me.

I run for the apartment door, cutting my mother off when it slams behind me. I pound down the steps and through the courtyard—the cold is worse, the wind is worse. In the back of my head is a voice telling me this is silly. But then I think of Mora, of her slick words and icy eyes, of the costume man in the parking lot she reminds me of. Of the beasts in Grandma Dalia's stories.

I reach Kai's door, grit my teeth, and rap on it.

Silence.

I knock again, my breathing slow, controlled, as if I'll be able to stop myself from panicking if he opens the door and she's standing over his shoulder.

Silence.

"Kai?" I call softly, almost inaudibly. Still nothing. I knock again, louder this time, then again, and I finally hear movement—from the apartment across the hall. I wheel around to see Mr. Underwood, wearing a painfully see-through white shirt and chewing on a thick cigar. His hair is so white it makes the hall look especially dingy.

"You're interrupting my news stories," Mr. Underwood says crossly.

"Sorry," I say. "I was looking for—"

"Kai, obviously. He's gone. So you can stop knocking."

"Gone?" I ask, voice catching.

"Hours and hours ago, with some pretty girl. Good for him, if you ask me. Better than sitting around moping over Dalia."

"Where did they go?"

"Hell if I know—point is he isn't here, so stop the commotion," Mr. Underwood says, waving a hand at me before he shuts the door.

For coffee. To a movie—are the theaters open in all this snow? Maybe for dinner. I feel sick hoping that they're just on some sort of date, but it's better than the alternative—I'm sure of that, even without fully knowing what the alternative is. Still, all I can think of is what I heard on the roof, Mora's voice all hypnotic and smooth. *Come with me.*

He can't have left. Not without me. Not with another girl.

I fumble with my key chain till I find the spare Kai gave me and slide it into the lock. The door creaks open; the apartment is pitch-black. Even though I know he isn't here, I call his name again before reaching over and flicking on the kitchen lights.

The kitchen looks like it always does. There are dishes by the sink, and a loaf of bread sits on the counter. I see one of Grandma Dalia's sweaters is still on the back of the armchair, and Mora's thick fur coat is laid across the couch.

Everything looks right here...I'm overreacting. I close the front door behind me and move through the house. Shoes in the hall. Toothbrush by the bathroom sink. They haven't left yet; there's still time to understand what's going on, to get Kai away from Mora and whatever...*spell* she has on him. I round the corner to his bedroom just in case and grope for the light switch. It springs on, revealing his bed—unmade, like normal—and a pile of dirty laundry on the floor, including a shirt I recognize from Grandma Dalia's funeral.

And then my eyes fall on the spot.

The spot where his violin is supposed to be. The spot where his violin always is. It's a void, an empty space on the otherwise cluttered carpet. I stare at it, unsure what to think, what to feel, what to do, because I know that this means he's gone. With her.

I call the police. It's the only thing I know to do.

"So wait, the violin is worth how much?"

"Thousands," I explain, brandishing Mora's fur coat at him, as if it's evidence. "But it's not that. If it's gone, he's gone."

"Is it insured?" he asks, ignoring the coat.

"I'm not worried about the violin!" I shriek. "He didn't steal it; it's his!"

"All right, all right, calm down," the officer says. We're standing in the courtyard, and I can see neighbors peeking out from their curtains to see what the noise is about. It's late—the police were so inundated with snow-related calls that it took them hours to get here. My mom stands beside me, arms folded, irritated not only that I called the police, but that, as far as she can tell, I'm being immature. Upset over a fight with my boyfriend. Childish.

She doesn't understand that I'm afraid.

"This, to me, looks like a kid freaking out over losing a relative," the officer says to my mother, as if I'm not standing right beside her, shivering. "Has his aunt shown up?"

"I don't know—" my mom begins.

"No. She isn't here. I don't even know if she's coming," I say dismissively. My tears have dried, but my voice is still stuffy and thick.

"Well, he's eighteen, so he's not a runaway. I wager he's taken the cello—"

"*Violin*," I hiss.

"I wager he's taken the violin," the officer says, looking weary, "to hock. Fast cash to hold him over till the will gets executed."

"That's not—"

"Honey," the officer says. "I have been driving through the snow for days now. Tomorrow it's supposed to let up. I get that this boy broke your heart and ran off with some blond, but he's a legal adult and can make his own decisions. Most of downtown's without power. Water pipes are frozen over. A few streets over, we've got a girl your age, murdered. Ripped to shreds. You really think I should be tracking down some boy instead of finding the monster who did that to her?"

"The girl who took Kai, I think she's done something to him," I plea. "He didn't just leave me. I think his grandmother—"

"He's a bum, Ginny—you'll meet someone else," the officer says firmly, and gives me a pointed stare. We're silent for a moment, still, him daring me to say another word.

"He's not a bum," I grumble, and spin around. I slip on the ice, a final indignity, before I stomp back inside. My bedroom is cold; I'm so tired of the cold. I turn the radiator on high, even though it fills my room with a sticky, plastic smell.

This is crazy. This is crazy, crazy, crazy. The magazine clippings are still assembled on my bed. I stare at them, trying to see someone other than Mora, but it's so clearly her. Her, on the Snow Queen page. Her, in Atlanta during a blizzard. Her, here the day Grandma Dalia died.

Mind the beasts.

I have to leave tonight.

MORA

The first week after taking a new boy was always the worst. The boys had questions, they clung to who they were, they got scared. Mora looked over at Kai as she pulled the car under the awning of the hotel drive. She knew what they were going through, almost exactly, and she also knew it would pass. And when it did? Things would get so, so much easier.

"Come on," she called to Kai as the valets came to open their doors. Kai stepped out, looking dazed as Mora walked around the back of the car to meet him. She frowned—he'd need new clothes, and soon; he looked shabby next to the car, the hotel, and her own silk dress. One of the doormen hurried to offer Mora his woolen coat—her shoulders were bare and exposed to the snow that was falling hard, clinging to the hotel windowsills like strips of icing. She waved the doorman off, pretending to shiver, and cursed herself again for leaving the white fur coat at Kai's house. Another could be bought, of course, but it was the convenience of the thing. She nodded for Kai to follow her, and they pushed through the dark oak doors and into the lobby.

Mora stopped, her knees locking as the memory hit her. Memories were strange for her now—just as she thought she had them all gathered up, under control, a new one would appear like a ghost from her former life. This time it was brought on by the smell of this particular hotel—like wine and floor wax and years of perfumes and cigars passing through. Kai stopped obediently beside her, waiting for her direction. *He's coming along nicely*, she thought.

"I stayed at this hotel when I was a teenager," Mora told him as the memory took shape in her head. She looked across the lobby. It reminded her of vintage dresses, pearl jewelry— pale pinks and creams and golden accents. There were pillars every few yards along the wall, leading up to a coved ceiling with inlaid carvings and stained-glass skylights. Someone played a grand piano at the far end of the lobby, classic songs that cut over the hum of conversation, the people in suits shaking rocks glasses, women with dangly earrings laughing. "It was for a wedding, I think," Mora continued, staring at a woman in a white cocktail dress. "Perhaps. Sometimes I can't tell what I've imagined and what's real."

"Why can't you remember?" Kai asked. His voice was hard, and if Mora were being entirely honest with herself, she'd admit she preferred the softer version, the one he used with Ginny. She rolled her eyes for thinking that, then answered.

"Because that life is long gone. It's like trying to remember something that happened when you were a baby. I remember . . . I remember that they made me go to the wedding with one of my father's friends. He was older than me, but he was rich. He was going to be a congressman, they said. I'm not sure if he became one or not—it was after I left. But, oh, they wanted me to marry him so badly. I think my father would have paid him to give me a ring."

"But he didn't?" Kai asked. Mora shook her head, regretting saying the memory aloud.

"He knew I didn't love him. There was another boy I wanted. . . ." Mora's eyes lingered on the piano player for a long time. "He played the piano."

"A musician," Kai said a little coyly, mistaking the seriousness in her voice for teasing. "I see why I'm here now."

Mora laughed a little, the sound broken and cheap. "Yes. He was brilliant, though, better than this one." She waved a dismissive hand at the pianist in the lobby as they passed him, moving toward the front desk. "But musicians aren't stable. Musicians aren't good choices. Musicians become poor drunks, whereas politicians become wealthy ones, according to my father. . . ."

Mora swallowed. It was easier, back when she didn't remember him. She stopped, turned to Kai, and ran her fingers along his cheekbone for a moment, a tender gesture that made a few people at nearby tables giggle in amusement. Kai was like the other boy, the one she loved. Talented. Beautiful. But the difference, the biggest difference, was that Kai would never stop being hers. The thought helped dull the ache of what happened with the other boy.

71

The boy she loved. The boy who broke her heart.

Kai turned his head to kiss Mora's fingers, a scandalous look in his eyes. She withdrew her hand just before his lips touched her skin; the act made Kai follow even closer behind her as she continued walking, hungry for her attention.

"My sister was here, too," Mora said. The memories of her family were less paralyzing, easier to talk about. "We shared a room. She had her own date, with some other rich man. My sister liked it, honestly. She wanted a house and a baby and dinner parties and boats. Maybe that's why she was the one who got killed. She hadn't learned to fight like I had." Mora shook her head and looked at Kai's raised eyebrows. "That's the way it works. Twins are two bodies with a shared soul. One of us had to die."

"Who killed her?" Kai asked, voice raspy—perhaps he was too new to hear this tale.

Mora stopped by an enormous arrangement of red roses, tilting her head to the side. "Have you ever had nightmares, Kai? About men who are monsters? Monsters who are men?"

He nodded faintly.

"That's what killed my sister. They're called Fenris. They're monsters, demons, creatures who eat girls—"

"Beasts," Kai said breathlessly—his voice was softer now. "My grandmother called them beasts."

"Ah," Mora said, sounding impressed, though she wasn't exactly shocked—every few years she ran into someone who knew about the Fenris. "Well, the Fenris killed my sister, so the single soul she and I shared was fractured. I suppose it's easier to turn someone broken like that into something dark, like them." She paused, and when she spoke again, her voice was quiet. "I could feel myself changing, forgetting my old life with my family. So I went to this beach we used to vacation at, because I was sure the ocean was the only thing big enough to make me remember. To make me feel again." She shook her head and looked up at the stained-glass ceiling, imagining for a moment that the watercolor-like swirls of glass were waves above her. "That's why all girls like me wound up there. We were ocean girls, adopted sisters, waiting to become as dark as they are. The Fenris waited until I was a shell, barely a living thing, then pulled me out of the water. They made me theirs." She forced her eyes back to Kai, gritted her teeth, and pleaded with her head to make the memory stop. It didn't work.

"What did they do to you?" Kai asked in shock.

"They kill their mortal lovers," Mora explained delicately. "So they need girls like me. They make us monsters, like them. They make us theirs. But you have to understand, Kai—I thought it was a curse, what happened to me, but it was a blessing. I was freed. Just like I'm freeing you."

"From what?" Kai asked, rubbing his temples as if he was waking up. Mora glanced at his arms and noticed chill bumps rising, then followed his line of sight over her shoulder. The roses in the vase, bright red and fully bloomed. He was staring at them, squinting now. Mora reached forward, grasping his hand forcefully. It was hot and sticky to her, and it was all she could do not to grimace at the feeling.

73

"From being mundane," she whispered, standing on her toes to bring her lips close to his ear. "From being ordinary."

"From Ginny. Where's Ginny?" Kai lifted his eyes to meet hers, and they were gold—too gold for comfort, too gold for Mora to overlook them. She leaned forward and pressed her lips to his. Kai's mouth was soft and gentle against hers; it felt as if she could crush him. She kissed him, licked at his lips, and slid her hand along his thigh until she finally felt his skin grow cold. When she pulled away, his eyes were dark, his skin fairer, a shade that matched her own.

"Come on," she said, motioning toward the front desk. "Michael and Larson have probably finished circling the building. I want to be in the room once they get here." She'd asked them to check the area for signs that the Fenris were nearby, that they'd followed her. They were in Atlanta, closer to her than she would have liked—she was almost certain they were responsible for the body found by Kai's building. If she hadn't taken Kai when she did, they'd probably have smelled her, if not *seen* her....

Mora swallowed the thought, took Kai's hand, and tried to pull him forward, but his feet were planted, a look of shock on his face.

"Mora," he gasped, squeezing her fingers. "I think I love you."

Mora smiled and wrapped her fingers underneath Kai's chin tenderly. "Of course, darling." She turned, pulling harder until he followed her. "You all do."

CHAPTER SEVEN

~o✦o~

Think. Think this through.

I leave a note for my mom saying I'm going to stay with Dad for a week or so, to get over Kai leaving. It'll buy me a little time, at least—she won't want to be the helicopter parent, telling me I can't go, and she won't want to call Dad to check that my story is true. Then I call the school, just in case the snow breaks sooner rather than later. I leave a voice mail with the attendance office in a voice that sounds like my mother's: *There's been a family emergency. Ginny will be out for a week.*

It's not a total lie.

Odds are good someone will notice Grandma Dalia's car is gone before they work out I'm gone, anyway, I think as I pull the station wagon out of the parking lot, opting not to consider what will happen if finding Kai takes more than a week. In the backseat, the dimes from the bowl rattle, now dumped in a grocery bag; I took them for luck. After all, if Grandma Dalia was right about the Snow Queen, she might be right about everything else, too.

The Atlanta skyline fades quickly, blotted out by snow clouds. I hardly ever drive, and the weather isn't making it any easier. The roads are slick and darkened by both the night and the power outages that dot my route. I can't go anything close to the speed limit—at times, I'm going less than half. My eyes are trained on the white dashes on the asphalt, so focused I feel hypnotized. I play a game in my head, pretending I'm leaping over the dashes, running toward Kai, running to stop him from . . .

From what?

Just find him, first. They can't have gotten that far ahead of me—a few hours, at most, and if they don't know I'm behind them they're bound to take their time. Plus, Mora doesn't seem like a road trip kind of girl. She'll probably want to stop in a hotel or something, and not a cheap one, either. It'll have to be one along this interstate—it's the only reasonable way to go north. Not that I really *know* she's even headed in this direction, but before leaving I looked at the weather forecast. Snow north of Atlanta, headed for Nashville. If I'm right, if Mora is the Snow Queen—a theory that alternates between sounding like the absolute truth and complete lunacy in my head—then she'll be where the snow is. I think. I hope. Please.

Strange how stealing a car suddenly doesn't feel like the craziest part of my plan.

76

Night begins to give in to the slightest implication of morning. The black sky becomes a shade of steel gray, though every now and then hints of the sun slip through, fingers of orange in an otherwise monochrome world. The sight snaps me out of my hypnosis a little, making me aware of just where I am and what I'm doing. I'm in Tennessee, somewhere near Nashville, I think. The snow here isn't deep, and cars are beginning to appear on the road, though the drivers look every bit as wary as me.

I yawn; my eyes burn and my throat is suddenly dry. *Has it really been five hours?* I'll have to stop and sleep soon, I'm certain—the very prospect feels like a betrayal, like my body is stubborn, defiant for needing rest. My headlights flash on a sign, indicating yes, Nashville is only fifteen miles out.

I take the closest exit, to a small but functional rest area hidden from the interstate by a swatch of pine trees. I dash inside to use the bathroom and buy a cinnamon roll from a faded vending machine. The trees in the adjacent forest sway in the wind, trying to lose the last few clumps of snow clinging to their branches—it's amazing how comforting seeing the greenery instead of stark whiteness is. I park the car, hug my coat around me, and climb into the backseat. I brought Mora's coat along—I'm not sure why, exactly, but I suspect it's to remind me that she's real, that I'm not crazy. Even though it looks warm, I kick it onto the floorboards.

One hour. That's all, I think, yawning again. I curl into a ball on the wine-colored upholstery and let my eyes drift shut....

My dreams include beasts with Grandma Dalia's voice, warning me to stay away. Every now and then my eyes creak open, unable to discern the difference between the dream world and the waking one. But with time, my dreams become more solid, warming into ones about Kai. In an apartment somewhere, one with old wood floors and wide windows. We're seated on either side of a coffee table, eating dinner with our hands and telling jokes and laughing and happy and together and home. Yet even in the dream, I remember what he said to me on the rooftop, all the cruel things. The memories taint our laughter, flooding out any comfort the dream might have brought me.

He didn't mean it. It was Mora; she's the Snow Queen. He didn't mean it.

My eyelids spring open. It takes me a moment to be certain the dream is over, that I really am wide awake. It's freezing, and snow is coming down, heavy and thick—so thick I can't see the interstate through the bowed-down branches of trees anymore. My bones feel like blocks of ice under my skin, creaking as I unwind my curled body and sit up. I hear a snap behind the car and whirl around to see a limb breaking off a tree, crashing to the ground under the weight of snow.

Then it's silent again, as if I'm the only thing alive here. As if I'm the only thing alive anywhere.

It's silent in a way that reminds me of the moments before Grandma Dalia's death. I scramble into the front seat despite how badly I want to curl back up and cling to whatever warmth I can find. I fumble with the keys, trying to look at the ignition and the forest at once—is it snowing harder, like

78

it was on the rooftop? The trees are giants pushing toward me; the road ahead is almost entirely hidden by the snowfall. My heart is beating faster, faster, faster; finally my numb fingers slide the key into the ignition, turn it forward.

The engine struggles to turn over, then fails. I lick my lips, realize I can see my breath. How cold is it out there? Air is raw and sharp in my lungs, I push the ignition forward again, again, try not to see Mora's face in my mind.

I push the key forward again, hold it this time as the engine sputters, struggles, and finally kicks to life. I crank the heat knobs to all the way on and all the way red, push the car into drive. The car lurches but stays put as sheets of snow and ice break and slide from the windows. *Damn it.* The heat is kicking in, burning then thawing me as I glance in my rear-view mirror—

Eyes. Bright eyes staring at me from behind the car, a man's shape in silhouette. My breath stops; I *can't* look away, but I reach over, lock the door—

I scream, because there's another man just outside my window. He has thick, wavy hair; a smooth face; and thick lips. The man at the window waves his fingers at me, and something about the motion isn't right. Something about *him* isn't right. I can't look away—

A scratch at the passenger door. I wheel around instinctively. There's another man there, then one by the front tire, two more behind me. They're everywhere, surrounding me, and I can't slow my heart down—

The man at my window smiles.

It isn't a real man's smile. It's the smile of a man in a costume. A smile I've seen before, on another face. A smile that terrifies me. What's worse is the recognition in the man's eyes—he knows that I know what he is, and his face gleams over it. I see him look to the back of the car; his gaze falls on Mora's coat. He frowns.

"You alone out here, miss?" the man says, his voice a hiss that somehow pours in through the closed window. I swallow. *Go, go, go*—I slam my foot down on the accelerator.

The tires spin uselessly, kicking up snow. I hear laughter from the men behind me. My lungs are shrinking, too small for my body. Every story Grandma Dalia ever told me about beasts is rushing through me, along with a feeling of certainty that this, this is how I'll die. I swallow.

The man at the window chuckles under his breath, a dark and raspy sound.

And then I can't stop screaming.

His eyes yellow, becoming smaller. His shoulders hunch over, and I hear a sound like celery stalks snapping—his bones are shifting, lengthening. With a resounding *crack*, his face juts out and becomes a muzzle. The noise is happening all around me—they're all changing. Sticky and wet-looking fur bursts through their skin; their fingers bleed as nails thicken into claws. They breathe out long clouds in the cold, and they're smiling—*smiling*—wickedly through mouths that are human, human lips, human skin breaking, tearing apart and bleeding.

My foot is pounding on the gas, the brake, anything,

please, please, please, please. One of the beasts with a still-human arm reaches forward, punches at the back window of the car. It shatters, and the others howl hungrily.

Lights. Something moves; something flashes. I hear tires squealing on gravel, and then, before I can figure out what direction the noise is coming from, I'm jolted forward as the back of the car gets clipped. I bounce, hit the steering wheel. I recover, turn around, and see a sleek red car sliding on the ice just behind me. The beasts are huddled a few dozen yards ahead of it—it's hit one of them.

I press my foot down on the accelerator again, and now that the car has been knocked around a little, it finds traction. I zip backward, unprepared for the speed; the rear of the station wagon crashes into the front end of the sports car. I cringe, throw it into drive, look in the rearview mirror.

Eyes meet mine—gray eyes, eyes that aren't a costume. Eyes on a real man. He looks out the window, toward the beasts. Something is happening—the monster lying on the ground, the one he hit, twists to one side. Darkness starts to rush across its body, as if it's being tied down by black ropes. More and more and more of them, and then suddenly the ropes are skittering away, shadows on the ground, and the monster is gone.

The others turn toward our cars.

The man in the sports car jumps out. I lunge over the passenger side, unlock the door as he jumps over his own hood, slides across mine, and grabs for the door handle. He yanks the door open, leaps inside, and slams it behind him.

The beasts run at us, grabbing for my car with claws and hands and something in between, broken nails and bloody fingertips. They slam against the already broken back window, clearing it of glass. Hands are on my hair, my coat sleeve, pulling at me—

"Floor it!" the other driver roars. I bring my foot down, throw the car into drive, and skid around in a circle. They're chasing us; one monster is still holding on to the back window, bracing himself as we fly away from the rest area toward the interstate. I slap the wheel to the right; it shakes the monster off and he falls away, his yellow eyes raging at me as we break out of the trees and onto the main road.

The other driver is panting, looking over his shoulder, shaken and sick-looking, though he doesn't seem as close to screaming as I am. My knuckles are white on the wheel, my eyes wide. I'm going to throw up, but I'm afraid to stop—I grab the window knob, roll it down, and lean my head out to empty the contents of my stomach onto the moving road.

"Better?" the man asks.

"Not really," I gasp, cringing at the taste in my mouth.

"You'll be fine. We got away. What's your name?" He extends a hand and, when I'm too flustered to take it, rests it on my shoulder for a moment in an exceedingly awkward way.

"Ginny," I say. "Ginny Andersen."

He nods, closes his eyes, and rests his head on the back of the seat. "Werewolf attacks aside, good to meet you. I'm Lucas Reynolds."

CHAPTER EIGHT

We creep along the interstate, our eyes mostly glued to the car's mirrors, certain one of the beasts is running up behind us. Lucas turns on the radio, spinning the dial back and forth until the little orange line finds a station not entirely obscured by static.

"...an additional six to eight inches are expected overnight. Temperatures are expected to drop below zero tonight, meaning roads will likely be impassable tomorrow. Be careful, Nashville, and stay home if at all possible. Stay tuned for more on the storm; we'll be bringing you updates on school and business closings every hour, or you can check our website for the most up-to-date information."

I inhale, looking at Lucas. "I have a question."

"Go for it," he says. Without his coat on, he's much less imposing—he's rail thin, and I'm pretty sure I could take him in a fight.

"The things in the woods—"

"Werewolves," he says. "Just call them what they are. You'll feel less crazy if you say the word aloud."

"Werewolves," I say, and he's wrong—I just feel crazier, talking about werewolves in a stolen car, in a blizzard, with a stranger. "You know about them?"

"More than I care to. Though I can't figure out why they're here right now. They're not usually around in the winter. Strange that there were so many..."

"Do you know about the Snow Queen, too, then?"

Lucas frowns, shakes his head. "Never heard of a Snow Queen. What's that?"

I lunge into the backseat, pull the cookbook out, and drop it in Lucas's lap. He opens it tentatively. "Flip...keep flipping...that page. There." I've stopped him on the pages about the beasts. Lucas looks at them, mouth parting a little as he flips the pages, past spells, warnings, and descriptions of monsters.

"Whoa," he says when he gets to the map. "Is this all of the Fenris packs?"

"The what?"

"The werewolves," he says absently. "That's what this is! I wonder if it's accurate. I know the Arrow pack is out of Atlanta now, and I think Sparrow is gone altogether. Is this yours?" he asks, motioning to the cookbook.

"No. It's my friend's grandmother's. And there was this girl, who is actually the Snow Queen, and she ran off with my friend—well, I guess...my boyfriend, sort of...."

"A girl ran off with your boyfriend and you think she's a magical creature?" Lucas asks warily.

"Not like that," I say. "There's more to it. She changed him, out of nowhere. Overnight, even. And right before his grandmother—the lady who made this book—right before she died, she warned him about a girl. And her picture is in that book."

Lucas looks entirely unconvinced, but he sighs. "And she's the Snow Queen. Huh. I don't know. Maybe I could call my brothers and ask. Silas hunts the Fenris—the werewolves—with his fiancée; maybe they've heard of her...." He drums his fingers on the seat for a moment, then points to an exit for someplace called Belle Meade. "Go ahead and get off here." I obey, turning the car and inching up the exit ramp, following the tire marks of the cars that went before me.

"Is that what you were doing out there? Hunting them?" I ask.

"Ha," Lucas answers. "Do I look like a hunter?" He motions to his slight frame, chuckling. "*I* was out getting microwave popcorn when I saw one, so I started tracking them. Making sure they weren't headed toward town, or to my house. And...turn again here," he says, motioning to a drive ahead.

"Wait...here?"

"Yep."

My hesitation is due to the neighborhood's entrance: a brick drive, framed by huge gates and a white guardhouse. It's the sort of place my mother would have sighed at wistfully,

85

perhaps making a comment about how the residents probably don't appreciate their good fortune. Lucas chuckles as a guard rushes out when he sees the station wagon coming—I can't exactly blame him. The car doesn't fit into a neighborhood like this any better than I do. Lucas waves from the passenger seat; the guard looks perplexed but opens the giant metal gates to let us pass.

Houses sit perched on hills, so big they could swallow my entire apartment building. The snow makes them look like they belong on holiday cards; they glow from the inside out in a way the places on Andern Street never could. Lucas guides me along, telling me when to turn. The houses change again—they grow larger, until the lots they're set on are so vast the houses loom like castles in the distance. Finally—

"Here," Lucas says. "This is ours."

It looks like something that belongs in the European countryside, cream-colored and sitting high on a hill. The magnolias that drip with snow along the drive make it hard to see for a moment, but I keep my eyes trained on the spot where it was; when we clear the trees, I can see the balconies on the second story with elaborate iron railings, and arched windows with snow piled along the sills like icing.

"What do you *do*?" I ask, amazed. We cross over a stone bridge; the road turns from brick to smooth cobblestone.

"It's not me," Lucas says. "It's my wife."

I immediately think of those men I've seen on TV, the ones who date older, richer women. I wouldn't have pegged

Lucas for one, but I suspect he is when we pull up to the house and it has a half-dozen garages.

"Come on," he says as he opens his door. "Speaking of my wife, she'll definitely want to meet you."

I park, grab my things, and climb out of the car. I gaze up at the mansion in wonder before tromping through the snow after Lucas, feeling dwarfed next to it, as if I'm a doll beside a human-sized building. Lucas leads me through the front doors, into a foyer with an enormously high ceiling. Mirrors on either side reflect my soggy complexion a million times back at one another, and everything is gold. Not *actually* gold, but the gold highlights and cream-colored travertine make the entire room look bathed in warmth, the exact opposite of the world outside.

"This way," Lucas says, looking a little bemused at my expression. He leads me through a formal dining room that must have twenty chairs at the table, sitting on top of a rug that looks old but I suspect cost more than the station wagon when it was new.

We finally stop in a kitchen full of stainless steel appliances and sleek, shiny countertops. Lucas rustles under the counter before emerging with a first-aid kit.

It's warm in here; I take my coat off, becoming increasingly aware of how shabby I look next to all the glossiness. I lean over the kitchen counter while Lucas dabs at the dried blood under his nose with a wet paper towel, then lifts the edge of his shirt to wipe off another cut.

"So, what does your wife do?" I ask when the silence becomes too powerful.

"She inherits money, mostly," he says. "She's excellent at it. You should consider it as a career option."

"Seriously?" I ask. "That's it?"

"She was also Miss Tennessee," he says. I raise my eyebrows without meaning to. "I get that a lot," he says, waving at my expression. "I don't look like the guy who ends up with the beauty queen. Believe me, I know."

"Then how did you?" I ask.

Lucas smiles. "I just ended up with *her*, and she happens to be a beauty queen. So, look—I need to soften her to the idea that I attacked a Fenris and wrecked her car doing it. So—"

"Which car?" a female voice says. Lucas wilts in front of me; I whip my head around to the speaker.

Lucas's wife doesn't look like a beauty queen, mainly because she's pretty. Really, genuinely pretty—I'm certain of it, because she's wearing sweatpants and a T-shirt and, as best I can tell, doesn't have any makeup on. Yet she still glows, not in the disconcerting way that Mora did, but in a way that makes me simultaneously judge and adore her. She pads across the kitchen, socks on her feet, and tugs the corner of Lucas's shirt up, revealing the cut he'd just finished tending to.

"The Audi," he says, trying to hide the wound.

"And you hit a Fenris with it? In this weather? I thought they were only in this area in the summer."

"So did I," he says as she frowns and wraps her arm around him. She looks ridiculously curvy next to him, like she's drawn in circles and he's drawn in sticks.

"But you're okay," she says, and he nods against her, his face ruffling her hair. The way they talk to each other softens the glossiness of the room—makes the space feel less like a castle and more like a home.

"This is Ginny Andersen," he says, motioning to me when she pulls away. "Ginny, this is my wife, Ella."

"Pleasure to meet you, Ginny," Ella says in a practiced but kind way. There's something a little guarded about Ella— something that makes her look as if she's giving an interview, the former Miss Tennessee shining through.

"Come on," Lucas says, walking over to the kitchen table. He and Ella drop into chairs; I stay at the counter, watching. "Have a seat," he says, motioning to the one beside him. "Tell her what you told me. About the book and...I don't know. Just tell us what you know."

I move to take the chair, trying not to think about Grandma Dalia and how she never offered me one, how she tried so hard to keep me locked out, a stranger. And yet here are *actual* strangers, inviting me in....It makes me blush.

I take a deep breath and start talking. I avoid their eyes, thinking instead about Kai, trying to let words fall from my mouth the way they do when I talk to him—after all, half-truths and nerves won't help me now. So I tell them *everything*. About Grandma Dalia, about her warnings, about her fear of the snow. I tell them about Mora and look down when I tell them about Kai, how he changed overnight into a cruel stranger, how he vanished. Then I open the book, skip to the pages about the beasts, and show them the sketches of fangs and eyes and claws. Then I reassemble the magazine clippings to form Mora's face.

When I'm finished, Lucas and Ella are staring—but not with the same guarded disbelief the cop and my mother had. Lucas and Ella simply look scared—which, I realize, is what I wanted all along. If they're scared, it means I'm right to be. The wind and snow howl at the glass doors leading from the kitchen to the snow-covered deck, threatening us. Ella stares at the clippings, reaches forward, and pushes some of them closer together.

"I've never heard of a Snow Queen," Lucas tells her. "I don't even understand how she's the queen of the Fenris if she's some sort of winter…entity? I never see them even in late September, much less on the rare occasion there's snow on the ground. And if she's their queen, is she a Fenris herself?"

"Grandma Dalia always said she was queen, but I don't know if she is one. She didn't look like the ones we just saw," I say. "They look like they're wearing human costumes, sort of. But she looked…she looked normal."

"And, just to make sure I'm clear—you think this girl might be the queen of hungry, soulless werewolves, so you decided to chase her down. Do you have a death wish?" Lucas asks, then shakes his head. "Do your parents know you're doing this?"

"Wow, Lucas," Ella says, looking up, eyes widening. "High school me would have punched you for saying that. What are you, ninety?"

"Well..." Lucas says, looking down. "I've seen what they can do. *You've* seen what they can do."

"True," Ella admits, voice wavering, and a new concern grips me—what if they call the police on me? I can't go home, not now. "*But*," Ella continues, "can you imagine someone trying to persuade me to stop looking for them?" I'm about to ask why Ella was looking for Fenris when Lucas answers.

"I *did* try to persuade you to stop. In fact, I think we got in a yelling match at the opera hall."

"Then you know how the conversation with Ginny will go—wait. The opera hall?" She looks down at the collage of Mora's face, and her jaw drops. "I know her."

"What?" Lucas asks, like he doesn't believe it. He leans in and stares at the clippings.

"I know her," Ella says again, then turns and bolts from the room. It's only a few moments before she returns, moving so fast she slides into the kitchen. She slams a framed photo down on top of the cookbook.

It's a magazine page. Ella and Lucas standing side by side—her a few inches taller than him. Then a boy I don't recognize, wearing eyeliner and theater makeup, with hair so blond it's nearly white. Beside him—

"That's her," Ella says. "Right?"

"Mora," I say, nodding. "Yes. That's her."

Ella taps the face of the theater boy. "And that's Larson Davies. He was an opera singer we were supporting."

"Supporting?" I asked.

"I like to take care of people," Ella said, shrugging. "He was great, going to be huge. And then he disappeared a few winters ago, during an ice storm—with her. I didn't know her all that well. He ditched the apartment we were paying for, and we never heard from him again. Kind of figured he was a run-of-the-mill asshole, and we just missed it somehow."

"She took him," I say, my heart speeding up. "Just like Kai. Kai is a violinist."

"What is she doing, starting a boy band?" Lucas says.

"I don't know," I answer, voice a little shrill. "I just tried to follow the snowstorm, and it led me here. So I think they're somewhere in Nashville, or close to it, or maybe they've just left. I have to find them. I have to find *him*."

"Don't worry," Lucas says, and he sounds larger than his body. "I can track her. With a face like that, it'll be easy."

Ella puts a hand on my shoulder, gentle but strong. "How long has he been gone?"

"A day and a half?"

Ella can't mask the grim look that flickers over her face.

"What?" I say, looking between them. "Tell me."

I stare, waiting, needing to know. Lucas squeezes Ella's hand, and she inhales, as if she's gathering courage. Finally, she speaks.

"I didn't know about the werewolves till a few years ago. I was with my best friend walking out of this club, and then...she screamed and everything went dark. No one knew where she went. It was like she just disappeared."

"And that's why you were looking for them?" I say softly, and Ella nods.

"Well, I didn't even know they existed at the time—I was just looking for *her*. Then I thought it was a serial killer or . . . something. I don't know. I changed my major to criminology. Made missing persons my pageant platform. Millie was like a sister to me, and I kept thinking if I did all the right things, she'd somehow come back and be fine. But...nothing worked. I heard about this guy, this guy who could follow any trail. Who could track anything. So I hired him to find Millie. And then I ended up marrying him." She laughs a little.

"Did Lucas find her?" I ask, looking at him.

"He did," Ella says. "Or at least, what was left of her."

CHAPTER NINE

✦

I ask to sleep on Lucas and Ella's couch; they
look at me as if I've lost my mind and put me up in a guest
room, one with a mattress I sink into and real oil paintings
on the walls. I don't want to fall asleep, to be honest, because
I'm afraid I'll wake up and discover I'm just in the backseat
of the station wagon, snowed in at the rest area. The next
morning, I make the bed, straighten the pillow, and wipe
down the bathroom mirror. No stranger has ever been so
nice to me, and I don't want them to regret it.

"How did you sleep?" Ella asks when I walk downstairs.
She's sipping coffee at the kitchen table and looks astound-
ingly *awake*. It makes me forget that I'm not much of a
morning person.

"Excellent," I say. "Better than I have in ages, honestly."

"You can try a different room tonight, if you want," she

says offhandedly, reaching for the carton of cream. She pours so much into the coffee that it's a caramel color. "I think the guest room you were in has the best mattress, but from the one on the second floor you can see for miles. Or, well, you'd be able to if it weren't for the snow and fog and general misery."

"Okay. I mean . . . if it's no trouble. Though I really should head out today," I say. "Not that I don't appreciate it—"

"Relax," Ella says, laughing a little at me. "It's just a place to sleep."

"Yeah, but you hardly know me," I say, shaking my head. I finally sit across from her at the table. "You don't have to be so nice to me."

"I'm going for Miss Congeniality," Ella jokes, but then adds, "Besides, the Fenris attacked you once when you were sleeping in your car. Think I'd let that happen again, when I've got a home full of queen-size mattresses?"

I blush a little and mumble thanks as Lucas walks past the doorway. He's in the adjacent room, walking back and forth in front of the studded leather couches. I lean in to listen close—he's asking questions, dialing, redialing, asking others. Things like, "My sister is supposed to swing by today—superblond hair, blue eyes. Have you seen her?" or "My drunk friend forgot where he left my car before the storm. It's a silver Lexus; is there one in your parking lot?" He looks like he's itching, a dog locked in a pen.

Ella sighs and explains he's been like this all morning—there's too much snow to go out and look for Mora himself.

The station wagon has no hope of making it out of the drive, and neither do any of Lucas and Ella's cars—though he tries each and every one. When the pink Hummer ("It was an impulse buy, but now it's just embarrassing to drive," according to Ella) stalls out at the bottom of the hill, Lucas gives up.

"I can find her," he tells me when he emerges from his den of investigation at one in the afternoon. "I can find anyone. She's playing it right, though—she's taking the same route back that she took coming down, following her own tracks. It makes it hard to know if she's still here or already gone. Raccoons do it, too, when a dog is after them—"

"Mora's acting like a raccoon?" I ask doubtfully.

"Don't knock nature," Lucas says. "If there's one thing it's good at, it's surviving. But I'll find her. I just need to get out of this house...."

Ella looks up from a tablet—apparently, she gets dozens of newspapers delivered daily and reads each and every one. With the snow preventing delivery, she's resorted to various websites and seems to be finding the entire process somewhat vulgar. "How am I supposed to stare at this thing to read the articles? It hurts my eyes. But Lucas—all this aside, we have to figure out what to do about food."

"There's no food?" I ask, remembering a fairly large assortment of cereal in the kitchen this morning.

"There's food," Ella says, "but Becky can't get here with the storm."

"She makes dinner," Lucas says a little awkwardly.

"You have a woman who comes every day just to make you dinner?" I ask.

"I guess we could eat cereal for the third time," Ella says, sounding sad. "Although after grad school I swore I'd never eat it for dinner again."

"Can I...see what you have?" I ask, trying to squash the bolt of laughter growing within me at Ella's helpless expression. She nods, and we walk to the kitchen. The cereal is still on the counter, and our bowls from breakfast and lunch are still in the sink. Ella wrinkles her nose at them, then opens the door to the pantry.

I'm pretty sure the Reynolds' pantry is as large as my entire kitchen in Atlanta. There's a glass pendant light hanging over a butcher-block table, and everything has its own separate, defined spot on the wire shelves. There's flour— wheat, pastry, self-rising, all-purpose—and rows upon rows of tiny glass jars full of different-colored crystals; it takes a moment before I realize they're salts from all over the world.

"We don't have any bread," Lucas says. "Ella doesn't eat anything with preservatives."

"Neither should you," Ella says. "Don't think I don't see the MoonPie wrappers on the Audi's floorboards."

Lucas shrugs, smiles, and doesn't look the least bit apologetic.

"Okay," I say, brushing past them. I open the refrigerator and find it's more of the same—lots of ingredients, but nothing prepackaged or precooked. "Give me an hour?"

"Oh, you shouldn't have to cook! You're our guest," Ella

97

says, a flash of the pageant queen emerging in her voice as she steps out of the pantry.

"Lucas ran over a werewolf to save me," I say. "We'll call it even."

Lucas and Ella insist on helping. Lucas seems to have a clue, as if he's at least seen someone knead dough before. Ella watches the entire thing like it's a cooking show, sliding ingredients and utensils across the counter to me when I ask for them. She looks mildly concerned when she sees me cutting butter into chunks, as if she's calculating the fat content of the dish. It's something Kai and I would have made fun of—he always thought it was hilarious when seven cheerleaders opted to split a single candy bar. But because the look on Ella's face is so endearing—and because she's so quick at converting the metric measuring utensils to standard and back again—it's hard to judge her.

I make what I'm good at—breakfast. Scrambled eggs and bacon don't require recipes, but for the biscuits, I use a recipe from Grandma Dalia's cookbook. The three of us carry the serving dishes to the kitchen table, where Lucas has already set up plates. The utensils are all in the right place, lined up perfectly, and there are even cloth napkins. Everything is loud, and the kitchen smells like bacon and is messy with flour and used bowls, and it feels...

It feels like home in the way that I thought only Kai could. I'm not sure how—it's been less than a day—but there's something around my heart that feels relieved, comforted, happy in a way that has nothing to do with the dozens of bedrooms or expensive paintings. It makes me smile; how can I smile when Kai is missing? But I can't stop.

"Maybe we should ask Becky if we can help her cook sometimes, too," Ella says, rubbing her hands together eagerly. "So we can learn things. Other than the microwave, I mean."

"It's not like you let me use the microwave anyway," Lucas says, half joking.

"That's because he wants to make Hot Pockets," Ella says, frowning. "Day and night. They're awful."

"You've never had one," Lucas points out.

"They smell like wax."

"Did neither of you ever cook at home, before you got married?" I ask.

Ella shrugs and reaches for the plate with the biscuits. "Not really. We had a cook there, too."

Lucas looks bemused. "I have eight brothers and sisters back in Ellison. We weren't allowed anywhere near the kitchen when our mom was making dinner—she'd chase us out with a spatula. And when I moved out, I pretty much exclusively ate Chinese takeout. Lots and lots of Chinese takeout. And Hot Pockets."

"Gross," Ella mutters.

"Eight?" I ask, probably too excited to hear about Lucas's family. The idea of growing up surrounded by sisters and brothers delights me.

He nods. "Eight. Three sisters, five brothers. We lived in this tiny house for ages, and then my dad implemented this

rule—if you want your own bedroom, you have to build it."
My eyes widen; Lucas laughs at the expression, then continues. "My dad's a woodsman. His dad was a woodsman. His dad's dad was a woodsman. Most of my brothers are woodsmen, even. So building a room isn't that crazy."

"Did you build one for yourself?" I ask.

Lucas hesitates. "As it turns out, I'm a pretty crappy woodsman. I didn't really fit in with my brothers, and my sisters went to boarding school early on. My brothers were big on fighting Fenris, actually. It was like this weird, twisted game they played, hunting them down, trapping them, killing them. I wasn't exactly cut out for it, but I could track them. I could track them anywhere, through any weather. It was the only thing that made me fit in." He says this with a smile, but there's a cool tone to his voice.

"I think it's pretty impressive," I say.

"Why? I haven't tracked anything for you just yet. Wait till I do. Then be impressed," Lucas says, grinning again. "Speaking of Fenris—all that talk of the beasts from this Grandma Dalia, and you never actually saw one till yesterday?"

"Not really—I mean, I'd never seen one like *that*," I say slowly, pausing to take a bite of bacon. "But when I was little, there was a man at the grocery store. There was something about his eyes that was wrong, and Grandma Dalia pulled me away from him."

"How old?" Lucas asks.

"Seven. Maybe eight."

Lucas tsks, shaking his head. "Must have been hungry. That's young." He pauses and leans back in his chair. "What I can't work out, though, to be honest, is how an old woman with a cookbook knows about this Snow Queen, yet I've never heard of her."

"Well, you heard *of* her, when she was dating Larson. You just didn't know she was some sort of evil ice witch," Ella points out.

"Fair point," Lucas says. They look to me.

I shrug. "I don't know. Grandma Dalia hated me—she never told me how she knew about any of this stuff. We hardly ever spoke, and when we did I was usually getting snapped at. It was like that from the moment we met."

"Grandparents are tricky," Ella says. "Maybe worse than parents. Though Lucas's father loathes me."

"My father has Alzheimer's. He doesn't even know who you are," Lucas says, waving a biscuit at her.

"He thought I was a hooker."

"He can't see well, and you were wearing that dress thing!"

"He offered me a hundred dollars to—"

"Stop!" Lucas says, slamming his hands over his ears, and I laugh with them. Ella leans over and kisses Lucas on the cheek as their laughter dies down. I hope she appreciates what it is to have him here, to kiss him whenever she wants. *She does. I know she does—I can see it in her eyes.* I inhale. *Kai. Focus. Figure out how to find Kai. Figure out how to find Mora.*

After a few moments, I look at my hands and ask, "What was Mora like, when she was with your opera singer?"

"Larson?" Ella says, frowning at the subject change. "She was pretty. Confident—but fake confidence. I know it when I see it; it's practically an airborne illness at pageants. You smile, show lots of teeth, touch people on the arm or shoulder and laugh loud and answer everything in complete sentences, but it's not real. It's just a pretty package to hide whatever you're really all about. Mora was oozing with that sort of confidence. Which is especially strange now—I mean, she can control the weather, but she's fake confident? Does that cookbook have anything else in it that might explain things?"

I shrug. "I've looked through it before, but it's hard to read and hard to tell what's real." I rise, retrieve the book, and set it down in the middle of the table. Lucas and I open it and flip through a few pages, but it doesn't take them long to see what I mean.

"There's a section on luck charms in here," Ella says, looking doubtful.

"Are luck charms any crazier than werewolves?" Lucas says, but he shakes his head and turns the page. "This is right," he says, tapping some text. "That wearing red attracts monsters. The wolves love it."

Ella flips to the last page of the book and, after reading a few inspirational quotes aloud, looks at the paper on the back cover. Her eyebrows shoot up as she traces the paper with her finger.

"How long has she had this?" Ella asks.

I shake my head. "As long as I can remember. Probably before Kai was born. Why?"

"Because," Ella says, "this book looks like it's, what, fifties or so? But this type of paper, all earth tones and stuff, is newer. Seventies, I think. Once my family bought a mountain house near Vail, and the kitchen wallpaper looked like this."

"So she repapered it?" Lucas asks.

"No," Ella says, wiping her butter knife with a napkin. She looks up at me. "Can I try something?"

"Um, sure," I say, hesitant.

Ella slides the knife between the paper and the back cover. "She didn't repaper the front or the pages or anything. Why just this interior?" I hear the glue giving as Ella seesaws the knife around the edges. When she's made her way around, she sets the knife down and slowly, carefully peels the paper back.

"Yes!" Ella says, grinning. She tugs something and finally removes a photograph, hidden between the paper and back cover. She lays it down on the counter; the three of us hunch over to study it. It's Grandma Dalia—a very, very young Grandma Dalia, maybe ten or eleven years old—standing next to a boy with bright red hair. His clothing makes him look poor, next to her, but their arms are wrapped around each other in a sweet way. She leans her hip into him, and he's grinning so widely that his eyes are little lines. I look over to his eyes, trying to discern the color, but they're hidden behind long lashes—

"I know who he is," I realize. "I've seen him before. He's Mora's work friend."

"Work friend?" Ella asks.

"Or something. I don't know—he was at Grandma Dalia's funeral with Mora. I remember. It was him and another guy. When this one," I tap the boy's face with my fingernail, "saw the photo of Grandma Dalia on her wedding day, he looked at Mora, and then she held his hand."

"What happened then?"

"Nothing," I say, shaking my head. "I was glad to see it, actually. I thought maybe it meant she was with him and that she wasn't interested in Kai."

"She took him—clearly—and then brought him back to go to Dalia's funeral," Ella says.

"She feels bad?" Lucas suggests.

"No," Ella says, shaking her head. "It's not guilt." She presses the paper back against the book cover absently, then speaks again. "Maybe I'm wrong. Maybe she's not faking confidence. Taking the boy she kidnapped back where he might be recognized? It's like a show of power. Like she's proving something to someone."

"No, wait," I say, shaking my head. "The boy at the funeral was maybe a few years older than me at the most. If it's the same boy, he should be Grandma Dalia's age. Right?"

Ella and I look to Lucas, who sighs and sits back. He rubs his mouth with his hand, and I can tell there's something he doesn't want to say. "She's done something," he says, finally. "The wolves—they don't age once they transform. Maybe whatever she's done to this boy—and Larson Davies, and maybe Kai—works the same way."

Something in my chest plummets.

I was afraid she'd kill him, afraid she'd hurt him, afraid she'd abandon him.

It never occurred to me she'd keep him.

CHAPTER TEN

Lucas is going to find Mora and Kai—*if* they're still in town. The snow has melted a little, making the roads somewhat passable, but there's still a snowdrift blocking the Reynoldses' garage; Lucas has to take the pink Hummer that he abandoned at the bottom of the hill a few days before. I watch him drive away, grimacing at the icicles dripping off the front porch—does the weather change mean the Snow Queen has moved on?

"You have to trust him. This is what he does, remember? Besides, if there are Fenris out there, you and I are just going to attract their attention," Ella says as we walk back to the living room and plop down on the leather sofas—Lucas insisted on going alone.

"They never attack men?" I ask. I remember Grandma Dalia's warnings about the beasts—was Kai only ever in danger from the Snow Queen herself?

"The Fenris don't, but it looks like Mora has that covered anyhow," Ella says as she flips another page of a thick book that appears to be written in Italian. I fidget for a few moments, looking at the clock. Ella lifts her eyebrows at me and smiles.

"He's just *finding* them. Then he'll come back and get us and you can go to work on persuading Kai to stay away from the Snow Queen, while I pummel her to find out where she took our opera singer. You have no idea how much money we poured into that kid," she says.

I nod. "I was thinking last night ... Mora told me and Kai once that she used to be wealthy, but that she was trapped. And something about how she wasn't allowed to dance."

"Huh," Ella says. "So she wasn't always the Snow Queen, then."

"No," I say, and shake my head. "And I'm thinking that's why she takes certain boys. Because now that she has this power, now that she's a queen—"

"She's using it to own the things she's always wanted. Artists. Bohemians. Rebels. The anti-tie crowd," Ella says, nodding. "Like Larson."

"Like Kai."

"I wonder what the other boy did—the redheaded one," Ella says.

"I wonder how many boys there are," I answer. I open the cookbook and flip through a few of the pages I haven't studied closely yet. The pages grow more confusing as the book goes on—the recipes toward the back are written in

107

shorthand so punctuated I can't fathom what they mean, and one page contains a weird shape outlined in pencil, something resembling a curled-up dog. There's text near it, but it's too smudged to read.

Read. I'm sitting here reading, while Kai is with her. While she's doing whatever it is she does to him, however she does it. Making him a collectible, all to prove something to the world, all because of some terrible past. Did she become the Snow Queen because of her past, or in spite of it? I look at Ella again. I trust her—I trust her and Lucas more than anyone other than Kai, even though I hardly know them, yet just sitting here while Lucas is out is making my head spin.

"What about you?" Ella interrupts my thoughts.

"Hm?"

"Kai plays violin. Larson sings. Lucas tracks things. The redheaded boy did something. What do you do?"

"I..." I trail off. I try to stop it, but my stock response, the same one I gave Mora, falls from my mouth, clunky and awkward. "I don't really do anything."

"Don't do anything," Ella asks, drumming her fingers on the sofa, "or don't do anything yet?"

I smile. "Is there a difference?"

"Huge difference," she says. "People who don't do anything annoy me. People who don't do anything *yet* excite me, because they can potentially do everything."

"Kai always said I need to find something," I admit, letting the idea that I can do everything sink in and rattle me pleasantly. "I think it bothered him that he knew he was a violinist, and I didn't know what I was. He said I should be something."

"You will," she says. "When you're ready. Don't let anyone rush you. Unless you're living in your parents' basement at thirty. Because then I'll personally show up and rush you. Don't think you can hide down there. Lucas can track anyone anywhere."

I laugh. "Don't you ever go with him, when he's tracking? Don't you want to?"

She shakes her head. "He's good at what he does. I'm good at what I do. But that doesn't mean that I'm good to have along when tracking. Or that he's good to have along when meeting the governor, because my god, he's not. Nor does he like wearing a tux, so it works out."

I'm not entirely sure if that's what I was asking. Kai and I have always done everything together, so I assumed all couples in love did so. Not that we *had* to, exactly, but we wanted to, before Mora showed up. I grimace, thinking about what Kai said to me on the roof, words that make my heart twist uncomfortably.

"What would you be without me, Ginny?"
"Nothing."

I know it was just Mora, that he didn't mean it, but the words still sting. We did everything together, because we were in love—but maybe also because I'm nothing without him. I'm just a girl, not a witch or a queen or a monster.

But then, once upon a time, Mora was just a girl, too. She told Kai that she wasn't all that different from him, but really, she's not all that different from *me*. At least, she didn't start out that way. She's just already figured out what she does— she steals boys. But right now, I can do everything. If Mora can steal boys, I can bring them back.

So why am I just sitting on the couch, like I'm nothing?

"Ella," I say, rising. "We have to go look for them ourselves. Or at least follow Lucas."

She frowns. "He'll call us—"

"I know, but . . . I can't sit here. I have to go. I trust Lucas, but . . . knowing he's out there and I'm here is driving me crazy."

Ella doesn't look happy as she puts down her book. "We can't get in the way."

"We won't. I just have to—"

"I know. Trust me. I've been there." She shakes her head and laughs a little. "You remind me of me, and I'm not entirely sure that's a compliment."

"I'll take it as one anyway," I say, smiling.

She nods, rising. "Come on. We should take your car— there's a better chance of Lucas recognizing one of ours."

I wonder if Ella wishes she hadn't said that when she climbs into the station wagon. It takes a few moments for the engine to get going, during which time we beat the caked-on ice and snow off the windshield. It breaks apart in big chunks, as if it's made of ceramic instead of water. The cold is, however, notably different today. It touches my skin but fails to kiss my bones, fails to make me feel I'll never, ever be warm again.

I wonder if it means she's already left.

"Does the engine always sound like that?" Ella asks, looking at me warily. "It sounds like one of your belts is bad." I back up; something under the hood knocks. "And it needs an oil change. How long has the back window been broken?"

"Since a Fenris smashed it. Do you want to take one of yours?" I ask, exasperated.

"No..." Ella says, though I see her look a little wistfully at the garage that, if memory serves, holds a gold convertible.

Ella guides me down the road, toward town; we pass someone riding on a tractor, and I'm a little envious of how well his tires seem to be gripping the road. I have to give myself a few dozen yards to brake, and we end up almost sliding into a ditch twice. Something about it is less scary than driving alone, like when I first set out—maybe it's Ella, or the end of that oppressive cold. Or maybe it's the simple fact that even when you slide off the road here, the worst thing that can happen is you end up in a cow pasture. It's an hour before we reach Nashville proper; Ella instructs me to pull over at an open McDonald's.

"There's no way Lucas would pass this without eating, not after three days snowed in without red meat," she says, jumping from the car. She wobbles on the ice for a moment and runs inside, and I see her talking to the cashier. Ella returns and points to the left. "The cashier says he went that way. Good thing Lucas took the world's most conspicuous car."

"Isn't that going to make it hard for him to follow Mora and Kai, though?"

111

"Only if they suspect Barbie is hunting them down," Ella says, rolling her eyes. "Seriously, Ginny, what was I thinking? It even has pink washer fluid. I don't know. It was a weird phase."

We ease along through town; it feels a little like the apocalypse happened while we slept. There are few people in the streets, and most are bundled up so much that we can't see their genders, much less their faces. We pass little shops that are still closed because of the storm and an enormous park crowned with a replica of the Parthenon—it's the liveliest place we've seen so far, dotted with kids building snowmen on the lawn.

A few more blocks, back to mostly desolate streets— "There!" Ella yells, so sharp that I almost slam on the brakes and send us skidding into a Starbucks. I whip my head around to see a flash of pink at the end of a cross street. I struggle to turn the car around, tossing snow up behind me, and hurry forward. "Slow down, slow down," Ella says. "He'll be pissed if he knows we're tracking him tracking them."

"Do you think he's close?" I ask, and there's an edge to my voice that surprises me, a hardness that feels stronger than the fear bubbling up in my stomach.

"I don't know—stop here, he's parking," she says, pointing. The pink Hummer slows to a stop in an empty public lot. Lucas jumps out, and for a moment, I think he's seen us. But no, not yet. He goes into a restaurant, the only one open on this street. Ella and I are perfectly silent as we wait....He emerges but leaves the Hummer, opting to walk down the street.

"Do I follow him?" I ask, though I'm already putting the car in drive.

"Maybe we should walk," Ella answers. "I think he'll notice the car. This place is like a desert."

I step out into the snow, gritting my teeth in case it's somehow become the bone-crumbling, painful type of cold again while we were in the car. But no, it's...it's just snow. Ella and I trudge along silently. Every now and then we pass an open restaurant, and the patrons stare at us, as if we're brave for walking in the weather.

We pause under a covered bus stop, and I notice it's snowing again—just a little, flurries at the most. Ella narrows her eyes at the street. Lucas is at the far end, walking slowly, with his hands in his pockets. He pauses for a moment, though he doesn't turn or look around, and then changes directions suddenly, cutting between buildings. Ella and I step out of the bus stop—

Wind, sharp wind—wind I know. Wind I felt on the roof when it first started to snow three days ago, when Kai and I ran for the door. Wind that I felt as Grandma Dalia lay dying a few floors below. Ella meets my eyes—this is different from a normal cold. It's oddly helpful to know I'm not the only one who feels the hate, the ice, the darkness in each gust. She shivers and, without speaking, we hurry forward.

It's nearly impossible to run, and as we move the wind grows stronger. The snow turns sharp, little needles from the sky, and we're forced to bow our heads to it. We find the alley

Lucas vanished into, abandoning the desire to stay out of his sight. It wouldn't matter, though; he's gone. The alley is empty, the lids of trash cans being blown off and tossed around as the storm picks up. The snow thickens, and I glance back—we're far from the car now, and most of the businesses we passed are either closed for the day or boarded up permanently.

Ella charges forward, and I see something in her eyes— panic. She runs, sliding, down the alley to the next cross street. I follow, my eyes darting to the roofs, the windows, behind the Dumpsters, certain that I'll see Kai or . . .

"Lucas!" Ella shrieks, but it's almost immediately lost in the air. I look up, but everything is white, as if our world is shrinking down to the size of an alley. She slides into the next cross street and stops so short I almost crash into her. I arrange my limbs, then follow her gaze to the storefront of an out-of-business deli.

It's Lucas. His hair is slicked back by the wind, his eyes narrow and his back pressed against the plywood covering the deli's door. And in the middle of the street, taking slow, deliberate steps, is a dark gray wolf.

It stares at him, ears pricked forward—there's something less monster-like, more wolflike about it than the things I saw at the rest stop, and yet for that it's all the more terrifying. The snow swirls around us as the wolf gets closer, closer— and I see someone is standing behind it.

It's Mora.

There's another wolf beside her, this one black, a total

contrast to the way Mora herself looks. She's wearing a sleek gown, silk and cornflower blue—I notice not only because she's so beautiful, but because it doesn't have sleeves; her skin, only a few shades pinker than the snow, is exposed. Yet Mora doesn't seem fazed by the cold; her hair spirals in the wind, her eyes are hard like jewels, and for the first time, I'm completely, undeniably certain that Grandma Dalia got it right. That Mora is the Snow Queen.

A shot—a gunshot. I whirl around and see Ella holding a pink handgun in both hands, her head tilted to the side to aim. She's not shaking; she's angry. Mora spins to face us. Her face darkens when she sees me, and the wind grows even stronger as her mouth twists into a cruel sort of smile. I'm not sure what Ella was aiming at—one of the wolves or Mora?—but she missed, and a heavy stillness sweeps across all of us, a stall before chaos.

Ella fires again.

Everything happens at once. The gray wolf, the one nearest to Lucas, lifts up on its back legs and falls—Ella hit it. Mora roars, her fingers tightening into icy fists. Lucas is running; Ella is aiming at the black wolf, and someone new, someone dark is stumbling toward Mora. I don't need to see his eyes to recognize the newcomer's posture, the way he carries his hands, the way his head bows into the wind. I whisper his name. Kai's chin lifts, and I see a sparkle of gold underneath his hooded sweatshirt as his eyes find mine.

Everything stops—at least, for me. Because for a moment, a small moment, he's just Kai, and I'm just Ginny, and we're in love forever. I know it with the kind of certainty that I know who my mother is, or where I live. I extend my hand toward him, certain love will break the spell, will draw him toward me.

He jolts backward. Mora—she's beside him and has wrapped her fingers around his wrist. She's yanking him away from me as if he's a child, while the world grows colder. I lunge forward, but the wind is too strong—all I can do is bend over and march through the gale. I yell his name this time, scream it. My eyes are hot and my lungs feel as if they're cracking with each breath, but he's here, he's alive, she—

The wind stops.

I fall forward, looking up just in time to see a silver car ease away down the street. Lucas is hacking, pounding against his chest as if he can't breathe; Ella runs to him and falls into the snow beside him. I drop to my knees and bury my face in my gloved hands. He was here.

He was here, and I wasn't strong enough to stop her.

"Ginny," Ella says. I don't look up. "Ginny," Ella says, this time louder. "Ginny, go to the car and go back to our house. You know the way?"

"Yes, why—" I inhale sharply, stomach twisting. The gray wolf that Ella shot is dead, lying in the snow among an ever-growing plume of blood. But he's also not a wolf anymore.

He's a man.

CHAPTER ELEVEN

Kai and I loved this book that we read in third grade, about a boy who befriended an Indian. One part in particular delighted us—when they became blood brothers. They cut themselves and touched the open wounds together so that their blood mingled, bonding them forever.

Of course, the idea of blood brothers was a lot more exciting before we were sitting in my bedroom, a pocketknife between us, looking equally green.

"Maybe you should cut my finger," I said, "and I'll cut yours."

"I'm not sticking you with a knife!"

"How is it any different from me sticking myself with a knife?" I asked.

Kai didn't answer but shifted uncomfortably. He looked from me to the knife and back again, then finally reached down and picked it up. "Maybe we shouldn't do our palms," he said. "Maybe something less...painful."

"Like what?"

"Maybe..." He twisted his palm around, finally pointing to the soft spot on the back side of his hand between his thumb and forefinger. "What about there?"

I shrugged. "Okay. Wherever."

Kai glared at me, held his breath, and then pushed the knife blade against his skin.

Six hours later, we finally left the emergency room. Kai had to get eight stitches, and I never got the chance to cut myself and complete the ceremony, since I was too busy screaming for Grandma Dalia. She blamed me, of course, and made Kai pudding for dinner.

The cut healed and turned into a thick scar with bumps along either side from the stitches. "All that," Kai said, regarding it a few weeks later in the rose garden, "and we didn't even finish the ceremony."

"I should have cut myself," I said, disappointed. "Before you went to the hospital."

"No. Then we'd both have dumb scars," he said, shrugging. But then his eyes met mine and sparkled, and I could tell we had the same idea.

Our blood never mingled, exactly, and we didn't get to say "now we're blood brothers for life" like the characters in the book. But I did drag a knife along my hand, cutting just enough to give me a scar that matched his—save the stitch marks. It hurt; when I cried, Kai ran home and got me a pudding cup.

"I'm so stupid," I said when he got back. "Look." I grabbed his hand and pulled it toward me—I'd cut my left hand; his scar was on his right. "They don't match."

"No," he said quickly. "See?" He took my left hand with his right, interlacing our fingers. "They match perfectly."

Kai was right—the line from his scar matched up to my cut, like a string wrapped around our hands, tying us together for life.

I feel numb, sitting in the house alone, staring at the flames in the fireplace. I'm not sure what weighs me down more—the fact that Kai got away, or seeing a man, bleeding, naked, and innocent-looking, where a monster had been.

And not just any man. I recognized him, his red hair, his cheekbones. He's the one from Grandma Dalia's photo, the one who was at her funeral. *I'm so sorry, Grandma Dalia*, I think over and over, as if she'll hear me, forgive me. I didn't even know his name. Losing him changed Grandma Dalia forever, made her afraid forever, and I don't even know his name. Did she hide his picture in the back of the book because she wanted to forget him, or because the image was just another reminder that she'd never be able to?

Did she love him? Did she know he became a . . .

I close my eyes. *Don't think it. Don't think it.*

I lie down on the couch to settle my churning stomach, though the position does little to stop the nausea or the weight of the afternoon from replaying in my head for hours. Could I have done more? I saw him. Kai saw me; he was right

119

there. Am I angrier at him, or myself? Does one of us not love the other enough to overcome Mora's spell?

It starts to rain—thick, fat drops that make the world feel even more miserable. I love Kai enough. I always thought he loved me enough. Am I wrong? The prospect is crushing, the weight of years and dreams bearing down on me until I feel I'll crumble. What if I was wrong all along? Maybe he doesn't love me, not the way I love him. Not completely.

And yet here I am, looking for him, wanting him, needing him.

I jump when I hear the door open and realize it's nearly eight o'clock—my jeans are still soaked from snow, and I haven't even taken my shoes off. Ella and Lucas walk in, looking tired. Her hair is wet from the storm, and she's shivering. And Lucas...Lucas is furious.

"You're all right?" he asks me, voice gentler than the lines on his face. I nod, and he continues. "Ella's lawyers came in. It was self-defense; they're not charging her. Naked in this snow, they figure he was some sort of psychopath."

"But he wasn't. He was...what was he, exactly?" I ask.

Lucas stops and drops his coat on an end table. It slides off and onto the floor. "I don't know. It's not normally like that." He pauses and watches as Ella slowly crosses the room, lowering herself into a chair as if she's in some sort of daze. He swallows hard and shakes his head. "You remember the one I hit with the car? They usually just turn into shadows, and...they're gone."

"Not this one," Ella says thickly. "Apparently."

"It wasn't your fault," I say, rising and crossing the room. I sit on the coffee table across from her chair. "Ella, he would have killed—"

"I know," Ella says, smiling weakly. "Pageant training— I'm collected under pressure." She laughs a little, but it dies in seconds. "I just wasn't prepared to see a body. I'm not sorry, and I don't feel guilty, exactly—he would have killed Lucas, then come for you. I just...I just wasn't prepared. That's all." She reaches forward and takes my hand in hers. I almost wince, her fingers are so cold. "Don't worry," she says. "We didn't tell the cops about you. So...no one's going to come and take you back to Atlanta. You're safe here."

I exhale. I hadn't really thought of that—a foolish oversight, I now realize—and I'm relieved to hear Ella and Lucas did. "Thank you," I say. "That sounds stupid, it's not enough—"

"It's plenty," Ella says gently. "Besides, if you're as much like me as I think, you'd just leave again looking for answers."

"Though I'm beginning to think there *are* no answers, to be honest," Lucas says. He sits on the coffee table beside me and props his elbows on his knees. "Whatever her guards are, they're not Fenris—and so I don't think she's one, either."

"So what is she, then?" I ask.

Lucas shrugs. "Scared. She could have killed me, but I got the impression she was afraid to do so. As if she didn't want to cause a scene—she just wanted to take your boy and go...." Lucas drifts off, as if he doesn't want to say something aloud. I keep my eyes on him, hard. He inhales. "The black wolf. I saw him before he changed. It's Larson Davies."

121

Ella's eyes jump up, horror etched across her face. She shakes her head and grabs the arms of the chair as if they'll hold her to the earth. "Are you sure?"

"Positive," Lucas says, then turns to me. "And the other was the boy from the photo. Which means..."

I finally allow myself not only to think it, but to say it aloud. "She's turning boys into wolves. She'll turn Kai into a wolf."

It doesn't sound like my voice—it can't be my voice. I wouldn't say something like that, because it couldn't be true. It couldn't possibly be true.

"She hasn't changed him yet, or she'd have used him today. *And* this means she's not killing them," Lucas says encouragingly, though I don't believe the confidence in his voice.

"But...if she's not a Fenris, what is she?" I ask, voice dull. It's taking every fiber of my being to not sink into the floor, weighed down with the idea of Kai becoming...

Don't think about it. Not right now.

"Maybe she's a witch," Ella suggests.

"I don't know about witches," Lucas answers, as if the idea might be a little childish.

"She magically controls the weather. She turns boys into wolves and back again. She keeps them from aging for decades—that red-haired boy should have been ancient. What do you call that?" Ella asks him.

"Fucked up."

Ella half laughs, with an expression that looks strained. Lucas rises, sits on the arm of the chair, and pulls her head to his chest. I see him shiver against her wet hair, but he doesn't move away; he lowers his chin and kisses the top of her head. After a long silence, Ella speaks.

"It doesn't matter what she is. They're gone. He's gone." I look at her, alarmed—not so much at the brutality, but that the words are coming from Ella's mouth. Romantic, hopeful Ella. Even Lucas looks surprised as she continues. "I'm not saying you should just give up, Ginny. But I looked for my best friend for years. I devoted my life to it. It changed me, it made me hard, it made me bitter. Lucas came along and helped me make sense of myself again, but... after all that, I still didn't get her back."

"But that's because she was dead."

"Exactly. You want to know what Lucas found of Millie? An elbow. That's it. Monsters don't give back the things they take, Ginny," she says. "Kai went with her—maybe it's what he wanted."

"That's not like him—"

"I know, I know," Ella says, shaking her head as if she's disappointing even herself. "I'm just saying, Ginny, you can't let the monsters take you, too." There are tears in the corners of her eyes, and I see she's gripping Lucas's hand tightly. I think about the gun, the strength on her face when she shot at the wolf, the fury. How impressive it seemed—and how fleeting. Is that how she lived during the years before she found Lucas? Angry and strong, powerful yet broken?

I'm not sure I can do that.

"Maybe," I whisper, but as the words leave my lips I think

of Kai. Old Kai, Kai who kissed me on the rooftop, Kai who sang songs with me across the courtyard through our open windows. Kai who I love. Kai who I want back.

Kai who walked away from me.

My chest aches as if someone is pressing down on it.

"Come on, Ginny," Ella says, sniffling as she stands up.

"Where are we going?" I ask.

"Your jeans are still soaked. They'll take forever to dry. I can lend you something in the meantime."

"I brought other clothes," I say, though it occurs to me that the single change of clothes in my bag is dirty. Based on her reaction to me cooking, I shudder to think of how Ella would respond to me using their washing machine.

"Please," she says, voice rocky. "I need a distraction. You need a distraction. And shopping is a distraction."

"We're shopping?"

"Please."

Ella now looks broken, so I nod. We walk upstairs, through the master bedroom, and into Ella's closet—it's enormous, as expected, with track lighting and cedar shelves. She opens up a closet and pulls a few articles of clothing out, laying them over my hands. I can practically see the stress rolling off her, the memory of the man in the snow temporarily masked.

"Okay. Okay," she says, swallowing hard as if this is a task that requires a lot of focus—and to be honest, it probably does take a degree of concentration to think about dresses instead of shooting a werewolf. "I've been meaning to get rid of things. You're about my size—maybe a little shorter, but you can always get it hemmed," Ella mumbles, yanking a top off a hanger and studying it.

I frown. "Are you giving me these?" I ask. Ella nods. "Wait, no. I mean...where would I even go in these?" I ask, though I confess, I badly want to try on the lavender dress she's holding up against herself.

"Wherever you want," Ella says. "Do you go to concerts? Or prom, maybe...though prom at my high school sucked. Was it decent at yours?" I look down. I wouldn't know if prom sucks; Kai and I never went to dances, opting to go bowling or to the movies instead....

"You know," Ella says, studying me, "you can stay here till the snow clears. Or a little longer, if you need. Lucas keeps watch; he knows when they're in the area."

I open my mouth to argue, but the words refuse to leave my throat. Kai walked away; Kai might not love me enough after all. But Ella and Lucas? They want me. They have everything I wanted with Kai. I lost one family when Kai left; how stupid would I be to leave another?

Ella walks across the closet to shelves that contain more shoes than I've seen outside a department store. They're all sorts of colors, with pearls and gems and strange fabrics and sky-high heels.

"These you definitely shouldn't give me. I don't wear heels," I warn her.

"Then you should learn," Ella says, dropping a pair of cherry leather heels into my arms. "I'll teach you."

Ella's back to dresses, dropping a flowery one over my

arms. The flowers are roses, big and red, so similar to the ones on the rooftop garden back home that I'd believe Ella if she told me the fabric was modeled after them. I stare at them and ignore Ella bemoaning how many sundresses she owns. I now have to try very hard to remember the feeling of Kai kissing me, of being in his arms. To remember the feeling of certainty, that we belonged to each other.

"Ginny?" Ella asks, and I raise my eyes to her—when did I start crying? "Oh, Ginny," Ella says, shoving the clothes out of my hands and pulling me close. I haven't been hugged this tightly in ages, and it makes me choke on my tears, inhaling Ella's perfume in big gulps.

"Sorry," I say. "It's just the roses on that dress, they reminded me—"

"We'll trash it. I'll burn it. Or both—we can cut it up, and we've got five fireplaces and a barbecue out back—we'll burn a piece in each one just for good measure."

She's trying to help, so I just nod, agree. But as we collect the clothing she's giving to me, as I make my way to my bedroom, all I can think about is the fact that the dress isn't the problem. That even when it's gone, the roses in my head will remain.

CHAPTER TWELVE

I barely sleep, plagued by a fight for my heart.
Staying with Lucas and Ella, being happy, being warm, being home. Or going after Kai, the boy who broke my heart. The boy who walked away into the cold. The boy who not only may never want me again, but might get me killed.

The boy who I love.

The roses in my head aren't going anywhere—the love I have for Kai isn't going anywhere, no matter what he's done, no matter if he still wants me or not. Besides— Grandma Dalia never found her boy, and she became... Grandma Dalia. I don't want that to happen to me, don't want to be looking over my shoulder, worrying, scared my entire life. I want to be with Kai. I have to go after him.

It's a decision I feel strong about until the following morning when I hurry downstairs and see Ella. She's in the kitchen, pulling out flour, sugar, multicolored salts, fancy oils—an entirely different person than the crying girl I saw last night. There's a stack of cookbooks on the counter beside her that look brand-new, and she's wearing a bright pink apron.

"What are you doing?" I ask, still sleepy.

"We're going to cook things!" she chirps.

"...Why?"

"Because you said you like to cook, and I figured you could teach me!" she says. "I got you an apron. You don't have to wear it, though. Help me find a recipe?"

I take the pink apron from Ella's hands. It seems so hurtful, so cruel to crush Ella's happiness by abruptly telling her I can't stay. She and Lucas have given me so much; I can give her a day, can't I? I'm stalling—for fear of Mora, of the cold, of whatever painful uncertainty lies ahead—but it's hard to be sorry about it when I think of Kai walking away from me. Staying a little longer feels like a way to even the scales between me and Kai, even if I'm the only one measuring.

Ella and I sit down at the kitchen table and begin to flip through the various cookbooks together. Many are signed, or written in another language, or involve ingredients that I'm fairly certain even Ella doesn't have in the pantry, like milk thistle and grapefruit curd. There's something soothing about paging through the books, though, looking at perfect photos of even more perfect food.

"What about this?" Ella asks, pointing to a page in a dessert book.

"That looks complicated," I say.

"But do we have all the stuff for it?" She looks over her shoulder at the counter.

"Probably," I say. It's a recipe for something called Chocolate Blackout Cake. Baking was never my thing, really, and this one involves a lot of steps for something I'm pretty sure we could make out of a box. Ella is persuasive, though, and twenty minutes later she's whisking eggs and oil together while I try to figure out if I can substitute some sort of fancy imported cocoa powder for melted chocolate chips.

"So I was wondering," Ella says, "do you know how to ride a horse?"

"I live in Atlanta," I say. "Shortage of horses there, except the ones pulling carriages."

"Because I've got four—they aren't stabled here, but it's close. We could go ride them while the cake cooks."

"It only cooks for thirty-five minutes," I remind her, smiling.

"Is that all? Why aren't I making these all the time?" she says, whisking so hard that some of the mixture spills out of the bowl. "Well, maybe when we're done, then. Or tomorrow. Though I was thinking we could go book shopping tomorrow."

"That sounds fun," I say, sliding a butter knife across the top of a measuring cup full of cocoa—I figure we'll just add a little more butter to make up for the substitution. Ella grins and helps me load everything into the mixer.

The cake turns out lopsided, and we're terrible at sprinkling the garnish around the edges like the picture. Ella is delighted, though, and insists on calling Lucas in to show him.

"We made it!" she says, whisking the top off the cake stand.

"I'm impressed," Lucas says, kissing her on the cheek. "I mean, you have three degrees, but...a cake..."

"Oh, shut up," she says. "I'm excited."

"Clearly," he jokes, and kisses her again, pulling her close so that her hip bumps his. We eat cake for lunch, so much that by four o'clock, all three of us are lying on our backs on the various couches in their "theater room."

"Is the ice better today?" I say offhandedly. I can't stall forever, but I want to ease Ella in to the idea of me leaving.

"Yes," Lucas says; I see Ella turn her head to him and glare, though I don't think she knows I catch it.

"I should..." I inhale. "I should go, then. Before Mora and Kai get too far ahead of me." I speak quickly, as if I'm ripping off a Band-Aid.

"But we're supposed to go horseback riding tomorrow," Ella says quickly.

"Yeah, but I can't...."

"She's a witch monster thing," Ella says. "Look, here's what I'm thinking: We'll call Lucas's brother Silas. We'll pay him and his fiancée to go run Mora down—they do it all the time."

"With Fenris, they do it all the time," Lucas says. "I don't think they even know about the Snow Queen. And I haven't been able to get in touch with him anyhow."

"Okay, but still. They kill werewolves. It's what they do. And he always calls back eventually."

"And what if Kai is a wolf by then?" I say quietly. Ella

goes silent, and Lucas sighs loudly. "Ella, I can't just...stay here. I..." I'm almost afraid to say it, especially after yesterday, but I force the sentence out. "I love him."

"I know you love him. But you dying won't bring him back. It'll just mean he's still a monster, and you're gone," she says. "Come on. Just let us call them. And we'll have a great time tomorrow. Besides—if you don't stay, I'll eat the rest of the cake myself."

"I'll help," Lucas says. Ella smiles, but it doesn't look real—it looks trained, like something she'd give a pageant judge. It looks desperate.

"And besides, Ginny, now that I know I *can* cook without burning the house down, I want to know how to make something other than chocolate cake. You know what I love? Quiche. Do you know how to make that?" Ella says brightly, sniffling back the last bits of her sadness.

"Sure," I say, fighting to keep my voice from breaking. I roll over to look at the scar on my hand. "We'll do one for lunch tomorrow."

It stops snowing at four in the morning. I know, because I'm still awake, staring at the clock. I feel delirious, drunk with imagined scenes where I punch Mora in her perfect teeth and pull Kai away from her—scenes cut with images of me and Ella horseback riding. Lucas and me driving around town. The three of us sitting at a dinner table together. They want me. I want them. I want this place. I want everything to be simple and beautiful and warm.

I want to stay so badly that for a moment, it feels as if my limbs don't work anymore—as if they're too heavy for me to lift, far too heavy for me to even consider something like getting up and walking. I squeeze my eyes shut. Kai. *You're all he has. You're the only one who will fight for him, really fight for him.*

Even though a future with Ella and Lucas is beautiful, one where Kai and I are the ones making quiche together is far more so. I can't stay.

I heave myself to standing and proceed to creep around in the darkness, throwing my clothes into a bag. It won't zip up; I finally pull out the red heels Ella gave me and tuck them under my arm. My bedroom door creaks open, the sound echoing through the darkened house. I ease down the stairs, inhaling the scent of cleaner and perfume that permeates this place. I try not to think of what Ella will do or say when she realizes I'm gone.

I bang my hip on the kitchen counter and curse under my breath. My phone is dead, so I turn on the little television on the kitchen wall and immediately lower the volume. After a few clicks I find a weather report and wait for the map to come up. Snow in southern Kentucky—record temperatures expected. That's where I'll go.

"You're leaving?"

I cry out and spin around, flinging my hair into my face. It's Lucas, standing in the doorway wearing a white T-shirt and sweatpants. His hair is rumpled—he was asleep. I catch my breath, blinking back tears of surprise. Lucas is perfectly still, waiting; finally, I nod in answer to his question. I'm trembling a little, both from being startled and worrying that he's going to stop me. Lucas inhales and looks at the floor for a moment.

"Are you sure you want to get even more involved in this?"

"If it were Ella, would you go after her?"

"Absolutely," he says without hesitation. "Give us a few hours to take care of things and we'll come with you." He turns to go upstairs—

"No," I say, louder than I intended. Lucas looks back at me, something like hurt in his eyes. "It's not that I don't want you to come," I say quickly. "It's that I can't let you."

"Is this some sort of 'I have to face her on my own' delusion? Because I'm happy to inform you just how bullshit that is."

"No," I answer. "You and Ella are a family. You're happy. You're together. You're..." I pause, looking down. "You're everything I want for Kai and me. So I can't let you come with me and risk your lives. You said the first night we met—I've got a death wish doing this."

Lucas looks thrown. He shakes his head. "But we can't just let you go. Ella's *definitely* not going to let you go. She's seen what wolves do to people."

I inhale. "Don't wake her up. Say I snuck out in the night."

"She'll see through that lie in a heartbeat."

"But I'll be gone," I say quietly. "Please, Lucas. I already might lose Kai. I wouldn't be able to handle losing you guys, too."

Lucas stares. He wants to call for Ella, wants to let her rush down and persuade me to stay. But finally he sighs and holds up a finger. "Wait just a minute?" Lucas turns and I hear him go back upstairs. I let my bag slouch off my shoulder while the weatherman continues to talk about Kentucky in the background. The channel has changed to some sort of countdown of the country's worst snowstorms when Lucas returns clutching something. He walks over to me, still a little bleary-eyed, and gestures for my hand. I open my palm; Lucas drops a money clip packed tight with bills into it. I've never had so much money in my life; my eyes widen.

"I had the back window of your car fixed yesterday, but still—don't sleep in your car again," he says, smiling a little. "Stick to the highways—people ask fewer questions. And when you find them again, Ginny," he says, shaking his head, "don't fight her. She's stronger and faster and a fucking snow witch. Just take Kai and run."

"What if I have to fight her?" I ask seriously.

He shakes his head, then swallows. "Don't say that. Ella's going to be mad enough at me when I let her know you're as good as dead."

Lucas's words make my throat feel swollen; my stomach feels tilted. I nod, though, trying not to think about them. I think about Ella instead, what she told me—that right now, I can do everything. I tuck the fold of money into my coat swiftly, meet Lucas's eyes for a long time, and then turn. He shuts the door behind me as I stumble out into the snow.

CHAPTER THIRTEEN

ᘓ

I became certain Kai and I were meant to be when we were eleven and I knew what our wedding would look like.

It sounds silly, but dozens of other eleven-year-olds were also inexplicably planning their own weddings—it was practically an epidemic at our elementary school. They talked about reality shows involving dresses and bridesmaids and threw around terms like *fit-and-flair* and *white bar*. One girl in my class even bragged about having a seating chart in mind. But the fact that I didn't know any of those terms and had far better things to think about than seating charts is what made me so certain that I was going to end up with Kai. Because, despite not knowing much about dresses or entrées, I knew that he would be there.

He was the only certainty.

I didn't say anything to him, of course, but I didn't need

to. A few weeks later, after the seating-chart girl got in trouble for starting a fight over her choice of maid of honor, Kai looked at me and said, "Can we just get married in Las Vegas, like they do on TV?"

I nodded, thinking myself lucky that this was settled sooner rather than later. It wasn't until I told my mom and she made a face that I realized it was a little odd, two eleven-year-olds shrugging with certainty over their wedding. I was embarrassed and wondered if I should talk it over with someone.

So I talked it over with Kai, until we decided to not care what the world thought. Vegas, limousines, and each other. That was all we needed.

It's beautiful. For a moment, just as I'm crossing into Kentucky, the sun is cresting over the hills and I forget about Mora and her role in the snow's presence. Chunks are falling from the trees, melting, though the promise of cold weather ahead remains. I wonder when I'll hit the storm—how far her power reaches. I look down at Grandma Dalia's cookbook, thinking about the mystery boy hidden in the back. Hidden away, as if she thought out of sight could render him out of mind.

It didn't work, obviously. I guess you can't forget love any more than you can forget the Snow Queen.

I recharged my phone with the car charger. There are two messages on it from my mom, one asking if Dad will be driving me to school, the other asking if I took her yellow shirt. I text her no to both and wonder if Atlanta has finally thawed.

I make it till about noon before my eyes burn from exhaustion and I realize I *have* to sleep. I pull off the interstate and look at the collection of chain hotels that dot the exit. One looks decidedly less expensive than the rest, making it my immediate choice. Just as I'm about to turn into it, I realize a teen girl checking in alone will probably rouse some suspicion, if I'm even *allowed* to rent a room without being eighteen. I frown, park in a McDonald's lot, and stare at the hotel's entryway, trying to figure out how to work this.

Clearly, I'll just have to lie about being seventeen. I lean into the backseat and grab hold of Mora's fur coat, along with the red heels. I yank my hair into a ponytail, tugging a few pieces down around my face, then bite at my lips until they turn red and flushed. I slide off my tennis shoes, put on the heels, and step out of the car. I focus on the details—the way Ella walks, the way her smile goes from the center of her lips out, the way she lifts her chin when she's asking a question. *Details, focus on the details and hope they're good enough to cover the lie.*

It's a miracle I don't fall down immediately in these shoes. Luckily, the snow gives me better traction than the ice, though it still provides an excuse for being somewhat wobbly as I walk toward the hotel lobby. Automatic doors whiz open as I arrive, bathing me in heat. I keep my eyes ahead, on the front desk. The clerk behind the counter is young, with a poorly drawn fairy tattoo peeking out from underneath her sleeve. I smile as I walk over to her.

"I just need a room for the night," I say, flashing a grin. "When's checkout?"

"Noon. Let me see if we have anything, though...yep, looks good. Okay, ID, please?"

I make a show over looking in my wallet, frowning. "Huh. I must have left it at the bar last night when I got carded."

"Sorry, I can't—"

"I can pay cash," I say, waving my hand at her as if our whole conversation is silly. "I'm not going back out in that storm. It's crazy out there."

The clerk looks at me for a moment, as if she isn't certain. Her eyes fall from my face to my clothes, down to the red shoes. I can see her assessing me: I'm put together. Polished. Nonthreatening. And I've got a handful of bills that it doesn't look as if I stole. She smiles and nods.

"All right—name?"

"Ginny Reynolds." I give Lucas and Ella's surname at the last instant—I don't think my mom is looking for me, and certainly not in Kentucky, but still. I hand over a hundred dollars for the room and tell the clerk to keep the change. The clerk opens her mouth as if she intends to argue, but it's purely for show. I can see her reflection in the elevator doors as I walk away; she pockets the entire amount. Just as well. I try not to be pleased with myself, but I can't help grinning when I get into the elevator. I can't wait to tell Kai this story someday, a thought I hold tightly in my mind so it doesn't slip away to the memory of Mora taking his hand, of them running away together. To the thought of a future where Kai doesn't care about me, much less my stories.

The hotel room is simple and clean, with abstract art on the walls and a white bedspread. I start the coffeemaker and turn the television on to some decorating show, the type of thing that's better for background noise than entertainment value. The sound of traffic outside is muted by the heater, making the room blissfully peaceful; I lie back on the bed and close my eyes. *Only a few hours*, I tell myself. *Then you're back to it*. I fall asleep.

MORA

Outside the penthouse windows, the storm heightened, turning roads and buildings and trees into a milky-white wonderland. Mora closed her eyes and willed the snow to increase now that they were in for the evening; impressive as her powers were, they couldn't help her car drive through feet of snow. It was best to find a place to stay, then bury the city in a blizzard, making whatever distance was between her and her pursuer impassable.

Pursuer. Ha. The girl was a child. Yet Mora was darkly impressed by Ginny, truth be told—she seemed so flimsy, so breakable back in Atlanta. Of course, all mortals looked flimsy to her now. Besides, she wasn't afraid of Ginny—she was afraid of what might be following Ginny.

Relax, Mora told herself. *The Fenris would probably devour Ginny before they could follow her to you. Self-control isn't their strong point.* Still, she worried. After taking so many precautions to keep the Fenris away, it was infuriating to think that a foolish mortal girl might lead them straight to her. She may have underestimated Ginny and her willpower, but she never, ever underestimated the Fenris.

"Shouldn't we have taken Michael's body?" Kai asked, his back propped against the headboard on the other side of the bed. Mora sighed, pulled the sheets up around her chest, and glared at Kai for ruining the mood. Larson was sitting in an armchair in front of a room-service tray of untouched wine and strawberries. *Perhaps I should have spent the evening with him instead*, Mora thought, looking his way.

"Mora? Should we go back for his body?" Kai asked again, like a child pestering his parent. He looked over at her, found her hand under the blanket, and clasped it.

"No," Mora finally answered. "Michael is gone. There's no point." *Besides*, she thought, *maybe now I'll just keep Edward*. Typically, six guards was all she could manage—any more and they didn't love her enough, weren't devoted. Edward had always been tricky to control; his memories were strong, constantly trying to surge up and reclaim his mind—she never took him out on excursions like this for that reason. The challenge had always been part of his appeal, really.

"How did Larson and Michael learn to change like they did? To become wolves?" Kai asked, sliding down till his hair spilled across the white hotel pillows like blackened vines.

"How did you learn to breathe?" Mora answered. She pulled her hand from Kai's, reaching onto the nightstand for her jewelry. "It just happens. All my guards can do it." She met

Larson's eyes as she tilted her chin to put the chain of a sapphire necklace around her neck, and they smiled at each other.

"You make it happen?" Kai asked.

"In a manner of speaking," Mora said. "I helped them become like me. Men like me become wolves."

"Does that make them Fenris? The things that killed your sister?" There was caution in Kai's voice now, fear, even.

"Not quite," Mora said. "The Fenris are monsters. Horrible things, entirely soulless. But men like you, Kai, you become warriors. My protectors. You become beautiful, so much more beautiful than you'd ever have been as a mortal thing. Talented and fierce and loyal. Perfect."

This seemed to satiate Kai; he stared at the ceiling, looking pleased. Mora always let her guards think they were her only salvation from the Fenris, and perhaps it was even true sometimes. But she'd escaped the Fenris all on her own the first time, another memory that was always affixed firmly in the forefront of her mind, reminding her she was stronger than them.

Even so, she *was* a Fenris once, a member of their pack. Back then, Mora couldn't remember her life as an ocean girl, much less her life as a human. Then one day the boy from her past appeared. It was all by accident, of course, and he was older—almost gray. She hardly noticed the change in his hair color, though, just as he hardly noticed that she was pale, her eyes dark, her face beautiful in a dangerous, smooth way. He ran to her and kissed her the way he used to, and with his lips came the memories, rushing back through her, colliding with one another in her mind. Her life as a human girl, her life as an ocean girl, the realization of what she was now—

Mora closed her eyes and remembered how sweet his touch felt, how she was at home in his arms. She fought a certain memory, though, the one of seeing a ring on his finger, a solid gold band that bound him to another.

"What's her name?" Mora asked. Her voice was strangled and not her own.

"Celia," he said. "Her name is Celia. We have five boys and a baby on the way. You were gone. I waited, but you were gone, Madeline."

Madeline. Her old name, her human name. In the ocean, she'd been Ry; as a human, she'd been Madeline, and now she was . . .

Now she was nothing.

"I would have waited," she told him. "I would have waited forever."

"It's been twenty-three years," he said, voice hard now, betrayed. "And you still look . . . you still look like you're seventeen." He seemed to realize this all of a sudden, looking down at his own hands to verify the wrinkles that were just starting to form around his knuckles. "Am I losing my mind? What's going on?"

"I would have waited," Mora said, mind reeling. It felt like waking up from a dream, only to find herself in a nightmare. "I loved you. I still love you."

He choked on words and shook his head. "I love you,

too. But I also love someone else now. I have a life. I don't understand what's happening, Madeline—"

"My name isn't Madeline," she said sharply. "Not anymore."

She turned and ran. Away from him, away from the Fenris, into the arms of her ghost memories, remnants from her life as Madeline, as Ry. She went to the ocean to see if she could return home there, but the water tried to drown her. She went to her family's home on Fifth Avenue to find it full of strangers. She went to her sister's grave.

"How is it," she mumbled to the gray headstone, "that you're dead, and yet still the lucky one?"

Her current life was perhaps the strangest, this one that lurked between monstrous and perfect. Three lives, human, ocean girl, and *this*, forced together ever since the moment the boy kissed her. *Three lives, three names. Too many for one girl*, she thought, intertwining her fingers with Kai's and leaning down to kiss him. He kissed her back hungrily, pulling her to his chest under the blankets.

"Tell me," she whispered in his ear before biting it playfully. "What do you remember about your first life? Before I found you?"

"I remember..." Kai paused to think. "I remember a rooftop. I remember an old woman, and that our house was dark...." He shook his head. "Wait, is that real?"

"Who knows?" Mora said sweetly. "Here." She stretched across him and tugged his violin case up onto the mattress. "Play me a song, darling?"

"What song?"

"Anything," she said. "Do you remember any?"

"Maybe," he said, removing the violin from the case. He fit it under his neck and dragged the bow across the strings. Mora winced as one squeaked loudly. That was the downside of changing them, turning them into something half dark like herself. As their memories left, so did years of piano, violin, voice, or cello lessons. The raw talent remained, as did those few songs ingrained in their fingertips, but it was always a bit disappointing to hear them play so poorly compared with what they once were.

She relaxed as Kai found the notes, finally, then beckoned for Larson to come over. He obeyed, wrapping his arms around her just the way she taught him to. Mora closed her eyes and exhaled. *They may lose their talent, but they're mine*, Mora told herself as Kai's song continued, notes that made her heart feel long and tender. *They'll never love someone new. They'll never leave me.* She thought back to her sister's grave, the way the acorns dug into her knees as she ran her fingers across the engraved death date.

In the hotel room, she looked outside at the storm-filled clouds and wondered if her sister could hear her. *You weren't the lucky one after all, Mora.*

CHAPTER FOURTEEN

❧

I wake up, disoriented, afraid for a moment—
it takes a few breaths to remember why I'm not at home, then
why I'm not in the car, then why I'm not at Lucas and Ella's. I
can hear the dull babble of the television in the adjacent
room, and the sound of the elevators chiming beyond that. Is
it four in the morning or four in the afternoon? I blink, a little dizzy, and peek through the blinds.

Four in the afternoon, as it's still light out—I haven't
been asleep as long as it feels like I have. The roads are more
crowded now, piles of dirty slush forming in the triangles of
intersections. The horizon is bright and pink, nothing like
the thick, white haze from earlier. It's warmer. The snow is
melting, however slowly. Mora and Kai are getting farther
away.

I feel like I should spring from my bed, but instead I
inhale. *Relax. You're no good to him without sleep*, I say to

myself in a voice with a cadence that reminds me of Grandma Dalia. I open my eyes, wrap the comforter around me, and step away from the window. The television is still on, muted; and the coffee I started earlier has gone cold. I reach in my bag for the cookbook, planning to flip through it absently while I work up enough hunger to warrant a trip to the McDonald's across the street.

It's not there—*right. Still in the car, in the front seat.* I jump in the shower instead—I'll grab the cookbook on my way to dinner at McDonald's. A half hour later, I regret not completely drying my hair as I step through the lobby doors and a gust of frozen air sweeps around me. I fumble to pull the keys from the fur coat's pocket as I walk to the car—

The car.

A group of boys my age stand around it, wearing beaten T-shirts and pants that don't fit right, with beads threaded into their hair. They laugh with one another, talking loudly, but I don't understand the words or what language it is they're speaking. They have the passenger-side door open, and one is leaning in, slowly dumping the contents of the car into the hands of another.

"Hey!" I shout, suddenly finding my voice. I don't sound nearly as threatening as I'd like, but I run forward. They look up at me, like wild animals caught with a carcass. "That's my car!" I snap. One of the boys—the one with woven bracelets up and down his arm—glances at the others.

And then, laughing, they turn and flee. Bracelets slides over the station wagon's hood, another jumps out of the backseat, and they spring away as if this is a well-rehearsed musical number. Bracelets, I realize, is carrying something I care more about than the car—the cookbook. It's tucked under his arm, with one of my sweaters and the bag of Grandma Dalia's dimes. I run forward, still yelling, stumbling in the red heels.

I stoop and take them off, and when I look up I see the four jumping into a beaten and ugly RV. A boy with blond dreadlocks takes the driver's seat, and, grinning, he starts the engine and moves the RV toward the McDonald's exit. I yell again, and people are staring—not helping. I chuck the heels into the back of the car, slam the door shut, and then jump into the driver's seat just as they run a red light and rumble out of sight.

No, no, no. I'm tired of people taking things from me.

I slam on the accelerator and squeal out of the parking lot. I feel blind, hot, as if someone else is living inside me. The light turns green again just in time for me to race after them—they're ahead, far ahead, going slower than expected. I supposed getting pulled over is more trouble than it's worth for them—probably for me, too, but that doesn't stop me from squeezing through two yellow lights until I'm just behind them, passing feed stores and tractor dealerships as we leave town.

They speed up as the town fades behind us, and I follow suit. The RV kicks out black exhaust, and we weave around minivans full of offended-looking families. *Go, go, go*—I see the boy with dreadlocks staring at me in the side mirrors, his expression growing more and more concerned as it becomes clear I'm not letting up. I hear a tiny voice in my head, begging to know what I plan to do when we stop—fight them? Not hardly. I squash the voice. I don't care about the voice.

The back of the RV is splashed with mud; two of the boys, Bracelets included, appear at the back window, staring at me as they relay information back to the driver. He cuts over suddenly, taking an exit. I almost miss it, but the station wagon handles better than the RV; I slide onto the exit ramp just in time, taking out a few of the bushes on the median in the process. Bracelets's lips form a string of curse words in response.

Right off the ramp, and we're on a tiny road now, one that becomes smaller and smaller as we travel. There's nowhere to turn, nowhere to hide, nothing to do but rumble along behind them. I'm low on gas, and the adrenaline is wearing off—I'm chasing total strangers through the middle of Kentucky. But the cookbook, I can't lose it—

The road becomes even smaller, scarcely two lanes—the RV barely fits, and it skids on the ice, which is far more plentiful here. I see Bracelets on a cell phone, yelling at someone. He looks like a child suddenly, the cocky, arrogant look I saw when he was robbing my car gone, replaced by fear. It makes me feel strong, makes my eyes narrow. Trees are flying by, the setting sun bouncing off the snow, flashing at me—

The RV slows, and for a minute, I think they're stopping, that I've won. But no, they're turning on a different road, a drive, almost—I follow, squeezing my eyes shut as the car slides a little; suddenly, the tires can't find traction. I mash the accelerator. *They're getting away, hurry, back out, hurry—*

Faces in the rearview mirror—there are people behind

me. Two men, wearing thick coats and strange hats, standing in my tire tracks. I cry out, remember the Fenris back in Nashville—this can't be happening again. I try to veer to one side, overcorrecting in my frenzy. The car lurches and begins to tilt; the front corner tire lifts up off the ground. I flounder, locking my door as the men draw closer; in the distance, I see the boys stopping the RV, springing out, and running toward me. I thrust my body forward, as if my weight will right the car, but nothing, nothing. I leave my foot on the accelerator, listening to the back tires spin uselessly, mud and snow flinging up in a wave behind the car.

Something clicks behind me—the back door, the one the boys broke in through; I forgot to lock it. I spin around and scream as one of the men reaches in; his teeth are yellowed, his face scraggly and bearded. I slink out of Mora's coat to avoid his grasp, but he isn't reaching for me—he's reaching for the door. He flips up the lock on the driver's side, and then it's open, it's open and people are grabbing my arms, hauling me out.

My teeth find someone's skin, my nails rake across Bracelets's face, people are yelling and shouting, and then something goes over my head, something dark that I can't see through. My hands are behind by back, tears stream from my eyes, and every story, every horror I've ever heard is coursing through me. I scream.

"Quiet down," Bracelets says. "No one can hear you out here anyway."

CHAPTER FIFTEEN

ༀ

My voice grows hoarse from yelling, and it's clear there's not much point anyhow. I stumble along, feet cold in the deep snow, led by someone—I'm not sure who, though I suspect it's Dreadlocks—into what I assume is the RV. It smells like pot smoke and incense, and I shake uncontrollably as I hear the engine start again. One turn, two turns, three, one more—I try to memorize them, just in case I get the chance to escape.

"What's your name?" someone asks, not unkindly but not comfortingly, either. Still, I don't answer. "Calm down. We're not gonna hurt you," the voice says. "But you can't follow us."

I keep quiet.

"Seriously, what's your name—"

"Stop talkin' to her," another voice barks—one of the older men. "Brigit'll be pissed." The man and the boy bicker for a moment in a language I don't understand—something with soft vowels, a steady rhythm. I listen carefully but don't speak.

I think about Lucas, about Ella, and feel stupid for leaving them. What was I thinking? I could handle this on my own? I lift an arm to wipe my nose through the thing over my head—a dark pillowcase, I think—and try not to whimper loudly. I don't want them to know how scared I am. I don't want them to know how to hurt me.

The RV comes to a stop; people are shifting around, moving, and then finally, someone puts a hand under my arm and helps me stand. They maneuver me down the steps, down to the ground; grass crunches under my bare feet, still iced over. I can hear generators banging, a chorus of them, and the rich scent of a campfire finds its way through the pillowcase, meat cooking and wood burning. More incense, cigarette smoke, and then I'm being pushed along. My feet burn in the cold as I take a step, another, another—

"Wait," Bracelets says—I think it's him, anyhow. I feel his hand on me, and for a moment the pillowcase flutters away from my arms and I can see his fingers, grimy and dark underneath the nails. He swoops a hand under my legs and carries me. I go stiff, like a rock, trying not to lean against him, trying not to inhale the scent of sweat and smoke from his skin.

I feel us duck into something, somewhere—not a door, exactly, but the sounds from outside are muted and it's warmer here. I can feel a fire nearby, hear it crackling. Bracelets—it's definitely him, I can feel the bracelets digging into my calves—stoops and lets my feet find the ground. It's a rug, thick and shaggy, and I dig my toes into it.

Someone, a new someone, shorter than me, tosses a blanket over my shoulders, then takes my hand. It's a woman; it must be a woman. She guides me across the room, someplace closer to the fire and then, in a fast motion, whisks the pillowcase off my head.

"Ah, *lashool greerse*," she mutters, lifting a lock of my hair. I blink furiously, the air stinging my eyes. *Look around, fast, where's the door*—it's behind me. I'm in some sort of tent, one that's clearly not meant to be moved often—more like a small version of the sort you'd see at a circus. I can see the flap where the door opens and closes, noting that there's a loose knot tying it shut. There's the rug beneath my feet, and a clay fireplace in the corner with a pipe leading out through a slit in the tent's fabric. And then there's the woman.

Her skin is freckled and darker than mine, her face wrinkled and her hair enormous, thick, and black—it makes her look so much bigger than she actually is. Her eyes are green, though I can only just discern that in the dim light, and she's wearing a strange combination of clothes—a sundress over jeans, boots, and a sweatshirt that's been cut into a deep V-necked coat. She's probably my mother's age, if not older, but her age is hard to discern exactly since she dresses so unlike any fortysomething I've seen before.

"What's your name, pet?" she asks, and there's an accent—Irish, it's definitely Irish—hinting around the edges of her voice.

Finally, I speak, though my words are low and nearly broken. "Ginny Andersen," I say.

"And you followed my boys?"

"They took something that belongs to me," I say.

"They tend to do that," she says, as if their breaking into my car is a lesser issue. She walks behind me; I turn a little, still sick and woozy from fear. There's a table back there, against the wall of the tent. She rifles around on it for a moment; when she shifts to one side, I see things from the station wagon are spilled out across the table. The cookbook, the red heels, the bag of dimes, Mora's coat, plus a few odds and ends like umbrellas and the owner's manual. She lifts the fur coat, admiring it.

"Daresay we'll need to take this," she says, smiling. "Payment for us giving you a ride over here, of course." She studies me for a reaction; when I don't give one she tosses the coat over the back of a chair, then gathers up the shoes, cookbook, and bag of dimes. "Anyhow. My name is Brigit, and this is my camp. And I don't care for strangers showing up, roughing things up for us."

"I didn't mean—"

Brigit's eyes go sharp, silencing me. She stoops on the rug at my feet and lays out the items from the car one at a time. She looks at me, then at the objects.

"You can take one back. Choose it."

I grab for the cookbook immediately, but she swoops in and whisks it away before my hands grasp it; I feel stupid that I fell for the trick. I groan, sit back in the chair, and close my eyes.

"This? I thought it'd be the money," Brigit says. "What's in here that's got you all worked up?"

"It's an heirloom," I say. "A family heirloom."

"That's not a lie," Brigit says confidently, without looking up at me, "but it's not the whole truth, either." She flips open the book, catching the clippings of Mora before they slide out and unceremoniously cramming them back in their spot. She scans a few pages, then looks up at me, eyebrow lifted.

"Who does this really belong to?"

"My boyfriend," I say.

"And yet you'll chase down a gang of robbers to get it back? Afraid he'll beat you for losing it?"

"No!" I protest, a little louder than intended. "It's just... I don't want to lose it."

Brigit rolls her eyes at me, then rises. She strides to the fireplace, opens the door, and holds the book in front of it. My eyes widen as I realize what she means to do. "All right, the whole story. Let's hear it. I've got a clan to run, and you're wasting my time."

"My boyfriend," I stumble over the words. "He's missing. He's with another woman—"

"A cheater, then? Fuckin' men—"

"No, she stole him. She's not a girl, she's something else—she controls the snow. It sounds crazy, I know, but it's in the book," I finish, pointing. My finger is shaking.

Brigit frowns, pulls the book back from the fire, and then tosses it onto the floor beside my other things. She doesn't look at me as she lowers herself into a chair across the rug, and I can't tell if she believes me or not. I really don't care, honestly—I just want to get the book and go. Actually, at this point, I might just settle for going.

"A girl who came with the snow?" Brigit asks. I nod, still unable to tell what she's getting at. She parts her lips, about to speak again, when there's a hissing sound, the knot on the door being pulled free. Two men walk inside, one gaunt and stringy, the other old and thick.

"*Sreego*," one says. "How are things with the buffer?"

"They're fine," Brigit says. "They're always fine. Out, both of you."

"This ain't the time to be dealing with buffers. Get rid of her so we can get back to the matter at hand," the gaunt one says.

"Unless Flannery has a ring on, there's no matter at hand yet," Brigit hisses. "And unless you want your gas share cut, you'll get out of my house."

"Look, Brigit," the other one says. "All we're gettin' at is Flannery is a bit hard to deal with without you, so rather than questioning this buffer, let's get rid of her and move on."

I swallow, not entirely sure what "get rid of her" means.

"I know how desperately you'd both like Flannery to marry your boy, and get my crown for your family," Brigit says threateningly. "Believe me. Everyone knows, with the way you two whine. And should my daughter have a moment of complete stupidity and choose one of your rats, then *perhaps* I'll want your opinion on matters like this buffer. But until then: You. Are in. My house."

156

They glare, eyes hard and angry, an expression Brigit reflects with twice the intensity. Finally, they turn and leave; a blast of cold air wafts from the tent flaps over to me.

"Assholes," Brigit mutters after them. "I give them the best twenty years this clan has ever seen, and they still can't get over the fact that I've got tits. And Flannery wonders why I say she's not strong enough to take them on alone...."

"What's going to happen to me?" I ask meekly, my mouth cottony and my lungs broken.

"For starters," Brigit says, rapping her fingers on the cookbook again, "you're going to tell me more about this snow girl."

CHAPTER SIXTEEN

I explain Mora as best I can to Brigit. I lay out the magazine clippings, tell her about Kai, about the Fenris at the rest stop, about Lucas and Ella—though I leave out the details there, to keep them safe. Brigit listens, barely moving, and when I'm finished she sits back on the love seat across from me. I notice there are tattoos on her arms and on the interior of almost every finger, symbols and shapes and words I don't recognize.

"That's everything," I say when she goes an uncomfortably long time without speaking. "And it's true. I swear."

"I didn't say it wasn't," Brigit answers. She reaches forward, flips around in the cookbook for another moment, and then speaks slowly. "I know about this girl. Your Snow Queen. *Grohkta-Nap.*"

She pauses and closes the cookbook gently. "She took your boy. Kai."

"Yes. So you believe me?"

"Unfortunately, yes," Brigit says. "I can't pretend I'm not angry. I thought she was only taking Traveller boys, lately. Didn't know she wanted buffers."

"Wait, what?"

"Grohkta-Nap. I won't question her choices, of course," Brigit says, casting her eyes to the ceiling for a moment. "I just hoped she'd choose another of ours when she needed a new guardsman."

"You...wanted?" I shake my head. "She *steals* boys. She turns them into wolves. She keeps them forever."

"No—she keeps them till she finds better ones. And she does far more than make them wolves. She makes them *gods*," Brigit corrects. "Like her. Well, not *like* her, but more like her than we are, anyhow."

"Are you crazy? She's the queen of beasts. She controls the other werewolves, the Fenris. They attacked me—"

"She's our only protection *from* the Fenris," Brigit says, and now her eyes light up angrily, as if I've said something deeply insulting. "And with the way you talk about Grohkta-Nap, it's no surprise she didn't protect you from them. It's by her grace they didn't kill you."

I fall silent, though I can feel a thousand words at a thousand different volumes trying to rise from my lungs. Brigit stands and crosses her arms.

"The question," she says, "is whether you've come to us as a blessing. Grohkta-Nap took your boy, let you live, and led you here. That's gotta be something. Or...are you a curse she's bringing down on my people? Sent to tell us she chose a buffer instead of my boys, to warn us about the Fenris coming…"

"I'm just Ginny," I say, voice breaking. "I just didn't want them to take the cookbook."

Brigit shakes her head at me, as if she pities my stupidity. "Nothing happens because of 'just.' So, you'll stay here until we work it out."

"You can't… I'm not just staying here," I say shrilly.

"Oh, no one here just stays," Brigit says. "Plenty of people here would kill for an extra pair of hands. It'll be a nightmare deciding who gets to keep you." She moves toward the tent flap to leave; I jump to my feet and sprint for the door. I'm running for it, I'm fast, I can make it somewhere. I burst past Brigit, stumbling from the darkness of the tent into the bright white world outside. My feet hit the snow, I don't care, I step forward—

And realize there's nowhere to go.

We're in a clearing surrounded by trees, tall, bare oaks that stretch their fingers to the now-dark sky. There are campfires everywhere, and I hear someone playing an instrument, a guitar maybe, backed by a harmonica. But mostly, I see people. People everywhere, dressed in worn but colorful clothes, smoking cigarettes and fighting, laughing, and singing. Hundreds of them, spread out among dozens and dozens of RVs and tents and campers.

Bracelets is in front of me, leaning against a post that holds the tent's "porch" up. He looks at me warily, silently asking me not to make him chase me into the trees.

"You can run," Brigit says, "but see those people? They'll stop you. And if they don't—" She points into the distance, to the line of trees. "See the forest?"

I nod.

"Those trees are full of teeth and claws. Run in there and see if Grohkta-Nap protects you from the Fenris a second time. She may be a goddess, Ginny, but I'd rather not test her patience, especially after questioning her power."

I sink to my knees.

"My parents will be looking for me," I hiss at Brigit. "They'll find me."

Brigit studies me for a minute, then brushes past me, walking out into the snow. As she moves away, she calls over her shoulder, "Don't lie to me, Ginny Andersen. No one's looking for you."

They've given me a pair of shoes to wear, and the fire is warm, at least. Everyone is gathered in a circle around it, a sea of smudged cheeks and shiny eyes. A blond girl with bright cheeks is wearing Mora's coat proudly, modeling it so other children can admire her. Across the fire from the girl, Brigit and a dozen boys my age talk. The boys have thick muscles and tanned faces, and old T-shirts peek out from behind scarves and coats. I feel as if I'm trapped in a movie, a play that isn't my life.

"Listen up," Brigit calls out. The crowd quiets, and all faces turn to her. "This buffer is staying with us for a bit, till I work out what to do with her." She pauses while two dogs get in a squabble, waiting for them to be calmed by their masters. When they are, she continues, sounding annoyed. "Name's Ginny. Don't know if she's any good at cooking or cleaning, but she's young, she'll learn. One from each family who can afford another mouth, winner gets her. No knives, no chains, no brass knuckles. Clear?"

Her words are blunt, though I'm still not quite clear what's about to happen. I look at her—she made no mention of the Snow Queen, of Grohkta-Nap, and from the way Brigit glares at me, I can tell I'm not to bring it up. I suppose that if she ends up thinking I'm a curse, she'll want to get rid of me easier, and if I'm a blessing, she'll want to keep me without a fight. My lips firm—*stop thinking like that. You aren't staying here either way.*

"Let's get on with it, then!" a portly man says loudly, and the crowd cheers raucously. Brigit motions for me to rise; I back up toward her, but Bracelets and Dreadlocks are once again blocking any escape route I might have taken. Boys from around the fire step out, tossing down their coats and hats. A dozen or so total, with a few stragglers opting in at the last moment, pushed by their mothers, who eye me greedily. The boys size one another up, rock back and forth on their heels. I see money being dug from pockets, exchanged between the crowd; small children push through the legs of adults to get a front-row seat.

Someone grips my arm, and I turn to see that it's Bracelets. "You'll want to step back," he says. "These things take up a lot of space."

"Ready!" Brigit shouts, voice ringing through the clearing. The boys vying for me tense. "Fight!"

They explode into motion, a flurry of hands and fists. The thick *slock* sound of punches meeting heads resonates over the roar of the crowd. People are screaming, shouting, encouraging the boys who fall quickly to get back up, to grow a pair and keep fighting. A boy's shirt gets ripped in half; another boy almost gets thrown into the fire.

I look over to Brigit—she's watching patiently, as if this bores her, even as a pair of wrestlers tumble forward and narrowly miss knocking her over. A few boys are staying down now, heaving into the ground with bloody noses and mouths red from busted lips. The crowd changes pitch, from cheers to gasps and laughter. I snap my head around, hearing Bracelets chuckle behind me. I can't see what's happening through the fire, and my eyes start to water from trying to stare through the flames. Finally I see something—I don't know what, but something—someone moving fast, darting around the boys' arms, ducking under their swings.

"Who is that?" I ask Bracelets.

"That," he answers, looking smug, "is Princess Flannery."

My eyes widen; I look to Brigit, who, though still, I can tell is seething from the stiff, hard angle her jaw has taken. The men are booing, yelling at Brigit, throwing their arms into the air in frustration. She ignores them, her eyes narrowed and trained on the fight—on her daughter.

I rise to my toes and finally see some of what's happening on the far side of the fire. Flannery moves fast, flickering around the boys as they wail on one another like clumsy giants. She ducks under a boy's arm, black hair flowing behind her, then rises up behind him to bring her elbow down hard on his head. He falls, and she sprints to another boy, sliding into the mud and taking a knee to her nose. It bloodies instantly, but she doesn't seem to notice, moving around the fire as she stoops and causes one of the boys to trip over her.

There're only a few boys left now—most are stumbling back into the crowd, enveloped in a sea of men slapping their backs and offering them flasks. Flannery dives toward the two boys closest to Brigit; they turn and see her, alarmed, and duck out of the way as she swings a fist at them. One of the boys grins, catches her hand, and flips her to the ground. Bracelets makes a growling sound that ends when she springs back up, leaps onto the boy's back, and wraps her arms around his thick neck. He flails and punches at her legs awkwardly, trying to shake her off, but she grits her teeth and holds tight.

The other boy runs at them both, hand clenched into a fist. He strikes the boy Flannery's holding on to, forcing him to stop fighting off Flannery and focus on his male opponent. The two exchange fruitless blows—one, two, three punches that sail through the air. Finally, Flannery's boy succumbs to the pressure she's putting on his neck and drops to his knees, red-faced and wheezing. Flannery releases him and looks up at the other boy, and I can tell he's thrown—he doesn't want to be the one to hit her, the princess.

She clearly has no such hesitation; she punches him, so fast he doesn't have time to flinch. He stumbles backward, rubbing his jaw, but before he can recover she's landed a solid kick to his stomach, then another, then a stomp to his instep. The boy falls to the ground and holds up his hands in surrender as she runs at him, foot drawn back, ready to strike again. She freezes just before making contact—there's no need. It's over.

The crowd erupts in a chorus of cheers, of boos, of conversation and dog howls. People are milling around; men are shouting over the wagers they placed. No one seems to understand what just happened, what this means—least of all me. Finally, an older man lifts his hands into the air in celebration and laughter.

"Take that, *mugathawns*! Flannery Sherlock is the winner!"

CHAPTER SEVENTEEN

⚮

I have no idea what this means, and am a little relieved to see no one else does, either.

Flannery, for her part, is grinning through the blood running down her nose. I'm finally able to get a good look at her face. She resembles Brigit, at least in her eyes, though her body is both curvier and shorter, something like a gymnast's. She runs past the crowd, encouraging them to cheer for her, but the people seemed mixed—the younger members are ecstatic and the older ones are scowling.

Brigit is talking furiously to an ever-growing mob of men, all yelling over one another. People start to take notice, quieting down so they can eavesdrop. Flannery, now on the other side of the fire and high-fiving a group of children, turns and cocks her head, listening.

"You'd better get control of your girl, Brigit. No man is gonna put up with this," one man growls.

"We'll handle it—"

"And what about my boy?" a man I recognize from Brigit's tent shouts. "God help me if his nose doesn't set right, Brigit. And besides, who gets the buffer now?"

"*I* get the buffer," Flannery shouts, storming toward her mother. "I won. I get her."

"Flannery," Brigit warns under her breath.

"What're you gonna do, add her to your damn menagerie?" an old man asks.

"You'll watch the way you speak to your princess," Brigit snaps.

"Maybe someone should've spoke to *you* that way, Brigit!" another says.

The crowd gasps, a murmur of threat, of indignation ruffling through them. Brigit purses her lips together and makes herself look taller, more regal than the man who last spoke. He seems to know he's said the wrong thing, shrinking back a little, casting his eyes downward.

"Flannery?" Brigit says, voice steely. Flannery steps closer, cowed by her mother's intensity. "Find Ginny a place to sleep. We'll figure out a way to handle this when Jameson apologizes. Make sure you watch her—she'll try to run." Flannery walks over to me, her gait bold, confident. Bracelets pushes me toward her, and Flannery grabs hold of my wrist tightly. She leads me away, out of the crowd; I look over my shoulder to see Brigit walking back to her tent, proud, as if she's uninterested in whatever squabbles the crowd of men might have.

"Where are we going?" I ask. Flannery doesn't answer.

"Hey," I say again, more forcefully. "What are we doing?" She doesn't answer, so I repeat the question again and again as we weave around RVs, generators, and charcoal grills.

"God, you don't shut up, do you?" Flannery finally says. We reach an RV close to Brigit's tent, a big, impressive one. Flannery walks up the steps, shoulders the door open, and leads me inside.

"I'm not...look, I'm not, like...yours or...I'm not going to be your..." I stumble across the words, embarrassed and confused.

"My own personal buffer?" Flannery asks, grinning wickedly. She laughs, loud and strong and a little lewd. "You are. I dunno what you'll do. Maybe you can help me—nah. Never mind. You'd just mess that up."

"I don't...I don't understand."

"What's to understand?" she asks, opening a cabinet and pulling out a bag of crackers, the fancy, name-brand kind speckled with seeds. "I fought, I won, so you're with me." She continues to mutter under her breath, in the language I don't understand. She tucks the bag of crackers under her arm and walks down the RV steps. I consider standing my ground, refusing to follow, but I reason that the more we walk around, the more of the camp I see—and the more likely I am to discover a way to escape.

People are heading back to their RVs and tents; fires are reduced to embers, and a haze of smoke covers the area. A few people congratulate Flannery, and a few others cuss at her; she unleashes a string of expletives back without hesitation, which usually results in her and the other person laughing together. Children watch us from inside tent doors, clustered together like nesting animals, eyes admiring Flannery while regarding me with a sort of wary fear. We're getting closer and closer to the edge of the camp, away from the bonfire light. The snow on the ground is still thick here, though there's a trail, as if Flannery has walked this path many times before. I turn my eyes to the tree line, wondering how far I'd make it if I got away and ran right now. After seeing the Fenris, the forest is infinitely more frightening, especially in the dark. Flannery looks over her shoulder at me.

"Afraid of the forest?"

"Yes," I mutter.

"You should be," she says. "Go in there and *they'll* eat you up."

"I know about them," I say. "The Fenris. And the Snow Queen—your mother doesn't want anyone to know, but—"

"*Quiet*," Flannery says, teeth flashing in the dim light. "I heard all about you. Talking trash about Grohkta-Nap, questioning her power."

"It's not that," I say, trying to pander to her a little. "I've just always thought she was the queen of the Fenris. But you say she protects your people from them."

"If she sees fit," Flannery says, pushing her hair over her shoulders—though there's so much and it's so thick that the curls flounce back across her face in seconds. "The snow slows the Fenris down," she continues. "She brings it down on us, tries to keep them away from our camp."

"And you don't care that she turns boys into wolves."

"That work for her," Flannery says, a spark of admiration in her voice. "And they don't back-talk and question her the way the men here question my mother. The Snow Queen has real power." I'm about to say more when up ahead, something near the trees moves. I jump, afraid, but no, this is small, thinner, lankier than a Fenris. We grow closer, closer, and I realize it's a deer, held captive by a fence made of chicken wire on one side and a very beaten VW bus on the other.

"Hello, *menthroh*," Flannery calls out; her voice is calmer now, as if the frenzy of the fight is falling away. The deer's ears flick toward us, and she immediately backs up to the far side of the pen.

"She's afraid of me," Flannery tells me, though she doesn't seem too sad about this. She reaches into the bag of crackers, tugs out a few, and throws them to the ground at the deer's feet. I see her silhouette, and her wide, eerie eyes flicker as she drops her head and sniffs, then ignores them.

"You feed her crackers?"

"I feed her whatever I can find that she'll eat," Flannery says, and turns. "Don't tell my mother. She gets pissed when she hears I'm giving them our food." I'm about to ask what she means by *them* when it becomes abundantly, ridiculously clear.

The fence holding the deer goes on for several yards, divided every few feet, and there's an animal in every section. The deer, then a fox, then a dog—no, not a dog, a coyote.

"I had an elk once," Flannery says forlornly. "But he trampled me and ran away."

"I'm . . . sorry?" I say, trying to keep the shock from registering in my voice. *She's crazy.* Not just strange, not just eccentric, but actually crazy.

"Nah. Good for him, being strong enough to break out," Flannery says, tossing some crackers into a pen with a badger. "Besides, now I have room for a bear, if I can catch one. It's hard—I need a really old one or a baby, and both are hard to come by. Especially since women aren't allowed to go *into* the woods. Gotta wait for them to wander close to camp, see one by the highway, that sort of thing."

Crazy.

"Why do you want a bear?" I ask, unable to keep the alarm from my voice this time.

"Because," Flannery says, drawing a knife from her waistband and running it across the chicken wire so it makes a tinkling sound. The animals' ears spring up and they begin to pace. "Wouldn't you be afraid of a girl who can catch a bear with her hands?"

I nod—but really, I'm fairly afraid of her as is. She doesn't need to catch a bear to scare me, though I'd believe Brigit and the rest of the camp might be harder to convince. We get to the end of the pens and walk to the back of the bus. It was once pale red—I think. Maybe blue or green—the paint is chipped and reveals that it's been many colors in its lifetime.

"This is Wallace," Flannery says, sounding pleased with herself.

"Why Wallace?"

"That's what it says," she answers, as if I'm stupid to not realize. She points to an assortment of faded bumper stickers on the rear door. Only one is still legible, the one that reads WALLACE FOR PRESIDENT in red, white, and blue.

Flannery opens the rear doors and climbs inside. There's a table and a few benches, and the pop-top roof makes it possible to stand up straight in certain areas. There's not room to do much else, though, because on every seat, every ledge, and every little table are cages, their occupants hidden in the darkness. Flannery reaches over and flicks on an electric lantern, temporarily blinding me. When I manage to open my eyes, I can't stop a gasp.

Possums. Raccoons. Squirrels. Some sort of mink, and, in a pen by what used to be a bed, a beaver. They scramble for food, and I'm overwhelmed with pity—they look well fed, cared for, but something about seeing a wild animal in a cage unsettles me.

Flannery reaches into the passenger seat and comes up with several boxes of cornflakes, which she dumps into the animals' bowls; they eat hungrily, the raccoons far more brazen than the deer outside.

Flannery raps on Wallace's wall fondly. "It runs and everything. My friend Callum and I stole it together last year. Took us six months to get it working. And another three to get my mother off my back about having a van just for my collection."

"She doesn't like it?"

"She says I'm greedy, wanting more while others have

less." She casts a hand toward the camp, fingers lingering in the direction of the smallest tents. "Says it's not our way, that I'm acting like a buffer."

"We're not like that," I say defensively.

"You'll have a hell of a time convincing me of that," Flannery says, laughing loud. "But I wager I'll have a hell of a time convincing you we're more than just thieves and vagrants, so we're square."

I'm not sure we're square at all, seeing as how I'm being held prisoner, but I keep my mouth shut. Flannery sticks her fingers into the possum's cage for a moment; when he ignores her, she speaks again.

"Maybe she's right. More proof I'll be a shit queen."

"Shit queen of *what*, exactly?" I ask, voice rising in something too akin to disdain for Flannery's taste. She whirls around and glares, and I see her fingers itch for her knife. It makes me jump backward; I trip over the console between the driver's and passenger seats, and my elbow hits the gearshift. I wince as she laughs at me, looking down. I'll probably have an imprint of the little numbers on the shifter bruised into my skin.

"I didn't mean it like that," I grumble, finding my feet. "I just don't get it. Who are you people? What are you doing out here?"

Flannery relaxes and smiles—her smiles look so wicked. "We're the Pavee. Tinkers. The Other Folk."

"I don't know what any of that means."

Flannery snorts, puts away the cornflakes, and flips off

the light. "We're Travellers," she says. "Well, mostly. We broke off from the other Traveller groups years ago, started a new clan when we came down to Kentucky."

"And so you're the . . . the princess."

"The Princess of Kentucky," Flannery says matter-of-factly. "But I'm shit at it, you know. So shit, in fact," she says, pausing dramatically, "that my mother thinks if I don't get married, have a husband to back me up when I inherit her title, that the clan'll overthrow me, take my crown before she's even cold in the ground." Flannery jumps out of Wallace and waits for me to do the same.

"Is your mother married?" I ask as my feet hit the dirt.

"Nope," Flannery says, snorting at the hypocrisy. "My dad ran off a thousand years ago, but when they tried to take my mother's crown, she fought back. I could fight back, too— hell, I'm stronger than my mother, braver, and I can handle a knife better. But she doesn't care. Thinks I'm weak. Says she'll just arrange the marriage herself if I don't pick someone soon."

"Would she really do that?" I ask.

"Damn straight," Flannery says. "She can't just leave well enough alone." Flannery spits on the ground and walks away. I follow her; we cross back into the more populated area of camp, though most people are inside now, silhouettes in their lit windows. There's a group of men drinking around a small fire in a pit; one points us out to the others as Flannery and I grow closer.

"Oy, there she is! The Princess of Kentucky herself, and

her prize!" He waves a bottle of liquor at us so emphatically that he topples over and nearly rolls into the fire.

"Better watch out, Flannery," another one yells. "Them boys won't forget about this. Might be inclined to teach you a lesson."

"They'll have a hard time doing that from the ground," Flannery says coolly, and we keep walking. The men are too drunk to be insulted, laughing and whistling. We're nearly out of earshot when one man calls out, loud enough that his voice shoots across the camp.

"Should've killed the buffer girl straight out. I bet we have to, to settle this whole thing."

Flannery keeps moving, while I struggle to keep breathing. She glances back at me, dark hair flying into her face from a breeze.

"Don't worry," she says. "I won't let them kill you." I nod meekly, feeling at least mildly comforted until she adds, "If you need to be killed, I promise I'll off you myself."

Everyone has a memory they treasure. A bright moment in the past to return to when things are too dark to live in the present. When I was small, it was a memory of dyeing Easter eggs with my mother. Then, when I needed something bigger, more powerful, it was the memory of finding the rose garden with Kai. Thousands of blooms in front of a graying twilight sky, a summer breeze, the feeling that we'd found our very own version of Narnia.

But now all I can think of is Kai destroying the roses, the

things he said to me, the way Mora sneered at my pain. So in the ever-darkening present, I turn to a different memory instead, one that's still pure, beautiful, perfect.

The second time Kai and I kissed.

The first time we kissed, we were excited, dreaming about the music intensive, about New York and the adventures we'd have there. Everything felt big, everything felt grand, and it was like kissing was the only way to get the joy out of our hearts and into the world.

But the second time, we weren't distracted. There was no letter, no dreaming, no plans. There was just me and Kai, and the knowledge that one kiss was a simple diversion, but two kisses were a pattern. It was evening in the autumn, the trees red and fiery and the air crisp. We were on the brick bridge leading into the park, watching the dogs in the fenced area below roughhouse. There were dogs barking, and there was the sunset, and then there was Kai's hand taking mine. He turned me toward him, and I reached up, wrapping my arms around his neck without thinking, and we were kissing as if it was the most natural thing in the world.

The memory is enough to light the darkness.

CHAPTER EIGHTEEN

☙☙

I'm given a sleeping bag on the floor of Flannery's bedroom. It's old, but admittedly warm and comfortable, all things considered. Flannery has a twin bed that's pressed up against a wall, which she leans against as she sleeps—I know, because I lie awake for hours. I think back to the hotel, how eager I was to someday tell Kai about lying my way in. Flannery snores loudly and rolls over. All this is going to make for a much more interesting story, if I escape.

I wake up the following day to Flannery tying her hair in an elaborate series of braids and buns and knots. She casts me a rather disdainful look as I stretch and stand. My hair is a mess of tangles, and finger-combing doesn't do much good. Flannery watches me, then sighs.

"Here," she says, handing me an elastic. "*Don't* lose it." I nod and knot my hair up into a ponytail. Flannery gives me a displeased look, but then rolls her eyes and wipes her face with the back of her hand.

"Come on," she says. "There're scones in the kitchen. Maybe."

I sigh and follow her. The knife is once again tucked against her waistband, threatening me if I don't.

There are, in fact, scones—spotted with raisins and delicious, clearly made from scratch. We eat them, then walk outside. It's still cold, but the ground is soggy from melted snow and the sun is bright—it's nearly midday, I realize. I follow Flannery across the camp, a far less threatening place in the daylight. Children are playing freeze tag, and women are lined up inside RVs, talking among themselves. I suspect the topic of conversation is Flannery and me, based on the hush that falls over people when we walk by. Most of the men, I notice, are gathered around a few RVs near the back of camp, running in and out like bees at a hive. They're repairing them—patching the roofs and ripping up carpet, arms elbow-deep in engines.

"Almost done?" Flannery shouts out to a woman standing near the closest RV.

"Two days!" she answers. She can't be much older than me, but there's a baby bundled in a knitted blanket on her hip. "Jolie can't wait to be out of the tent."

"Wager that's true, in this weather," Flannery answers, grinning as we take a sharp right.

A few moments later we reach a massive structure that's part tent, part camper—like the owner built an addition onto the place out of tarps and metal rods, with a few moving blankets on the interior for insulation. We duck through the makeshift doors, growing warmer as each layer is pushed aside. Five layers deep, we reach the center—a room illuminated by camping lanterns, covered in beaten rugs and cheap furniture. Three people sit at a table in the center—Bracelets is among them, along with another boy I think I recognize from yesterday. They welcome Flannery and offer her the last empty seat at the table; Bracelets rises, grabs a chair for me, and drags it over without a second glance.

"Ginny, this is Callum," Flannery says as I sit down. She points to Bracelets. "And all you need to know about him—well, all of them, really"—she motions to the other two at the table—"is that they're Kentucky nobles, and their money is about to be mine."

The other two boys jeer at Flannery for a moment, then introduce themselves—Declan and Ardan—Ardan is one I recognize from yesterday at my car. Bracelets—Callum, rather—pulls out a battered deck of playing cards and begins to distribute them among the others, passing over me.

"All right, bastards: Aces are high, lucky hearts, and bets in before the drop. And I swear to god, Ardan, if you're opening your mouth to suggest one of your candy-ass rules, we'll throw you out and let the buffer play instead. What the hell, Declan, already?" Callum says when Declan passes him a beaten thermos. I can smell the alcohol inside from across the table.

"What? It's almost noon," Declan says, grinning.

Callum rolls his eyes. "You make us look bad. But I can't have that shit anyway. You know that."

"Then pass it here," Ardan says, lunging across me to reach for the thermos. Callum sees me watching the exchange as he shuffles the deck again.

"You drink, buffer?" he asks.

"Ginny," I say firmly, patience worn. Callum raises his eyebrows at me. "My name's Ginny, and I'm getting tired of being called *the buffer*."

Flannery snickers, and Callum, for a moment, looks as if he's going to mock me again. Instead, he shrugs. "All right, then. You want a first name, that means you want to be like us. People like us play cards."

"What's the game?" I ask, trying to sound bold. I *feel* bold, honestly—I'm good at cards. And I really, really want to win at something right now.

"Widow's Lover," Callum says, dealing me six cards.

"I don't know that one," I say.

"You'll be easy to beat, then. You betting Flannery's money, or your own?"

"She's not betting my money!" Flannery protests, looking astounded that Callum would even suggest it.

"She's got money," Ardan says. "Hang on." He rises and sprints out into the melting snow. A few moments later he returns with a pillowcase. He empties its contents out on the floor; the bag of dimes hits the ground with a solid *chlank*, followed by the red heels and the other odds and ends from the backseat of the station wagon.

"Don't look so surprised," Ardan says to me. "Just because we kidnapped you doesn't mean we're grifters."

180

"That's hardly going to be enough for a half-dozen hands," Declan says, pouting a little as he points to the bag of dimes.

"Look at those shoes," Flannery says, eyes widening. She reaches forward and runs a finger along the cherry-colored leather. "Where'd you get those?"

"They were a gift," I say, suddenly protective of them and the memory of Ella and Lucas. I snatch the shoes up, along with a sweater and a flowery umbrella that I remember seeing under Grandma Dalia's passenger seat, and stick them behind me. *I wonder what the hotel has done with the rest of my stuff.*

"What would you do with shoes like that, Flannery?" Declan teases. "You'd look ridiculous."

"Not when I used the heel to stab you in the throat," Flannery snarls, and Declan quiets but continues to smirk. Callum finally smacks him on the side of the head, wiping the smile from Declan's lips.

"I," Callum says, clearing his throat, "think you'd look fine in those shoes, Flannery."

"Shut up, Callum," Flannery growls. "Just play."

They bet fifty cents a round, starting with Callum. The game is some strange combination of poker and hearts; they drop cards into a pile, trade them for new ones, and fold out of the hand—though when anyone folds, the other Travellers mock him or her for being spineless.

"I'm staying in," I say on the first hand, keeping my cards close to my chest.

"Riding," Callum says. "You're riding the hand, *buffer*." I glare at him, drawing another card when he offers me the deck.

We go around the table twice more, and I ride another hand, and then we reveal our cards to one another on the count of three.

I lose—Flannery squeals in a more feminine way than I'd have expected and slides everyone's money toward her.

It's four rounds before I have a clue what's going on; I watch the others carefully, and when cards are revealed I backtrack and remember how they reacted, how they used them. The bag of dimes is getting depleted quickly, but finally—

"You won the hand," Ardan says, looking dumbfounded. I reach in and slide the money toward me, ignoring the daggers in Flannery's eyes—and the one on her hip.

"Beginner's luck," she says, and we play again.

But then I win a second hand a few rounds later, then a third, and I'm back to where I started money-wise. I focus, watching where Callum places the discarded cards in the deck. I'm not good enough to count them all, but I keep an eye on when several hearts or high cards are put down at once, betting higher than the fifty-cent minimum when I think they're about to reappear. It works, and after a few hours, I'm slightly above Flannery and Callum. Ardan and Declan are teetering on bankruptcy.

"Where'd you learn this game?" Ardan says accusingly. He turns to Flannery. "Did you teach this to her last night? Brigit's gonna be pissed."

"Sit down," Flannery scolds. "I didn't teach her anything. I know better than that."

"I'm good with cards, is all," I say quickly. And then, while I have their attention: "Thought your people would be, too."

It gets the reaction I'm hoping for; Ardan snarls and rises, and Declan has to force him down. Callum and Flannery make eye contact and go uncomfortably still.

"Our people?" Callum says. "That's the thing about you, you buffers. You think you know all about us. But fine—you're so good at cards? Up the wager."

"Okay," I say. "To what?"

"Three dollars a hand."

I shrug. "That's it?" My stomach is in knots. If I lose a few hands at that high a bet, I'm out—and not just of the game. Of bargaining tools.

"You have a better idea?"

"We're not letting you go," Flannery says before I can speak. "If that was your idea—play for your freedom? Not a chance. We'd get shunned. Thrown out. Travellers don't just betray their family."

"All right," I say, trying to look disappointed. I'm not—because I'm not surprised. I never planned to ask for my freedom; that's clearly something that will have to be stolen, not won. I pretend to think for a moment, then raise my chin a little. "Information. I win, you tell me what you know."

"About what?" Declan asks. I can tell Flannery knows where this is headed before I say the name.

"About Grohkta-Nap," I say.

Callum laughs out loud. "You think you can walk in here and win our history from us?"

"I just want to know what you know about her," I say.

"Well…you know, we've got a song about her. Legends

about her, stories that would make your head spin. I know what buffers think about legends, though—the same thing they think about us." She motions to herself and the boys. "That we aren't real. But listen here, Ginny Andersen: We're real, realer than anything you've got in your world. Real enough that it'll cost a lot more than three dollars," Flannery says, voice sharp.

"Five," I say, and Ardan shifts, looking as if he's about to agree. The others glare at him.

"What? Our stories aren't *that* great. And you hate our traditions more than anyone, Flannery," he says.

"But they're *our traditions*," Callum says firmly, and Ardan falls silent.

I exhale. "All right..." I reach behind my back and pull out the red shoes. "What about for these?"

Flannery twitches a little, and Ardan rolls his eyes. "What would I want with ladies' shoes?" he asks.

"I wouldn't think to tell you what to do with your winnings," I say, "but I think a girl might be grateful to get these as a gift."

"Very, very grateful," Declan says, grinning mischievously. I decide not to dwell too long on what he means.

"Red's against the rules here," Flannery says. "Draws the monsters in." I didn't notice it before this moment, but now that she's pointed it out I realize she's right—the camp is blue, green, yellow, purple, a million colors, but not red. I shrug.

"If you're worried—"

"Don't you try that on her," Callum threatens, glowering at me. Even as he says this, though, he puts down a few coins, counting himself in. Ardan finally relents as well. It's down to Flannery, who looks at the shoes for a long time.

"Come on, Flannery. Hey—maybe we can sweeten the pot. You marry the winner?" Declan waggles his eyebrows at her in a way that makes me want to slap him.

Flannery's face tightens. "You'll be inclined to remember, Declan, that while I may be the Princess of Kentucky, I'm still a fuckin' lady." She looks at me. "Deal. Three rounds, two drops."

The cards are dealt, and the table is quiet; outside, we can hear the muffled sounds of roosters and dogs and children. I lift my cards, surveying them for a moment. It's not the best hand, but I've had worse in the past few hours. I save my hearts and a single ace, and drop the other cards. I draw the queen of hearts, trying not to let my relief show—it's a good hand, an extremely good hand.

"I'm done," Ardan says, putting his cards down; Declan follows. Callum studies me, and then glances toward Flannery.

"You're a bunch of asses. It's the first time she's played. Don't let her scare you off." Callum says. He draws a card on the third round, but I ride it out—the hand is already strong enough, I think.

"Right, then. One, two, three—" We slap our cards down on the table.

Callum whoops and throws a hand into the air. He won. He reaches across the table, grabbing my winnings and the shoes, and I feel as if I'm withering in front of him. Flannery sighs; Declan takes another long swig from the thermos.

And outside, someone screams.

CHAPTER NINETEEN

꤮

The boys and Flannery leap to their feet. I follow them to the tent flap; when it's raised, there's chaos. People are screaming, parents are hustling their children toward the center of the camp. I hear shotguns being cocked, people crying and shouting. Ardan and Declan dash from the door of the tent. A man with Declan's sharp nose and chin tosses him a rifle. There are whistles, and a crowd of men is gathering at the edge of the RVs, staring into the forest, their eyes locked on the trees ahead.

Flannery grabs the shirt of a crying woman who runs past, yanking her around. "Who's gone?" Flannery shouts at her.

The woman is quivering, eyes wide and filled with tears. "Keelin," she says. "The little one."

"Keelin," says a voice behind me—Callum. "They never take girls her age. She's too young."

"Apparently not," Flannery says, releasing the woman, who stumbles away toward her RV. Callum vanishes back into his tent.

"What's happening?" I ask.

"Fenris," Flannery hisses, as if she hates even the word. "Took one of our girls, seems."

My lips part in surprise. "He could be with them," I say, ignoring her as my heart rate rises. "Kai could be with them. He might be a wolf now; he won't know what he's doing. Flannery, I have to—"

"You have to do nothing," she answers. "If he's a wolf, if he's got a little girl out there, you really want us to go easy on him just because he used to be your boyfriend? And besides, you said Grohkta-Nap took him. Her guards don't take girls like this. Hers are tame."

I'm about to respond—though I'm not sure how—when Callum pushes past me and Flannery. He brushes his hair back with one hand and slings a rifle over his shoulder with the other, takes a few steps forward—

"Callum!" Flannery says, and there's a desperation in her voice that surprises me. He stops, turns back, and looks at her. The eye contact seems to break whatever pain was rising in Flannery's eyes. She shrugs a little, glancing at the ground. "Bring one back alive, and we'll add it to the menagerie."

Callum laughs and shakes his head, but he can't totally hide the nervousness in his voice. Then he turns, running to the hunting party. Finally, the group moves forward as a single unit, determined, strong. I can't help but feel a strange twinge of jealousy—when Kai went missing, the cops, my mother, the neighbors barely even listened to me. Flannery watches them disappear into the trees; she reaches down and wraps her fingers around her knife enviously as the last one disappears.

"What happens now?" I whisper.

"Well..." Flannery says, turning her head toward the center of camp. The other Travellers are gathered there, children in the center of a circle. They're all on their knees, and I hear one word louder than the rest—*Grohkta-Nap*. They pray for her protection, her grace, her will to bring Keelin back. Flannery looks back at me, studying me for a moment, and I find myself hoping we'll join them. I want to be a part of this. I want to do *something* to help.

"Follow me," Flannery says, then turns and sprints away from the others. I follow, swallowing my disappointment. We cut around behind the RV, till the noise from the center of camp gets quieter and quieter. We're headed toward the trees, and it makes my hands tremble. We come to a stop by the menagerie.

"We should get inside," I say, panting. "I've seen the Fenris, Flannery, and I don't really want to again."

"This lot is the best alarm system in the camp," Flannery says, motioning to her animals. They're stretched out in the sun, lazily flicking their ears. Their legs are caked with mud from where the snow became water and soaked the ground.

Flannery ducks into Wallace, emerging with a bag of cheap dog food. She empties it into the pens; most of the animals ignore it. Flannery leans over the fox's pen and extends her fingers toward it; it shies away, making an angry hissing noise at her. She stretches her hand farther, and the animal suddenly lunges, its teeth nearly grazing Flannery's palm. She yanks her hand back to her chest.

"Did it get you?" I ask, bouncing my eyes between her and the tree line.

"Nah," Flannery says. "It never does. Keeps trying, though. It's getting stronger." The last word rolls off Flannery's tongue in a voice that sounds like Brigit's.

"Why not let it go?" I ask in a pleading voice. "All of them. They're miserable."

"Because," Flannery says, looking at the fox a little admirably, "if they can survive me, they can survive anything."

"I know how they feel," I mutter.

"You think you know what it is to be trapped, Ginny?" Flannery says, shaking her head as if she pities me. "Who has you locked up?"

"Um, you, for one."

"Yeah, but *really*," Flannery says, rolling her eyes as if I was kidding. "Trust me. These animals and me, we know more about being trapped than you'll ever know." She pauses and looks back at the fox. "But one day we'll be strong enough to bust free."

I frown, almost uncomfortable with how sane Flannery just sounded. I'm about to speak, but I get cut off—something deep in the forest howls. The animals tense but don't panic. Flannery's face becomes hard.

"That far off already..." she says under her breath.

"Do the men who went after them always come back?" I ask, taking a step back, away from the trees.

Flannery chews her lip and looks at me. "Usually." She pauses, staring at the forest. "Sometimes it's too late for the girl."

I nod, wanting to say something, but I can't find the words. Flannery takes a few steps closer to the trees, her arms to her sides as if she's approaching a cliff. She closes her eyes, waiting, waiting, daring something to snatch her. When nothing happens, her arms fall, and she shakes her head and turns around, looking irritated. I can't stop the sigh of relief from escaping my lips.

"If she dies, we're supposed to be happy for her. Grohkta-Nap wanted it," she says, giving me a hard look. "And if she lives, we're supposed to celebrate Grohkta-Nap, too. And if she takes one of our boys to be on her guard, well...then we're suppose to really celebrate. She always takes the best ones. The most handsome or the most clever or the most talented. Once we saw one of our boys with her, after she'd made him..." She pauses. "*Different*. He'd forgotten us. Even forgotten how to speak Shelta. But most of the time, we just never see them again."

"You're afraid she'll take Callum," I realize aloud. Flannery whirls around, eyes flickering dangerously. She yanks her knife from her belt and charges forward. I curl my toes, lock my feet into place, and try not to breathe as she lunges at me. I lift my chin and clench my fists as she holds the blade to my throat.

"It would be an honor for Callum to become one of her guards," she growls.

"You don't really think that. You don't want him to go, to forget you."

"Shut your mouth, buffer. No one would be angry if I killed you."

"Why not just marry *him*?" I choke out, wincing.

Flannery glares at me, pressing so hard that I can't believe the blade doesn't draw blood. But then she cusses loudly and pulls the knife away, though she doesn't sheath it. Her cheeks are red and her eyes are glowing as she turns her gaze to the forest. Another howl; the animals curl into balls now, burying their heads by their haunches. Flannery takes a step toward the trees again.

"It's complicated," Flannery says, voice low.

"It seems easy to me. Your mother wants you to get married. You're in love with him. Does he not—"

"That's not it," Flannery cuts me off. "Look, if I marry Callum, or anyone, it'll be because I want to. Not because it'll shut my mother up, or because it's convenient, or because of some stupid tradition. I'm not using love as a means to an end."

The argument I prepared while she was talking almost leaves my lips—I loved Kai, but I also loved the idea of what we would do together. Of how his talent would mean me leaving Atlanta, finding a new home. Did I use him as a means to an end, as an excuse not to create my own plans, my own life?

"Tell me about your boy," Flannery interrupts my thoughts quietly.

"Kai?"

She nods.

"He . . . plays the violin. He's amazing at it—he's better at playing the violin than I'll ever be at doing anything. But the thing about Kai is underneath all that talent, he's normal. He's not arrogant; he's not waiting to become famous or rich. He just loves playing the violin for what it is." I pause, because everything I'm saying seems stupid, mundane. "That's how he loves me—for what I am. Kai makes me feel like myself. Like for the rest of the world, I'm pretending, but with him, I'm real."

"So what happens if you don't get him back? You're a paper doll for the rest of your life?"

"I used to think so," I say. "Part of me still thinks so. I never pictured a version of my life without him."

Flannery spits on the ground, rolling her eyes. "Goddamnit, Ginny. You don't realize how lucky you are. I'm the Princess of Kentucky no matter what. But you can be whatever you want to be; you can do whatever you want to do. You can be . . . I don't know. A teacher. Or a drunk. Or both, I don't know."

"You really don't like being the Princess of Kentucky?"

"Of course I like it," she says, looking a little offended. "It means I'm gonna be queen someday. This is my home. And that aside, it's my favorite place in the world. I mean, you should see it at Christmas. Everyone turns off their trailer lights at night, and we use all the generators to run thousands and thousands of string lights all over the camp, connected to every single trailer and tent. Like a knot between every one of us. It's the most beautiful thing you've ever seen." She runs her tongue along her teeth and shakes her head. "What kind of leader would I be, though, if I got married just to hold on to the crown tighter? Nah. If I'm not queen enough on my own, then ... maybe I'm just not queen enough."

"What would be your first order of business?" I ask, lifting my eyebrows. "I mean, day one. What do you do?"

"Well, I bury my mother, I guess, since if it's my first day, that means—"

"Okay, okay. *After* that. What's the first nondepressing thing you do?"

Flannery grins wickedly. "I tell all the women here they don't have to clean the entire trailer every damn day. Or at the very least, they don't have to mop every day."

"Every day?" I ask, shocked.

"Most of them," she says. "And let's see, second order of business..." She looks toward the woods and drops her voice. "We go after the Fenris. *Really* go after them. And not just when a girl's taken, not just when Grohkta-Nap steps in." Her second order doesn't surprise me, but the way she says Grohkta-Nap does—as if it's a joke. My eyebrows lift, and Flannery shrugs at me.

"My mother says you think she's the queen of the Fenris. That she's as evil as they are," she says. "Is that true?"

I exhale. "I don't know what she is, really. I don't know how she does what she does. You're the only people I've met since leaving home who already knew about her. That song, Flannery..."

"I'm not singing it for you," Flannery says, shaking her head. "It's ours. Besides, I know you just want it so you can use it to find your boy. Grohkta-Nap claimed him, he's hers—"

"You don't really think she's a goddess, though, do you?" I ask, and Flannery stops short. She cracks her knuckles and presses her lips together.

"I dunno. Me and some of the other Travellers our age have our doubts. No one will say it outright, 'course. But... the Fenris take our girls. Grohkta-Nap takes our boys. Seems like the same thing, different name, and some of us are getting tired of it." Flannery looks at me for a while, then back to the trees. "I've walked along the edge of the woods before. Worn all the red I could get my hands on. The Fenris have never taken me." She drums her fingers across her knife. "Wish they'd try. Maybe then I'd get some answers. Get a chance to fight one. See if my mother thinks I'm weak after *that*."

"Why not go after them, then?" I ask seriously.

"You think I'm afraid?" she asks, eyebrows lifting. I shake my head, and she exhales. "Maybe I should. Take a page out of the buffer book, go after the monsters with a cookbook and a pair of high heels." Flannery kicks at the ground a little

194

before speaking again. "Difference between you and me, Ginny, is you're chasing after your family. I'd just be running from mine."

The hunting party returns three hours later, at twilight. They exit the forest shadows of the men who went in—they look tired, sweaty, and hungry. Beaten. Flannery, Brigit, and I are standing at the door of their RV letting news filter back to us. The Fenris were sluggish in the snow, and they ran instead of fighting back. Still, there was no sign of Keelin—though one of the men has a scrap of the scarf she was wearing, the ends frayed and bitten off.

"Come on, then," Brigit says quietly. We follow her to her tent, where she unlocks a large steamer trunk. Inside are unopened bottles of liquor. She hands one to me and one to Flannery, and holds on to the other herself. Together, we walk to a small black tent, one that's near the boundary of the camp.

There are dozens of people here, but no one speaks; the sound of feet padding across frost and mud suddenly seems loud and imposing. Inside the tent, I hear crying, but not the loud, hysterical sort. A gentle noise, like a rain that will last for days instead of a storm that will last an hour. There are dozens and dozens of bottles at the front door already, some with silk flowers tied to them, or scarves, or charms. The crowd steps back as Brigit approaches—I see Callum among them, looking grim.

Brigit says something in Shelta—something that includes

the word *Grohkta-Nap* and inspires the others to clasp their hands and look to the sky. She then sets her bottle down with the others; Flannery does the same. I walk up and place mine down, letting my fingers trail along the top of the bottle.

A piece of paper flutters in the wind, stuck under a candle. It's a photo, I assume of Keelin. I lean in closer to see it, my eyes widening a little. Long blond hair, sunny face—I remember seeing her.

My heart stops.

She was the little girl wearing Mora's coat.

Keelin was too young to be taken. They usually want them older—that's what Callum said. Unless they didn't mean to take Keelin, unless they thought she was someone else. Lucas said it was strange for them to be around in this sort of cold. I think about the way Mora ran back in Nashville rather than fighting, about the way the Fenris at the rest stop looked at her fur coat in the back of my car. About the fact that the snow slows the Fenris down.

They thought Keelin was Mora.

"They're chasing her," I say under my breath. "She makes it snow to slow them down. They're—"

"Quiet," Flannery hisses at me, and I go red, dropping my eyes in shame. But there it is, the realization, unfurling inside me. I'm not the only one who wants to find Mora.

No wonder she's running.

CHAPTER TWENTY

ⓔⓧⓞ

The Travellers are mostly quiet the following day. There's no music echoing over the camp, no laughter, and every now and then someone paces along the edge of the forest with a shotgun, waiting for a target that never comes. A rainstorm sweeps through in the afternoon, cold and miserable; I fall asleep to the sound of it pelting the RV's roof.

When I wake up a few hours later, Flannery is at the kitchen table. She's fiddling with a music box she's taken apart, broken into a million pieces; the little plastic ballerina lies on her face on the kitchen table across from where Flannery is sitting. Flannery moves the pieces around as if she means to put the box back together but doesn't know where to begin. She looks up at me.

"*Shoru*'s tonight," she says dully, then answers my question before I can ask it. "Funeral. Well. Sort of. There's no body, so..." She shrugs and looks back at her music box.

"Should I . . . do you wear black?" I ask.

"If you've got a black dress hidden somewhere, feel free," Flannery says, and I'm sad she doesn't grin to punctuate the sarcasm.

A knock at the door; Flannery looks up, confused. She rises and goes to answer it.

"Flannery," a male voice says.

"Callum," Flannery says. "What're you here for?"

"I, uh . . . came to apologize. No Fenris for your collection, I guess."

"Yeah." Flannery exhales and looks at me. "'S for the best, I guess. Better you be alive and all. I'll get one someday."

"You will," Callum says with enough certainty that even I believe him.

A long silence again, in which I can tell Flannery and Callum are making still, perfect eye contact. Finally, he exhales and moves a bit. "I brought these for you." I see his arm extend; he's holding Ella's shoes. They're even shinier than before, as if he buffed them.

Flannery's face forms a strange expression; her eyebrows dip down, her lips part, and for perhaps the first time I see she's not entirely unlike the girls I go to school with—save the knife. She reaches forward, hooking her fingers into the heels.

"Why'd you want to give these to me?" she asks.

"I dunno," Callum says, sounding sheepish. "Figured maybe the red would bring the Fenris to you, finally. Besides, it's not like there's someone else I want to give them to."

"No one else?" Flannery asks immediately, pointedly, and there's so much weight on the question that even I sink under it. It's a long time before Callum answers.

"Nah. No one else." He exhales. "I should go."

"Yeah," Flannery says. "There's no point...I mean..."

"Yeah. Enjoy the shoes."

The door shuts.

Flannery walks over to the table, eyes cast down, hair wild and tangled around her face. She puts the heels on the table and sits down, staring at them, then looks up at me.

"Do you know how to wear these?"

"I know the basic idea," I say.

"They're stupid. I mean, seriously—who the fuck designed these? You can't run. You can't even walk on anything but pavement. That heel'll sink right into the dirt."

She's quiet again, crossing her arms, but her eyes keep flitting to the shoes.

"Do you want me to show you how to walk in them?" I ask quietly. Flannery scoffs and shrugs her shoulders, but then stands and takes her shoes off. She holds on to the table as she steps into the heels. They're a little too big, but not horribly so. Once she's in them and balanced, she looks up at me hopefully. I rise.

"Try to take a step," I say; Flannery obeys, almost immediately toppling to the floor. "No—don't slide your foot. Just step and—yeah. Only instead of hitting heel first, kinda hit toe first. Sort of." Flannery wobbles across the RV's tiny kitchen and back. I'm glad Ardan can't see her.

"How do you keep from . . . damn it," Flannery says when she wobbles to the side and has to grab onto the oven.

"Pull up from your stomach," I say, though I'm not sure I have a clue what I'm talking about. Flannery lifts up, and I raise my eyebrows—she looks regal, like Brigit. Less like a girl, more like a queen. She takes a few more wobbly steps, then a handful of confident ones before she grins and sits down, sliding her feet out and rubbing the arches.

"They're still ridiculous," Flannery says, though it doesn't wipe the smile off her face. She picks up the music box figurine and makes her spin between her fingers for a few moments.

That evening, at the shoru, the Travellers cook dinner over the campfire, potatoes and meat—I'm not entirely sure what type—wrapped up together and left on the rocks surrounding the fire until cooked through. Declan plays guitar, songs that start out somber and pick up as the night wears on. There's liquor, but also milk with honey stirred together, and cakes with hard shells but soft centers.

"Not all our traditions are bad," Flannery tells me under her breath as she stuffs a few cakes down her shirt for later.

By sunset, most of the crowd is drunk and dancing, save Keelin's parents; they sit beside Brigit at the head of the fray, eyes glistening with tears in the firelight but faces firm. Yet by the time Brigit and Flannery disappear together a few hours in, Keelin's parents sink even farther down in their chairs, as if they're hoping to melt into the ground like the snow.

No more stalling. I'm going to have to run for it, and

soon. I begin to consider when—are the wolves more likely to get me in the daylight, or at night?—when Callum walks over and sits down in the dirt beside me.

"Wager I can't talk you into another round of Widow's Lover, can I?" he asks.

"Not a chance," I say. "You'll forgive me for still being bitter that you won."

"Ah," Callum says, grinning. "You might've had me. The secret to that game—to all games, really, if you ask me—is to always have the upper hand."

"In a game of chance, that's easier said than done."

Callum nods a little. "Always have the upper hand, and if you should find yourself in a situation where you don't… create a new upper hand. You had me there, at the end, till I reminded you it was your first time playing. Made you bolt. Got me my upper hand back."

I consider this. "Just as well," I finally say. "Flannery likes the shoes more than I did anyhow."

Callum instantly goes red, staring at the fire. It's a few moments before he speaks again. "So she…she did like them? Really?"

"Yeah," I say. "I taught her how to walk in them."

"Good," Callum says, looking relieved. I can't decide who is more pathetic among us—me, kidnapped and desperately in need of a shower, or him, ridiculously in love with the Princess of Kentucky.

"I wanted to find one for her," Callum says, changing the subject. "Wanted to bring it to her alive."

"Has *anyone* ever caught one?"

"Killed one, yes. Not often, but yes. Caught one? No one's done it yet," he says, running his fingers through the dirt. "Truth is, Flannery's probably the only who's got the skill and strength to catch one, even though she doesn't believe that herself. She's never allowed to go after them anyway, so I guess it doesn't matter." He stops and smiles at me. "Did she tell you she's waiting for a bear to wander into camp, so she can catch it?"

"I heard," I say, rolling my eyes. "And she doesn't think she's strong...." Callum laughs aloud.

There's a toast going on for Keelin's parents; Callum and I lift our glasses, take obligatory sips, and then fall back to silence for a few moments.

"Truth is," he says, "nothing good can happen from going after monsters. They don't live in our world; they don't play by our rules. I don't mean Traveller rules—*human* rules. You're going after your boy, Ginny, but even if you find him... he's not going to be the same boy. You can't live with a monster and walk out a person."

"Maybe," I say, nodding slowly. "But maybe it's just no one's done it yet."

Callum frowns, but before he gets a chance to respond, Flannery is behind me. I'm not sure if she says anything, or if it's the daggers in her eyes that make me turn around and look at her.

"You okay, Sherlock?" Callum asks. Her hands are in fists and her hair is even more of a knotted mess than usual. She

202

stares at Callum for a moment; her hands relax and it looks as if she's going to reach for him. Instead, she exhales and turns away.

"I'm fine. Let's go," she says to me.

"Where?"

"To sleep. Does it matter, for fuck's sake? Come on," she snaps, and spins on her heel. I rise, slowly; Callum looks at me and raises his eyebrows, but I shrug.

"All right. Night, Flannery," he calls across the few yards between us. "See you tomorrow, Ginny."

I open my mouth to answer him, but he's already turned back to the fire. I hurry to catch up to Flannery.

"Are you all right?"

"Don't talk to me," she says.

"Okay—"

"Don't talk, period," she says. "I just want to go to bed, all right?"

I nod. We reach the RV door, which she flings open. She goes into the bathroom for a moment, leaving me in the kitchen. I absently open up Grandma Dalia's cookbook, still on the table with my other things and Flannery-slash-Ella's heels. My fingers drift along the pages—

"Stop looking at that," Flannery snarls, and I look up—she's standing in the doorway, face red.

"Why?" I ask.

Her hands are shaking. I don't understand why she's so angry. "Because there's no point. You're not leaving. So you can stop acting like some lovesick little girl. Better to stop looking at it, and stop talking about him, and stop thinking about him. He *left you*, Ginny."

My eyes widen. "You think I don't know that?" I snap. "But I don't love him just because he loved me back, so I can't hate him just because he's stopped. And besides, she's not a goddess, Flannery—the Fenris are chasing her down. She's running from them, not leading them."

"Don't be stupid. Just because there's a bigger monster chasing Grohkta-Nap doesn't mean you're like her. Doesn't mean you can beat her. You think the fact that you love Kai means you'll win?"

"No," I say slowly. "I think the fact that I love Kai means I'll fight for him."

Flannery balls her hands into fists, and for a moment, I'm certain she's going to punch me. But no—she storms into her bedroom and flops down on her bed, pulling the mismatched flannel blankets up to her face even though it's stuffy in here. I'm not tired, but I climb into my sleeping bag and stare at the ceiling, trying to ignore the spark that Flannery's words caused to leap up within me. *He left me. Our love wasn't strong enough. What makes me think any part of me is?*

"You didn't congratulate me," Flannery says after a half hour, her voice flat.

"On what?" I ask, spitting the words. I'm angry at her, even angrier with myself for letting her stir up doubt in my chest.

She inhales, and I can practically see the eye roll in her words. "On my engagement."

CHAPTER TWENTY-ONE

Flannery and Callum are getting married.

"There's nothing at all wrong with him—besides, everyone knows you two want each other. Will you stop slouching like that? We'll never get it to fit," Brigit says as Flannery stands in her tent, staring at herself in a mirror. Flannery is wearing a wedding gown, a big, sparkly sort of thing that looks like a high school prom dress on steroids. Other Traveller girls hover around Flannery, offering suggestions as to how she should wear her hair, or who among them should be her bridesmaids. They brag about the dresses they own, how they're sparkly but "not so much that it'll overwhelm yours, Flannery."

Flannery doesn't seem to care. Not about them, or the dress, or the engagement, or anything. She won't make eye contact with me, instead staring at her own reflection as if she loathes it. I pull my knees up on the love seat, the same place I sat when I first arrived, and watch, mesmerized, horrified, next to the pile of her regular clothes that have been discarded in lieu of the gown.

"Is Sal really gonna be able to take it in fast enough? It's just that it's about four sizes too big in the waist. Though it fits just right up top—god, Flannery, when did you grow these tits?"

"I wonder what Callum's doing right now."

"Probably getting drunk. All grooms get drunk before the wedding."

"Are you sure you don't want to switch and marry Ardan? I saw him naked once...."

"I hope he cleans his house a little. I wouldn't want to spend my wedding night in Callum's place as is."

Flannery's hair looks stupid in the weird updo one of the girls is tying it into. I want to say something, but I don't. *Besides, this'll make it easier. If she has to stay with Callum tonight, I'll be able to run for it since Flannery won't be guarding me.* Just as I'm thinking this, Flannery finds my eyes; she doesn't say anything before looking away. I reach across the love seat and slowly, carefully pull Flannery's knife and Wallace's key from her discarded jeans' pocket. It takes me only seconds to tuck them into the back of my bra strap. It takes me even less time than that to be certain that if I need to use the knife—against a werewolf or a human—I will.

Kai and I first heard the story of Emperor Nero from his third violin teacher. He went through them quickly, getting a new one each time he surpassed the previous's skill. Kai was ambivalent, but I loved the story. A man, standing amid flames, playing the violin. Fearless, so enamored with his music that he didn't care about the danger.

Of course, then we were told that some suspect he set the fire. He let Rome burn so he could tear down the charred shells of homes to build a new palace. Nero lit the stadium where they held chariot races on fire first, but the rest of Rome was quick to follow. The fire burned for days. I wondered if Nero played the violin the entire time. I wondered if he played it because he didn't care, or if he didn't set the fire and played it because it was the only thing that kept him from going mad, watching his empire become ash.

Kai didn't wonder anything like that. To him, it was just a story—and a likely untrue one at that. He got hung up on the fact that violins weren't even around in ancient Rome, so Nero couldn't have played one. It was a detail that didn't matter much to me, so while Kai practiced and I sat in Grandma Dalia's mauve recliner, I thought about Nero. I thought about him as a villain, as a hero, but mostly as a man.

Maybe all you can do, when your world is burning, is hold on to the thing you love the most.

The bonfire is huge, the crowd feasting on fresh bread and roasted chickens. Flannery and Callum sit in throne-like chairs a few dozen yards from the bonfire, where people run up to give them gifts and advice, or to make lewd jokes to Callum. His face looks as contorted and uncomfortable as hers; they clasp hands tightly, as if they're afraid to let go. Callum is wearing a dress shirt, though the collar buttons are missing and he has the sleeves rolled up, and I have to admit, Flannery looks beautiful. Awkward, but beautiful.

Brigit conducts the ceremony, speaking in Shelta, asking Flannery to repeat after her. She's misty-eyed, happy, as if she doesn't notice that her daughter appears to be dying a slow, chiffon-induced death. The couple exchange simple silver rings, and then Brigit binds Flannery's and Callum's hands with bits of scarf and declares their hearts and minds tied together like their wrists. And then it comes time to kiss, and Callum leans toward Flannery—

She flinches, pulls back, and a ripple of dissatisfaction goes through the crowd. Callum watches Flannery for a moment, then leans forward and whispers something to her—not something sweet or poetic, I can tell by the lines of his face. He pulls back and I see him tap her hand with his thumb, counting down. One. Two.

They kiss on "three," short and quick, but it's enough that the crowd cheers, stomps their feet, and throws artificial flower petals in the air. Brigit instructs the couple to sit back down and urges the musicians—a handful of guitar players—to play something snappy. Couples dance, liquor drinks are poured, and the revelry begins. I hang toward the back of the crowd, by Ardan and Declan, who are placing bets on how long it'll be before Flannery gives Callum a black eye. I consider getting in on the wager.

If it weren't for the fact that the bride and groom look

utterly miserable, the wedding would be pretty amazing—the sort of homegrown thing that those brides on the reality shows my classmates watched are always trying to emulate. The guests look happy and well fed, the music hardly stops, and the sky above is clear and diamond-studded. A few hours in and the liquor is still flowing, encouraging the frenzy. Callum waves for someone to bring him a large cup of beer. Flannery eyes him, shakes her head, then slumps down in her chair. Her eyes narrow, as if she's thinking very hard. She exhales, looks at me as if she wants to say something, and then—

"Hey, boys?" she calls across the fire to the musicians. "How about 'Winter's Keep'?"

I see Callum's eyebrows shoot up. He looks at me and, for a moment, I think he's going to call out for them to stop. But Flannery somehow pulls his eyes to her, and there's a silent conversation between them. Callum sits back in his chair as the musicians begin to play.

Come along, my brothers,
stay your drink and calm your words.
It's comin' on the season,
bring the ice and go the birds.

And with it comes a lady,
from the great wood, strong and bright.
She tames the fangs and fur and claw,
we honor her, tonight.

She lives among the selchs and snow,
she knows her magic well.
She'll call the very best to her,
The rest she'll send to hell.

So climb into your beds, my friends,
But think before you sleep, of
the beauty and the terror
of the Lady Winter's Keep.

I inhale, close my eyes, and replay the words in my head over and over until they're memorized.

CHAPTER TWENTY-TWO

It's late—three or four in the morning, and my breath forms bright white clouds as a group of Travellers escort Flannery and Callum back to his RV. It's covered in Christmas lights, and someone has painted flowers on the door frame. Flannery looks pale, and I want to follow her, but Brigit is watching me carefully. I swallow, turn my back on Flannery, and head back toward Brigit's RV. I hear Brigit finish her conversation; I glance over my shoulder casually, looking just far enough to know she's following me. When I reach the trailer I walk immediately to Flannery's bedroom, pull on one of her hoodies to fight the temperature, and get in the bed on the floor. Brigit opens the trailer's main door, and a series of sounds tell me she's taking jewelry off, opening cabinets and drawers. I jump when she suddenly flings open the door to Flannery's bedroom, her shape illuminated by the lamp in the kitchen.

"You can sleep in her bed, you know. She lives with Callum now," Brigit says, then shuts the door. The brusqueness of her words fully ignites the feelings that have been smoldering in me all day. I jump up and follow her out into the kitchen, letting Flannery's door bang into the wall behind me. Brigit is steeping a cup of tea, rubbing her temples. When she sees my expression, she scowls.

"Gonna come in here and go all buffer on me?" she says, motioning to me. She sounds as if she's prepared for this argument. "Call me a monster, a bad mother? Save it—I see your news programs. I know what you think of traditions that aren't like your own."

"She didn't want to marry him," I say, shaking my head. "That has nothing to do with tradition. She doesn't want him; it's simple."

"She loves him," Brigit says. "You know how lucky she is, that she loves the man she's marrying?"

"But she didn't *want*—"

"Don't think for a second you understand us after a few days," Brigit snaps, sloshing the tea from her cup. "Most of these Traveller girls, they're not going to be professors or lawyers or surgeons. They're going to be housewives. Except for Flannery. She's the one with a real future—she's going to be queen. But there's not a man in this camp that wouldn't take it from her. They see a single woman as weak, while a married woman as strengthened by her husband. Trust me"—she points to herself—"I know. Flannery deserves better than the reign I've had. Isn't that what every mother wants for her daughter—a better future than her own?"

I stay quiet; if Flannery herself can't convince Brigit that she's strong enough to rule *anything* on her own, from bears to deer to a clan of Travellers, then I doubt I can. I swallow as Brigit sits down at the kitchen table.

"What's going to happen to me?" I ask.

Brigit lifts an eyebrow, then shakes her head pityingly. "You haven't already decided? That's the problem with buffers, Ginny Andersen. You let the world determine your fate."

I firm my jaw. "So I'm a blessing, then?"

Brigit shrugs. "You're a curse. I wanted to leave you in the woods, let the Fenris have you, but Flannery made a bargain. She marries Callum without pitching a fit to the clan, and you stay here."

I nod faintly and walk back to the bedroom, shutting the door behind me. I lie down in bed—the one on the floor, not Flannery's—and stare at the ceiling. I hear Brigit finish her tea, put the cup in the sink, and then pause at my door for a moment, listening. I lie still, and Brigit eventually goes to her own bedroom. The trailer falls silent, though I can't tell if she's actually asleep or not. Any minute now, threads of gold and violet will appear in the sky. There's not much time.

I sit up in bed.

I don't know if Brigit's right—if I'm a curse, or a blessing, or neither. But she was definitely wrong about one thing:

I'm not letting the world—or anyone in it—determine my fate. Not anymore, at least.

I pull Flannery's window open; the cold air rushes in, biting my arms and neck. I can see the forest from here—are the Fenris there, waiting? I have to move either way; there's no time to dwell on the fear. The window frame is sharp—I can feel it bruising my hands as I heave myself up onto it. I hold my breath, listening for the sound of Brigit rising, moving, coming after me. Nothing.

I drop to the ground. It's so cold I feel a shock run from my feet to my hips as I hit the dirt. I reach into the hoodie pocket and find Flannery's knife—I stashed it in there hours ago—then run.

The camp is quiet, and I'm grateful for the snow that's still thick between trailers—it mutes the slap of my feet. I'm exhausted, my vision watery, but I keep moving. There, ahead—Callum's trailer. It's dark and still, like everything else, but I grip the knife even tighter in my hand as I approach. Something in the woods rustles, and my breath catches in my throat; I hold the knife ahead of me, keeping my eyes trained on the branches. I exhale. It's nothing, just snow falling from the trees. I turn back to the flower-painted door. *Now or never.* I hold my breath, turn the handle, and then push the door open.

I jump back. Flannery and Callum are awake, sitting at the head of the bed with a foot or so between them. They're wearing the same clothes I saw them in last—Callum in a dress shirt and Flannery in her wedding dress. There's a candle lit on the nightstand, making their bodies soft and shadowy.

"Ginny?" Flannery asks, making a face.

"Hi," I answer, because I don't know what else to say.

"What are you doing here?" Flannery says slowly. I step through the door frame, and her gaze falls to my right hand. "And what are you doing with my knife?"

"I'm . . . I'm kidnapping you," I say, brandishing it a little.

She raises her eyebrows and looks over at Callum. For a moment he's still, but I can't tell if it's because he's surprised, or because he's working out how best to fight me off. But then he laughs, a quiet sound, under his breath and guarded.

"What's so funny?" Flannery asks.

"I was just thinking about what I'll tell everyone tomorrow," he says. "My wife ran away with a buffer. While wearing her wedding dress."

Flannery laughs this time, and I can hear the relief in the sound. In lasts only a moment, though, and then they're still, staring at each other, as if I'm not in the doorway wielding a knife. Callum moves first, throwing his legs over the side of the bed.

"Go on. I'll buy you some time," he says swiftly, calmly.

Flannery looks at Callum incredulously. "I can't just . . . I can't just leave."

"You can," he says firmly. "Unless you want to stay. Do you?"

"Yes," Flannery says automatically. "This place is mine."

I'm not sure what she means by *mine*—her kingdom? Her home? I'm not sure she knows, either.

Callum pauses and asks a different question in a softer voice. "Do you want to stay if it means you're forced to marry me?"

And Flannery hesitates.

"Go," Callum says.

"I was that bad in bed?" Flannery says, trying to joke. The tears in her eyes betray her.

"Look, our first fight as a married couple," Callum says drily, and this finally gets a laugh from Flannery's throat. He smiles at her. "Also, you'll need to punch me."

"Why?" I ask.

"It needs to look like I fought back," Callum says. "If they think I let her leave, they'll shun me."

"How about instead of getting punched in the face, you come with us?" I suggest. Callum falters, looking away.

"You still don't get it," Flannery says, shaking her head at me. "This is our home. These people are family. And the world out there . . . well. It's not a world that makes it easy for a lone Traveller. But . . ." She looks down, balls her hand into a fist. "I . . . I just . . . I *can't* stay." Flannery then swings her fist forward, punches Callum hard in the face. The impact makes a loud *crunch* sound, and Callum goes down, crashing onto the floor of his trailer. Flannery lifts her chin and studies him as he wobbles to his feet.

"Is that gonna bruise?" she asks hurriedly. "I can do it again."

"It'll bruise." Callum winces. "Goddamn, Flannery. You never do anything halfway."

"All right," Flannery says, spinning around to me. "Let's go." I nod and dart for the door. I can already see the idea of the morning on the horizon. I jump from the edge of the trailer's door to the ground, icy and crunchy under my feet. I look over my shoulder to say something to Flannery—

They're kissing, Flannery's arms slung around Callum's neck, his hand resting on the small of her back, and I find I can't possibly speak and ruin it. Flannery looks small beside him, a body at odds with her personality, and when they break away they look at each other for a moment that lasts for years. Flannery inhales and shakes the sentiments away.

"Put some ice on that," she says, rubbing his eye with her thumb so hard he winces again. Then she springs out of the trailer after me, and we dash away together.

CHAPTER TWENTY-THREE

We weave away from the camp, around pockets of stragglers finishing off the last of conversations and beers. Flannery moves quickly, less sneaking, more prowling. It isn't until she hears the snuffling sounds, however, that she figures out where I'm headed—the menagerie. As we get closer to the animals—and therefore farther away from human ears—Flannery speaks again in a low voice.

"Well done, buffer."

"I try," I say, fishing the keys from my pocket and waving them at her.

Flannery inhales, then walks into Wallace. I hear a rustling, a clanging, and then there's a flurry of movement. I jump back just in time—the possums and raccoons stream out together; a few moments later, the rabbits cautiously hop down the steps and into the trees. Flannery reappears at the door, eyes locked on me, as if she can't bear to see the animals going.

"So are you driving, or am I?" she asks.

"You have to drive," I say. "I can't work a stick shift."

"That's the sexiest thing you've ever said."

"Stick shift?"

"No, 'you have to drive.'"

I would laugh if my heart weren't finding its way into my throat. I drop into the passenger seat as Flannery hitches up her dress and kicks off the red heels in order to work the pedals. It takes a moment for the engine to turn over; Flannery encourages it in Shelta. When it finally gives, she pats the dashboard and whoops. I almost fall out of my seat when Wallace jolts forward.

There's a screeching, ripping sound; I look out my window and see the deer leaping into the woods, then the fox, then the badger as we wreck the pens leaning against Wallace's side. Flannery slams on the brakes, twisting around to look through the back window. I see her watch the animals vanish into the forest, something akin to pain streaking across her face. The deer is the last to vanish, its white tail flicking up, a spark of bright in the black.

"Good luck," she murmurs. "Hope you're strong enough."

She stares a moment more, as if she expects the animals to reappear, then turns and grips the steering wheel tightly. "I hope we both are."

Flannery slams her foot down on the accelerator. Wallace flies forward, smoking, rattling, *running*. We curve to the outside of the camp; everything in the bus slides to the right as we tilt a little, one set of wheels riding along the incline leading to the trees.

"They're up," Flannery says sharply, her voice focused and clear. I look in my side mirror, grimace. People are stepping out of their homes, curious as to who has an engine running. As we progress I can tell people recognize the bus. They point, and then—

"What are they doing?" I ask in disbelief.

"Same thing I do if one of my animals gets loose," she says, then stomps on the gas. "I chase after it."

We lurch forward, fishtailing a few times when we hit slick spots. A car appears behind us, a rattly El Camino. It takes me a moment to recognize who's behind the wheel— Brigit herself. Behind it, I see other cars lighting up, people shouting and jumping into them through open windows. They're angry, swerving behind us, plowing through the edges of tent porches and sending tarps flying. Flannery takes a hard right turn, nearly toppling us to one side.

"Keep driving! Your mother's behind us!" I shout as I jump up and stumble my way to the back of the bus. Holding tight to a crevice by the roof, I fling open the back doors. The sound of engines and glare of headlights hits me, disorienting me for a moment; I almost fall out when Flannery takes an especially wild turn.

More time, more time. I look around frantically. There's nothing here, nothing except—

"How's it looking?" Flannery yells, punching the shifter into a higher gear.

"Perfect!" I yell back as I position one of the raccoon cages by the back door. *Wait, wait*—I kick it out just as the El Camino speeds up. It clatters to the ground; Brigit swerves to avoid it, but the cage hits the windshield of the truck behind her, shattering it.

The main road is up ahead—I see the station wagon just off the embankment. Faster, faster, though the bus is pitching dangerously. My heart speeds up, and my eyes narrow. I kick another cage out as we round another bend. It bounces along the ground toward the El Camino. Brigit avoids it but loses valuable seconds by braking to do so; I think I hear her cursing in the wind that's whipping hair into my eyes. I turn back to grab another cage—

I'm out. There's nothing else here, nothing to throw, nothing to do, and at least four vehicles chasing us. Flannery meets my eyes in the rearview mirror briefly; she speeds up in response. There's nothing left to do but drive—

I hear a kicking sound, and something about the drone of the engines changes. I whirl back around and see several sets of headlights growing smaller and smaller behind us, until we go over a little hill and they disappear entirely. The El Camino continues closing in, but suddenly its engine quiets as well. I narrow my eyes at the darkness—did Brigit give up? Surely not.

"What happened?" I shout to Flannery, cautiously making my way back to the front.

Flannery taps the brakes quickly, hard enough to cause the back doors to slam shut, then laughs. "Looks like they're all out of gas."

"So Callum did buy us time," I say.

"He did," Flannery says. "He bought us the rest of our lives. For the low, low cost of two raccoon cages."

I laugh, but then we're silent for a moment as it sets in. We're free. Both of us. This won't just be a good story to tell Kai—it'll be a good story to tell anyone, everyone. I feel like shouting, like celebrating; Flannery, on the other hand, looks shaken. Broken, even. She keeps looking in the rearview mirror as if she wants to see something familiar, something she loves, but it's empty.

"So," Flannery says, swallowing hard. "We're going to look for Grohkta-Nap. Us and the Fenris, too. Huh." It isn't a question, and I can tell that despite her doubts about Mora's divinity, Flannery is still afraid of her. I can also tell that having this plan, this mission, is the only thing stopping her from feeling totally adrift.

"You don't have to come," I remind her, just in case I'm reading her wrong. I want to give her an out.

"I know," Flannery answers. "But I spent my whole life thinking she was a goddess. My whole life being the shit Princess of Kentucky and being threatened with marriage and being told lies and..." She shakes her head. "I'm free. I don't have anywhere else to go now. And truth be told, I'd really like to stab something, so your Snow Queen will do."

MORA

Home. We're home.

It seemed an odd title for this place, when compared with homes in her other lives—the apartment on Fifth Avenue and the depths of the Atlantic Ocean. Different as those were, strange as they were, they felt like places she belonged. Places she loved. This place felt no more like home than the hotel rooms—a place to stay, nothing more, no matter how hard she tried to change that.

Mora let her fingers dance along tree trunks, watching frost climb from the roots to the tops of limbs at her touch. Despite there being no signs of Ginny or the Fenris on her trail, a nagging worry lingered in the back of her mind. She closed her eyes, focused on the water in the air, and made it cooler, cooler, until it became rain, then snow. It poured from the sky on her command and coated the ground, covering their tracks and freezing the Fenris out, should they be lurking somewhere close.

It almost amused her, how the Fenris probably thought they were taking any power she might have when they stripped her of her humanity. But in the ocean, her new sisters showed her how to listen to the water, how to use it for her will. Not control it, exactly, but to work with it, like persuading a wild horse to let you on its back. It was a skill Mora temporarily forgot when she first emerged from the waves and joined the Fenris. Now, it was easy: water in the sky to rain, rain to sleet, sleet to snow. The Fenris had inadvertently given her the very skill she needed to keep herself hidden from them.

Mora kicked at the ground, watched the snow turn to ice as it struck her boot, and then opened the front door. As expected, the cottage was disappointingly unwelcoming. She'd hoped moving into a small place, something that a grandmother or an artist might live in, would make it feel more... *real* than the high-end apartments and New England mansions she often took over. No such luck. *Perhaps we should move again*, she thought as the other members of her guard rushed to greet her at the door. They kissed her hands and the insides of her wrists, letting their fingers trail along her back. She allowed it for a moment, then stiffened; they stepped back and cast their eyes downward obediently.

"Gentlemen," she said fondly, "this is your new brother, Kai." She stepped aside and motioned to the doorway. Kai was there, silhouetted in gray light. Snow dusted his shoulders and his bare forearms, even clung to his thick lashes, something so attractive it made Mora press her lips together hungrily. She resisted the urge to kiss him, allowing the others to shake his hand instead. She often wondered if they really saw themselves as brothers, the way she and the other ocean girls saw themselves as sisters.

"Michael, unfortunately, didn't make it back," she said, dropping her head respectfully.

"What happened to him?" one of the boys—Edward— asked.

"He was shot," Mora answered. "By hunters. And they could be following us."

"We'll go stand lookout," Edward said immediately, and the others nodded in agreement. They were easily excited— there wasn't often much to do here, few ways for them to prove their love and devotion.

"Excellent," Mora said, smiling at them. Controlling the water was something Mora had to be taught, but controlling boys, teaching them to love her above all else? That came naturally. Perhaps it was something primal, or perhaps it was something that came from the darkness around her heart. The Fenris, after all, were all males and terribly good at persuading girls to love them, trust them. And then in the water, when she was an ocean girl, boys were hypnotized by the sound of her voice. Primal or dark, it wasn't a skill she fully recognized until well after the boy she loved kissed her.

If you'd known back then, you'd have him here with you. But now he's just dead in the ground. A corpse who can never love you. It was a disheartening thought, one that occurred to her daily—she could have had him, right there, and yet she had missed the chance.

That was the only thing she hated herself for.

The guards turned to go outside and begin setting up the lookout. Kai looked confused, bumbled around behind them, and shivered for a moment in the snow. Mora watched him carefully; he swallowed, and the chill bumps on his arms disappeared. He stood up straighter, now seemingly unfazed by the temperature, and walked off with another guard.

Mora sat down in a linen armchair and exhaled. Ginny wouldn't come—they never came, in the end. A few others had gotten close, of course—Michael's girl, Dalia, found the island even, but turned away when he broke her heart; he didn't remember her. Mora tried, once, to choose boys who weren't loved, who weren't adored, but they never made good guards. It wasn't their fault; it was just hard for her to love a boy who wasn't a challenge. Taking an unhappy, unloved person was so much easier than taking someone like Kai. Perhaps that was why it was so simple for the Fenris to take her, change her.

She'd considered killing her boys' lovers dozens of times. It would make it easier, but it would also draw so much attention. A trail of missing boys didn't attract the Fenris—they targeted girls. A trail of heartbroken girls didn't warrant their attention, either. But a trail of young, dead girls? There was nothing that would attract the Fenris quicker. Mora admired the girls who followed her, sometimes—after all, the boy she loved didn't track her down, didn't move heaven and earth to find her fading on the ocean floor—

226

Perhaps he didn't love you enough.

She clenched her fists, then reached over to sweep a lamp onto the floor in anger. It crashed, bits of colored glass skittering across the floor. *Stop it*, she scolded herself. *Enough.* Mora stomped to the front door and looked out at her storm. The Fenris were her concern at the moment. They were the threat. And they were smart enough to follow Ginny to her.

You're just a girl, Ginny, Mora thought, looking out at the clouds. *You're like I was, once upon a time. Innocent. Sweet. I don't want to kill you, but I will if you make me.*

CHAPTER TWENTY-FOUR

❦

Kai was the first one to recognize our love for what it was.

We were on the way to school and stopped by a doughnut shop on Ponce. It's one of those places that attract all types: blue shirts on their way to the office, the poor who just want an inexpensive breakfast, stoners who have been awake all night, and tired-looking mothers with babies in their arms.

We got up to the counter right as a new batch of doughnuts came out of the kitchen, and so, instead of ordering two apiece, Kai ordered a dozen, laughing aloud about how we should race to see who could eat their six fastest.

"Six?" asked a woman to our left. She was tall and blond, with skin that looked like leather and coral-colored lipstick. "Better watch how you eat now. It'll catch up to you," she said, giving me an especially long look.

I made a face at her; she made an *ugh* noise at me and turned around to place her order (some sort of smoothie and a bagel, neither of which I realized the doughnut shop carried). Kai and I sat down at a table near the back, silently agreeing that we'd skip first period in order to enjoy our feast. We each lifted a doughnut and pretended to toast.

"She's right, you know," he said in faux seriousness. "We're going to end up like those people who get removed from their houses with forklifts, if we keep this up."

"Not me," I said. "They're going to have to just tear my house down around me."

Kai laughed. "Then we'll go on a talk show, one of the trashy ones. Where we're both huge and weird but talk about how we've been in love since we were little kids so we don't care that combined, we weigh as much as an adult elephant." I choked on a doughnut laughing, and as I regained my composure Kai grew a little quiet, realizing what he'd just said.

"Not in love since we were little kids," I corrected, and Kai looked down, embarrassed. I continued, "Since we were *seven*. Seven is just straight-up 'kid.' Anything under six is 'little kid.'"

He exhaled and grinned. "Oh, I disagree. Under six is baby."

"It is not! No one remembers when they're a baby, but I remember life before I was six. Bits and pieces, anyway."

"Fair point. I guess I do, too," he said, starting on a second doughnut.

"What do you remember?"

"Little things. Nothing important. Going to school, the red lunch box I loved. Oh, and the Easter my cousins came to town. I got into a fistfight with the older one."

"Who won?"

"She did," he said. "That's pretty much all I remember, though, from that age." Then he shrugged, blushing hard enough that his ears turned red. "There wasn't much worth remembering before you, Ginny."

Eventually, I wrap myself in a blanket I find under a seat and fall asleep on Wallace's floorboards. I expect Flannery to join me at some point, but when I wake up, we've parked and she's sitting on the bench in front of the little table. More impressively, the table is piled high with bags of groceries, blankets, and clothes from Goodwill. She's changed, now wearing a long-sleeved T-shirt and jeans that have so few holes, they look strange on her.

"Where did this come from?" I ask, squinting in the sun. It's got to be early afternoon, maybe even later.

"This? There's a Goodwill just around the corner."

"That's not what I meant," I say. "Where'd you get the money for all this stuff?"

"Easy," Flannery says. "There's some sort of indoor pool-waterslide-thing up the street. Full of tourists—seriously, who needs to swim in November? That's the whole point of November. You don't have to swim. But anyway, it was easy. Picking wallets was like picking apples, for fuck's sake."

"You stole people's wallets to buy us clothes?"

"No," Flannery says, rolling her eyes. "I stole people's wallets to buy us food. And blankets that don't have raccoon fur on them. And then I stole us some clothes."

I frown but don't protest too much when she hands me something from the grocery bag—beef jerky. It's not exactly my favorite breakfast item, but I'm definitely not going to be picky at the moment.

"So," Flannery says once I've changed clothes—she greatly overestimated the size of my chest, so my shirt is huge. She's in the driver's seat and motions to the radio, which is playing quietly. "They say it's snowing in Minnesota."

"Then that's where we're headed—"

"And also Illinois and Wisconsin. Which storm is hers?"

I exhale and sit down on one of the seats in the back. "I don't know. Hers feel different. The cold is . . . darker."

"They don't much report that sort of thing on the weather," she says drily, and I glare at her.

"Sing the song again?" I ask Flannery. "Just the part about where she lives."

She sings without hesitation, her voice more elegant than she is.

She lives among the selchs and snow,
she knows her magic well.
She'll call the very best to her,
The rest she'll send to hell.

Perhaps hearing the song wasn't as helpful as I expected.

"Is there a map in here?" I ask, flipping down the visor and finding nothing.

"No," Flannery says, "but I know where some of the states are."

"Hang on," I say, trying not to look piteous. I reach down and grab the cookbook. "There's a map in here, somewhere...." I flip through the cookbook hurriedly, finally finding the page on the Fenris near the middle.

"Those aren't the states," Flannery says, leaning over my shoulder.

"The blue lines are the states, the light ones," I say, motioning to the faded marks. "The black ones are where the Fenris packs are. Just ignore those; look at the state lines."

Her eyes widen. "Whew, look at Kentucky," Flannery says, clucking her tongue. "We're infested."

"No kidding," I say, glancing down at the state. The thick marker lines that separate the different packs converge on the state into a blob of black that looks foreboding even just in ink. I look up, squinting to see if Grandma Dalia left any notations in pencil that I somehow missed.

"Remind me," Flannery says, folding her arms, "to move to Montana." I look over and see that Montana doesn't have any marker drawn through it. Few of the northern states do, really, save the Northeast—as if the Fenris prefer the raw heat down south.

"Weird," I say. "All that forest? Seems like paradise for a Fenris."

"No point living in paradise if there's no food," Flannery answers, and Keelin's face races to my mind so quickly it unsettles my stomach. I let my eyes wander toward the three places expecting snowstorms—Illinois, Minnesota, and Wisconsin.

"All right, there's that line about forests earlier on, right? *And with it comes a lady, from the great wood, strong and bright,*" I sing off-key. "The biggest forests out of the three are in Minnesota or Wisconsin. I don't think there are forests in Illinois—not 'great' ones, anyway. And Minnesota and Wisconsin probably have more snow, too."

"*She lives among the selchs and snow,*" Flannery says. She runs her finger along the map, toward the Great Lakes and along the edge of Minnesota and upper Wisconsin. "Water. Gotta be here somewhere."

"Do I want to know what the selchs are?" I ask.

"It's what she used to be—that's the story, anyhow. She was a selch, a water girl, and rose out to become Grohkta-Nap. That's why she can control the snow—she controlled water for so long," Flannery explains. "Dunno if it's true, but either way. If her power comes from water and if she 'lives among the selchs,' she lives near a lake or river or something."

"She talks like she used to be human, though," I say, shaking my head.

"Maybe she was both. Don't ask me," Flannery says.

I look back at the map. Water, trees, a snowstorm in both places. I narrow my eyes, trying to see past Grandma Dalia's black lines, but it's impossible.

And then it hits me. I sit back, laughing under my breath that it's taken me this long.

"What?" Flannery asks.

"We're going to Minnesota," I say. "Up in the north. Near Canada."

"How'd you work that out?" Flannery says, folding her arms.

"This," I say, tracing my finger along one of the thick lines that slices through the top of Wisconsin, then divides Minnesota in two, indicating that much of the area below belongs to the Mirror pack. "Mora's running from the Fenris, right? This little corner, here," I say, pointing at the northeast corner of Minnesota, on Lake Superior. "It's the only place she'll be safe from them. That area doesn't belong to a single pack."

"She could go farther north and get even farther away from them," Flannery says. "Into Canada."

"She could," I admit. "So we need to hurry. Maybe she can get across the border, somehow, but there's no way two girls in a stolen VW bus are making it over. But this is a start, anyway. We can go up through here," I say, drawing my finger up the border between Minnesota and Wisconsin.

"And then what?" Flannery asks.

"And then we're there."

"No," she says. "Then we're on the edge of a huge fucking forest looking for a goddess. And besides, that route takes us straight through a mess of cities."

"It's the fastest."

"People will see us. All sorts of people."

"Like who?"

"Like cops. Other buffers. Government."

"They're not going to arrest us for driving through a city. Go the speed limit, signal. Don't steal anything else. We'll keep a low profile, won't give them a reason to look twice at us."

"Yeah, thing is," Flannery begins, "I'm not saying this for convenience's sake. I *can't* get arrested. For starters, I have a record. But second off, my mother will be looking out for me in the papers. Waiting to see my mug shot, to figure out where I am. She'll drag me back kicking and screaming. Or dead."

"It'll be fine," I say. "I promise."

"All right," Flannery says, looking doubtful.

CHAPTER TWENTY-FIVE

❧

Hotels are excellent places to pull over, not because we can afford a room, but because they've got massive parking lots. This hotel, in upper Indiana, has been repainted poorly—all around the fake shutters, you can see where the stucco was once avocado green instead of creamy white. Flannery and I sit in the back of Wallace, rear doors open, watching traffic on the interstate fly by.

"How much gas do we have left?" I ask, flipping through the last of our money.

"Half a tank," Flannery says somberly. "Used to be able to steal it, easy. Not anymore. Had to go make everything complicated by making you pay first."

"Wonder why they did that," I say. When I go to tuck the money into the cookbook—we figured it'd be safest there—Flannery's knife flips out of the sheath on my hip for the third or fourth time today.

"Stop it," Flannery says. "You're gonna break the blade."

"Here," I say, sighing. As much as I like the idea of having it, we're probably safer if it's with Flannery anyhow. I take the sheath off and go to hand it to her.

"Keep it," Flannery says. "I've got my own." She reaches down her shirt, between her breasts, and pulls out a knife exactly like the one I have. "Part of a set," she says. "I don't much care for having one in each hand, though. Makes it hard to throw a punch."

"How long have you had that on you?"

"Never take it off," she says, shrugging.

"So you let me break into Callum's RV and threaten you when you were wearing a knife the whole time?" I ask, and Flannery grins.

"Aw, don't be mad! You looked menacing!" she says when I fold my arms. "Come on. Let me show you how to use a knife, at least. It'll help in case you need to kidnap me again."

It takes some convincing on Flannery's part, especially since my pride is a little wounded. But a few minutes later, we're standing outside, shivering every time the wind gusts through. Flannery has me start a few feet away from her, my back toward the open rear doors. She removes her knife and motions for me to do the same.

"All right," Flannery says, flipping the knife and catching it squarely in her palm. "What do you already know?"

"About knife fighting?" She nods. "Nothing." Flannery sighs and rolls her eyes at me.

"What can you do? Run? Jump? Are you super flexible?"

I raise an eyebrow.

"Christ, Ginny. All right, here." She reaches over and grabs my wrist, shaking it until I tense my muscles. "Hold it tight. But don't treat it like it's your hand or anything. Remember that it isn't stuck in one spot. Yeah. Hold it tight but loose."

I nod, as if I understand.

"So, the trick," she says, "is to cut the other guy."

"So I gathered," I say, and she gives me an irritated look. "What? I mean, that's pretty obvious. Isn't there something more to it?"

"I'm getting there," she says. "So, here. Try to cut me."

"What? Right here?"

"What's wrong with right here?"

"You're afraid of getting arrested, but you want me to try to stab you in a hotel parking lot," I point out. "What if someone sees us?"

Flannery laughs dangerously. "For starters—I'm not *afraid*. It'd just be an inconvenience. And second, you're making excuses. Let's do this."

Before I can answer, she runs at me, arms out, flailing, hair streaming behind her head like a crazy person. I jump out of the way and she flies by, slamming her hands onto Wallace's back floorboard.

"Ginny! How the fuck am I supposed to teach you if you won't try to cut me?"

"I don't want to hurt you!" I protest.

"You won't—you're not actually gonna get me!"

"What the hell? I might!" I say, indignant, though I suspect Flannery has a point. She puts her hands on her hips impatiently as I adjust, ready myself. I nod, tense; she flails at me again. Right before she reaches me, I can't help wondering what someone looking out the hotel window will think is going on.

I lunge forward, stabbing my wrist out as if the blade is a sword. Flannery dodges it, laughs at me, and slows.

"Shut up," I say.

She ignores me. "You're trying to stab me. Why?"

"You told me to!"

"No, I told you to try to *cut* the other guy. That's different. Don't try to stick the other guy like a pincushion, because then you've only got one shot—you stick out your knife, you miss, and then he guts you while you're recovering."

I try not to cringe but fail; Flannery, as expected, gives me an exasperated look for it.

"Instead," she says, "just try to touch skin. Slice around, keep your arm moving, re-angle the knife. You just want to hit skin. Because . . . what do you do when you cut yourself?"

I frown, thinking about the many times I've nicked myself with a kitchen knife. "I stare at it," I answer. "Put a hand over the spot."

"Exactly," Flannery says. "Cut them the tiniest bit, and you'll almost always get a moment where they're staring at the spot you hit, or where they have to fight one-armed, 'cause the other palm's pressed against the wound."

"And that's when I stab them?"

Flannery studies me. "If you've got the stomach for it, yeah." She lifts herself into Wallace, lunging across the floor to grab an apple she stole from a roadside stand. "There are two secrets to fighting, though—any kind of fighting," she says as she sits back up. "The big secret and the little secret. The big one"—she pauses to stick her knife into the fruit—"is to not get in a fight to begin with."

"Really?" I ask, alarmed to hear something like that come out of Flannery's mouth.

She shrugs, slices off a bit of apple, and chews it noisily. "I'm assuming that what's most important to you is surviving, right? In that case, don't get into a fight. Bam. You survive."

"What about when you fought for me?" I say accusingly.

"Surviving wasn't the most important thing," she says darkly. "And besides, that wasn't a real fight. You think they'd have killed the Princess of Kentucky in front of her clan? Not that I couldn't take them in a real fight, of course. Fuckers wouldn't know what hit them—"

"What's the little secret?" I cut her off.

Flannery cuts off another piece of the apple and studies it in her fingers for a moment. "Before you start, figure out who's going to win."

We make it to northern Illinois before we finally pull over in a shopping center parking lot for the night. We stop the car in the back, near a closed bookstore, and spread out on Wallace's floor. Flannery is leaning against the rear doors, letting them press against her the same way the wall of her bedroom would have back at the camp. She's happily eating from a drum of cheese puffs.

"So, what happens when you find him? When this is all done?" Flannery asks, licking the cheese dust off her fingers.

"I...go home," I say.

"What really happens?" Flannery says.

I look down, tucking my arms into my sweatshirt to get warmer. "I go home," I repeat, and then continue, "but I don't stay there. Not for long. I don't think I could after all this." Truthfully, it feels strange even calling Andern Street "home." Kai was my home, *him*, not the building, but now even that seems strange. After all, I've made it this far. I've escaped monsters and kidnappers and been brave without him. Maybe he's my old home, the childhood one I love, but not the one I live in anymore....

"Look how quickly we turned you into a proper Traveller." Flannery laughs, cutting off my thoughts. "No place is your home, so every place is. So where will you go? What will you do?"

I pause for a long time. "I don't know," I say. "I adopted Kai's dreams. I never really had my own."

"And that made you happy?" Flannery asks warily.

I frown. "It did, but I'm not sure how. I guess it was enough for me then. I still want Kai back, of course, but..." I swallow and can't believe what I'm about to say. "I don't think I'm afraid to be without him now." I think I should feel guilty about thinking that, much less saying it aloud, but I just feel strangely free.

"Well," Flannery says as she screws the lid back onto the cheese puff drum, "I for one think you'd make a stellar spy. Creeping around, car chases, hunting down monsters...if I were hiring spies, you'd get the job."

"What about you?"

"That," Flannery says, "is a mystery. You gotta understand, Ginny—you walk out on the Travellers, the way I've done, you walk out on them for good. I can never go back. But..."

"Callum."

"Yes," Flannery says gruffly. "And that's my home. Those are my people. I'm supposed to lead them one day. I dunno. My mother thought I wasn't tough enough to rule alone. I thought I'd feel free, running away. Happy. But instead I just feel like she's right. Like I ran because I wasn't strong enough, in the end. Forever the shit Princess of Kentucky..."

"I watched you take down a bunch of guys with your fists, Flannery. You're plenty strong. Brigit is *wrong*."

Flannery doesn't answer, but her fingers move to a chain around her neck. It takes me a minute to realize what the necklace charm is—her wedding ring. She catches me looking and shrugs, tucking it back under her shirt. "I've got a question for you," she says slowly. "You knew Wallace was a stick shift. Which means you knew you couldn't drive it when you stole the keys."

"That's not a question—"

"Why'd you take the keys, then?" she finishes, staring at me.

I laugh and darkly enjoy the fact that it irritates her.

"Because," I say, "I planned on making you come with me the moment you announced your engagement."

Flannery is quiet for a long time, so long that I think she's fallen asleep. But then she speaks, voice small. "Why?"

"Easy," I say. "I'm going to fight werewolves, and you throw a mean punch."

Flannery laughs. "True. And with the way you handle a knife, you'll definitely need me."

CHAPTER TWENTY-SIX

We make it two more days before the snow gets so thick that we can barely drive. The roads aren't becoming slick, necessarily—they're just becoming impassable, as if they've been paved in pillows instead of asphalt. The trees on either side of the highway are covered in ice, as if they've been candied, and headlights bounce off the snow and blind us every mile or so.

"We have to pull over," Flannery says. "We can't drive in this. Not into the forest, anyway."

"We can't pull over, we'll lose her," I answer, shouting—the snow is so heavy on the windshield, it sounds like a thunderstorm.

"Don't be so stupid, Ginny. We're not going to find her if we're dead in a ditch somewhere. This thing's got practically bald tires as it is. It can't handle snow this deep."

I grimace as Flannery takes the closest exit; Wallace

struggles to make it up the off-ramp and onto the main road. There's little here—it's the sort of stop that's geared to truck drivers, I think. There's a Flying J gas station that advertises hot showers, which is attached to a fish restaurant and...not much else. We pull Wallace into the parking lot, struggling to find a space—we weren't the only ones who decided to stop, apparently.

Flannery turns the bus off and we sit for a moment, watching the snow rain down as if it wants to suffocate us. We creep to the back and sit; Wallace becomes colder, colder, and colder still. It's a million times worse than Atlanta, than Nashville—I guess Mora has less to fight in Minnesota, given how cold it is up here even without her influence.

"Let's go inside," Flannery finally says. "We'll dine and dash. I'll talk you through it. I'm a pro."

"How are we supposed to dash when we can't actually move the car?"

"You worry too much."

I give her a tired look, but I have to admit the idea of real food instead of crackers sounds appealing. We bundle up as best we can, layer upon layer of thrift-store clothes. I grab the cookbook just before we step outside.

"You're bringing that?" Flannery asks, perplexed.

"Last time I left it in a car, I ended up getting kidnapped," I point out, and Flannery laughs.

Together we tromp through the parking lot to the fish restaurant. There're a few inches of snow on the ground already, and at the rate it's coming down there'll be a foot before it gets dark. The bottoms of my jeans are soaked, and my lungs ache from the temperature.

I reach for the restaurant door, fling it open, and am punched by a wall of sound and wave of heat. People are huddled over tables, nursing enormous plates of food and cheap beer. They cast wary looks out the windows every so often, shake their heads, and go back to it. A harried-looking waitress calls out to us as she sets a basket of bread down.

"Two?"

I nod. She bustles over, grabs some paper menus, and leads us to a seat by the back wall.

"Order something," Flannery says, fiddling with a wood-and-golf-peg game in the center of the table. "Don't think about it, just do it. They'll never even notice when we slip out." When a different waitress stops by I order a fish sandwich without hesitation. Flannery orders the most expensive thing on the menu, and smiles at the waitress so genuinely that I'm impressed.

"How much farther?" Flannery asks.

"Maybe two hours if the roads are clear," I say. "*If* they're ever cleared of all this." I'm about to say more when something catches my eye. A photo near the top of the wall, wedged between an old pair of skis and a signed painting of basset hounds.

"Ginny? You listening?" Flannery asks.

I ignore her and rise, standing on my chair to get a better look. I reach up and pluck the frame from the wall. It's a photograph, an old one.

A photograph of a pack of wolves.

I lower myself, setting the photo on the table. Flannery leans over me to look; the animals are a few dozen yards away from the photographer, and though they give the camera hard stares, it's impossible to tell if anything in their eyes is human—if they're just wolves or if they're Mora's guard. But something about the way they're standing, the formation they're in, the curve of their shoulders...

"This isn't them, is it?" I say. "I think I'm just—"

"Desperate?" Flannery says, giving me a skeptical look. The waitress drops by our table and sets down two waters.

"Thanks," Flannery tells her, grinning. "Hey—this photo. What do you know about it?"

"Uh, nothing," the waitress says. "I mean, I've never really noticed it before now. Why?"

"Just wanna know where it was taken."

"Well...I can ask the manager?" the waitress says, looking confused.

"That'd be swell," Flannery answers sincerely.

"Swell?" I ask when the waitress walks away.

"Don't buffers say *swell*?"

I shake my head, and Flannery looks crestfallen. She's just recovering when the waitress walks back over with an old woman. Her eyes are tiny blue gems in a sea of wrinkles that only deepen when she smiles at us.

"This is the owner," our waitress says. "Liz. They wanted to know about the picture?"

"This one!" Liz says, looking surprised. She leans over

247

the table to get a closer look, though it doesn't take much, given how short she is already. The scent of lotion and perfume temporarily overtakes the smell of cooked fish. "My husband took that. Years ago. The wolves on Isle Royale, I suspect."

"Isle Royale?" I ask.

"It's a park, just off the coast here. Middle of the lake."

"Is there a way over by car?" I ask, and hear Flannery groan.

"Oh, no," Liz says. "You'd have to rent a boat or catch the ferry. I think they start running again in April."

"April?" I ask, my heart sinking.

"You don't want to be going over there this time of year anyhow," Liz says, looking at me as if I'm crazy.

"She just gets excited," Flannery says.

"It's a lovely island," Liz says. "Huge population of wolves. Hang on, I'll get you a brochure."

Flannery scowls at me. "You're not thinking right. Come on. I thought we were going into the forest."

"I know." I move the photo off the table as our food arrives. It's hot and burns my tongue, but that makes me like it all the more. The shaky, vibrating feeling that was buzzing inside me dissipates as I eat, until finally I'm full and tired and relieved that Flannery insisted we stop here. She orders strawberry shortcake for dessert and is eating it greedily when Liz makes her way back to us, a few coloring books tucked under one arm and the promised brochure in the other.

"Here you go. If you want to book a trip sooner, just call that number on the back to schedule a plane. They're not cheap, though," she adds, looking from Flannery to me. She walks away as I unfold the brochure.

"What are you expecting to see?" Flannery asks. "A werewolf theme park or something?"

I ignore her, studying the first flap. Nothing exciting—a national park, no permanent inhabitants, largely impassable terrain except for a few picnic areas. Wolves, moose, foxes, mink. There's a picture of a wolf on the second panel, but it's clearly an animal—eyes that are watery, intense, but not human. I flip to the back and see a map of the island, showing ferry and plane routes. It looks a little like a curled-up dog.

I inhale.

"What?" Flannery asks through a mouthful of strawberries.

"The island, the shape—" I grab for the cookbook, nearly knocking our drinks off the table as I slam it open. Flip, fast, fast, I know this shape. *There.* In pencil, on a page stuck between dozens of shorthand recipes. I squint in the dim light to be sure. *Yes, yes. Grandma Dalia, you knew.*

The pencil line. Just an odd shape, one I thought so little of. I press the map down beside it and follow the lines. Curled-up dogs. I look at Flannery.

"The island. Mora is on the island."

Flannery's eyes widen. "I guess we need to find a plane."

CHAPTER TWENTY-SEVEN

✑

"Can I use your phone?" I ask our waitress, clutching the brochure in my fist.

"It's out," she says. "Gas station next door is probably working, though—newer building."

"Thanks," I say, and rise.

"Whoa," Flannery hisses. "This is not how you dine and dash, telling the waitress where you're headed."

"I need to call this pilot!" I say. "We've got to go."

"You go," she says. "I'll sit here and order more food."

"Why?"

"Because if we keep ordering, we're paying customers, not squatters," she says, as if this is the most obvious thing in the world. She flags down a waitress and simultaneously waves me out the door. I bury my head to my chest and brace myself for the cold—

I didn't brace hard enough. This is Mora's weather, I know

it. The sick kind of cold that makes my skin feel brittle and my bones feel bruised. I glance back at the restaurant and see our waitress delivering a cup of coffee to Flannery while customers seated close to the windows watch me in disbelief.

I pull my hands to my face to warm my nose and lips and stumble toward the gas station, lifting my feet up high. A foot of snow already, at least. The sky is dark gray above— what time is it? I can't tell what's night and what's weather. The gas station shines bright ahead, cars parked under the awning. People are milling around inside, killing time. No one looks panicked—I suppose Minnesotans don't freak out over snow the way Atlantans do. My theory is proven when I finally push open the gas station door and see someone's purchased and opened a twenty-four pack of beer, which is being passed around to everyone inside.

"Er, no thanks," I say when it's offered to me on the way to the register. "I just wanted to use your phone?"

"No tow trucks," the attendant says. "They're all booked. Better off just to wait till they come along and plow it. They move pretty fast, typically."

"I actually wanted to call a friend," I lie. The attendant hands the phone across the counter. I huddle back in a corner and dial the number on the brochure.

"Hello?" a man on the other end says.

"Hi, I was calling about booking a plane to Isle Royale?" Silence.

"*Now?*"

"Soon. I mean, not *now*, obviously. There's a blizzard."

The man laughs in relief. "Oh, all right, then. So, when were you thinking?"

"Maybe tomorrow?"

Silence again.

"Look, it's not really tourist season. No good place to land when there's ice on the water. Maybe we could look at April or so?"

"No, no, it has to be sooner than that," I say. "Just two people."

"Yeah, look, it's not even worth the gas with just two people," he says. "And definitely not worth the risk."

"How much do you need to make it worth it?" I ask. I don't know *why* I'm asking—whatever the amount is, it's too much.

"Say you'll pay it."

The voice makes my breath catch in my throat. I lower the phone a little, turn around slowly, slowly, afraid and excited at once.

"Whatever it is, you'll pay it—double it, even, if he can go tomorrow."

"How'd you find me?" I ask, dumbstruck.

"Come on, Ginny," Lucas says. "I told you. I can track anyone."

Lucas is unshowered, his eyes red and full of sleep. He smiles at me, and then, before I can stop myself, I fling my arms around him. I'm embarrassed and start to pull away, only to find him hugging me back, chuckling under his breath.

"Why'd you come? I told you not to!" I say, torn between frustration and happiness.

"Well," he says slowly, "two reasons. For starters, Ella gave me the silent treatment for three days. But second, well...like you said when you were leaving. Ella and I are a family. And we decided, now that we've tracked the Snow Queen, made breakfast, and essentially committed a murder together, that you're family, too. Family sticks together."

My lips part. I know I should laugh at some of what he's said, but I'm too struck by the rest of it to speak. Lucas blushes, and instead of speaking I'm hugging him again.

A half hour later, we have a plane booked. Two days from now—that's when the pilot thinks it'll be warm enough that the lake isn't frozen over. We'll get only two hours on the island. I can't decide if that's too little time, more than enough, or simply too late for Kai. Next Lucas puts me on his cell phone with Ella, who yells at me for leaving before promising that she's getting on a flight this evening—she'll be here tomorrow.

"We'll help you get him back, Ginny," Ella says seriously. "Not just find him—*get him back*." We hang up, and then Lucas takes the phone and shoves it back into his pocket. We sit on the floor in the back of the gas station, between the soda cooler and a display of pork rinds. The spot gives the illusion of privacy—the rest of the crowd is keeping vigil by the windows, growing ever rowdier as they take bets on who will see the snowplow first.

"I lost you for a while, in Kentucky. Trail went cold," Lucas says, shifting so that the pork rind bags crinkle behind him.

"I was lost for a while," I admit. "This group of Travellers—"

"Travellers?"

"Gypsies, kind of?" I try to explain. "Anyhow, they sort of . . . kidnapped me."

Lucas's eyes go wide. "You got kidnapped by gypsies?"

"For a little while, but it's fine now. The Princess of Kentucky is over in the restaurant, actually. We stole that VW van? The one in the front of the parking lot?"

Lucas's face contorts to an even stranger expression.

"I guess when I put it that way, it sounds crazy," I say under my breath. We're silent a few moments, pretending to look at the rows of sodas in the cooler across the aisle. I rock my feet back and forth, wondering how Flannery is faring at the restaurant. I should go back soon.

"So this island," Lucas says. "You have a plan, once you're on it?"

"No," I say simply. "I've got nothing. No more than I had when I left Atlanta, anyhow."

"Except me and a VW bus."

"And a Traveller," I remind him. "And I still have the cookbook. And I know a little more about Mora than when I started, I guess."

"Like what?"

"Well," I begin, staring at the cooler ahead. "For starters, she doesn't rule the Fenris—she's running from them." I tell him about Keelin, about Mora's coat.

Lucas's face darkens. "What if the Fenris have beaten you to her?"

I cringe. "I'm trying not to think about that, actually. But the Fenris aren't up in this area—the map in Grandma Dalia's cookbook shows the packs stop farther south. It's too cold for them here, I guess."

"That doesn't mean they can't throw on a coat," Lucas says.

"Lucas..." I sigh. "I'm going after her either way."

Lucas is quiet a long time, considering this, but then nods. He rises and offers me a hand. I accept it and stand up, just in time to hear cheering from the crowd by the window.

"Is that the plow?" I ask the other stranded customers.

"Yep," a fat man says, hoisting his pants up a bit. "And a bunch of cops."

"Doing what?"

"Got me, something at the restaurant."

"Oh god," I say, and dash for the door.

"What?" Lucas calls from behind me, but I don't get a chance to answer before I'm out in the cold. I run as best as I can, stumbling through the snow. Blue and red lights bounce off of it; even squinting, all I can see are silhouettes ahead. Lucas is shouting behind me, but I can't take the time to turn around and explain—

"Get your fucking hands off me!" Flannery shrieks. "I'm the ex–Princess of Kentucky!"

"Enough," a large female cop says, sighing under her breath. "Keep it up and we'll charge you with resisting. That's a lot more paperwork than I want to fill out. Don't make me do it."

"You bet your ass I'm res—"

"Shut up, Flannery!" I snap. She lifts her head, deflating a little when she sees me. The cops look over, raising their eyebrows.

"And you are?" the one leading Flannery asks.

"She's my prisoner." Flannery laughs. "I fought an army to win her."

"Quiet," I repeat. "I'm her friend. Sorry, she's—"

"Under arrest," a male officer finishes.

"For dining and dashing?" I ask in disbelief. "Can't she do dishes or something?"

"For lifting the wallets off about twenty-three people in there," the male officer corrects me.

"Oh, Flannery," I groan.

"Easy pickings," she says, lifting her chin at the cop defiantly.

"Seriously, shut up," Lucas says firmly. Flannery opens her mouth to cuss at him, but I glare hard enough that it keeps her quiet. "Where are you taking her?"

"Wesley station. You can post bail for her there."

"Got it," Lucas says, then looks at Flannery. "Cooperate."

"Who are you?" Flannery asks, sounding annoyed.

"He's trying to help you. Just listen," I say as they manhandle her toward the car. Something is sinking in me—they'll book her, take her photo. Even if we get her out, her mother will know where to find her now, just like she was afraid of. I can see the fear in her eyes, a layer mostly hidden by anger.

The cop shuts the door, answers a radio call, and then climbs into the front seat. Lucas drops a hand on my shoulder as the car eases forward and turns down the road the snowplow just cleared.

"That's your gypsy princess?"

I sigh. "That's her."

CHAPTER TWENTY-EIGHT

They're holding Flannery for twenty-four hours and refuse to make an exception—primarily because she wouldn't stop singing Shelta songs at the top of her lungs on the way to the station.

"She'll be fine. We'll pick her up tomorrow when they open," Lucas tells me as I drop into the passenger seat of his car. It feels strange and low to the ground after riding in Wallace.

"I know," I say. "I just . . . I shouldn't have left her."

"You can't be responsible for everyone, you know," he says, starting the car. I don't answer.

Lucas books a hotel room on the edge of Lake Superior. I can't see the island, given how dark it is, but I can feel it. That's where she is—does she have a private boat to get there? Her own plane? I wonder how long they have, before she turns them to beasts—how long Kai will have.

I wonder if it hurts.

"How does she do it, do you think?" I ask Lucas absently as I sit in a chair by the window, knees drawn up to my chest.

"What?"

"Turn them into wolves. How does it work?"

"How does anything work?" Lucas says, shrugging. When I look unconvinced, he tries again. "There are some things in the world that defy explanation." Lucas looks out toward the island. Every so often I think I can see its outline in the darkness, but it's a trick—there is nothing but shadows outside at the moment. He clears his throat and speaks again.

"What are you expecting to happen on Thursday?"

"I . . . I guess I expect her to cause a blizzard or something and—"

"Not from Mora," Lucas says. "From Kai."

"I expect . . ."

I don't know what to say, because I can't quite separate what I expect from what I simply want. I want Kai to run to me. I want him to renounce Mora. I want us to get away and never think of her again.

But I expect it to be much harder than that.

"I expect him to be different," I finally say softly. "He must be. Even if he hasn't . . . changed. Do they ever change back, once they become wolves? I mean, permanently change back."

"I . . ." Lucas extends the vowel for a long time, and I can tell he doesn't want to say the truth. I look at him pleadingly, and he relents. "When someone becomes a Fenris, they aren't really the person you knew anymore. It's like...the monster lives in their body. Uses their voice and their eyes. But if he's changed, it won't be him. Not really."

"What if it's different with her? I mean, you didn't even know she existed. The wolves with her look different—" My voice sounds whiny, childlike.

"Maybe," Lucas says, holding up his hands. "Maybe. But you have to remember that they're very, very good at what they do. The wolves will manipulate you. They'll play to your emotions, make you vulnerable. And then they'll kill you." His voice is gentle when he says this, but it does little to soften the blow. "So if he's changed, Ginny, but you think the boy you knew is still in there somewhere..."

"I'll be wrong," I finish for him.

"You'll be taking a risk I wouldn't take," Lucas corrects. "So the real question, I guess, is...if he's changed, do you want him alive as a monster?"

"*He* wouldn't want that," I say. "I know he wouldn't." Kai—the real Kai, not the one Mora has created—wants to be a musician. He wants to live in tiny apartments and take trips to foreign villas and drink coffee in shops tucked away from the masses. He wants to make the world more beautiful, and he wants to do it with me.

He doesn't want to be a monster, and I love him too much to let that happen, even if it means I have to live without him forever. That's what the loudest voice in my head is saying; a cool, collected voice, one I know I should listen to. But there's another voice, a softer one, that's crying in the back of my mind. *Maybe he'll be fine. Maybe he won't have changed. Maybe it'll all be okay.*

Please, please let it all be okay.

Lucas looks so grim that I have to avoid his eyes; I look out the window at the darkness as he speaks. "I was never much of a hunter. I mean, if you need me to...I'll try. But if you're waiting till he gets close enough for you to be sure, it might be too late to do anything."

"I know," I say, though I'm not sure I *really* knew until this moment: Kai might kill me.

No. Not Kai. The monster, the monster who killed Kai might kill me. The monster Mora created, controls.

"I've got a knife," I say weakly. "Flannery taught me how to use it."

"*Will* you use it?"

I swallow. I can't answer.

"All right," Lucas says, exhaling loudly. "I've been driving all day—I've got to get some sleep. You should, too."

"I will," I say. "I just can't. Not yet. Will I keep you up?"

"No," he says. "You're fine. Let me know if you need anything."

"You've done more than enough."

"Well. Still," he says, and smiles. He walks to the bed on the far side of the room and yanks the spread back, then buries himself in the blankets. It isn't long until his breathing becomes rhythmic and slow. I reach to the side and flick the lamp off; the room vanishes into complete darkness for a few moments until my eyes slowly adjust. There's a glow outside, the smallest bit of moon combining with a few streetlights. I can see the red light where the hotel's dock ends, but I don't know where the horizon is. Everything in front of me is black. Black and cold, as far as the eye can see.

Sometimes, when my mom's work schedule meant she came in late and left early, Kai would spend the night at my house. It was an accident the first time—he fell asleep while we were doing homework and we didn't wake up till six o'clock the next morning. It even started as an accident the second time. He was frustrated with Grandma Dalia for embarrassing him at the store—shouting at the produce manager when he didn't know what St. John's wort was.

"It's crazy. She's crazy. Can't she just let it go? I feel like I have to spend my life looking over my shoulder just to make sure she's not looking over *her* shoulder," he said, falling onto my bed and staring at the ceiling.

"She's just scared," I said. "She's always scared."

"You believe her? About the beasts?" he asked in disbelief.

"I believe it's real to her," I said—I'd never told him about how the man in the grocery store parking lot looked at me, about his costume face. "I don't know. She seems so normal, other than all the beast talk. What if she's right?"

"And St. John's wort can stop shape-shifting beasts from attacking me?" Kai said warily.

"Well. Maybe not right about everything," I said. I sat down beside him with my back propped up against the headboard. It was already late, my room illuminated by a lamp on

262

my nightstand with a crooked shade. We talked for another hour, then two, about Grandma Dalia's eccentricities, before the conversation lulled and I yawned.

"Are you staying?" I asked. He looked at me, then at the clock. One thirty in the morning.

"Yes," he said. I reached over and clicked off the light, and suddenly there was more space between Kai and me than there'd ever been before. We were pinned to opposite sides of the bed, each of us afraid that any touch would make things awkward. I fell asleep that way, stiff and uncomfortable from trying to stay in a perfectly straight line.

But when I woke up at four, Kai's arm was around me, my head against his shoulder. He was breathing slow, still asleep, his face turned toward mine so that I could feel his breath across the top of my head. I hesitated, then draped an arm across his chest and drifted off again. It was always like that, afterward—we would start the night splitting the bed in half, but always woke in the middle, pressed close.

In the dark we always found each other.

MORA

Mora stared out over the ice, leaning against the door frame of the cottage. As immense as her powers were, she couldn't thaw the lake instantly, return the ice to violent, deep water that few would venture across. Freezing was easy enough—she just pulled heat away from the water. But thawing? Thawing required the sun, warmth, things that were beyond the scope of her talents. The best she could do was crack the ice here and there, break it into smaller and smaller pieces until it collapsed.

Kai and two other guards walked up the hill together and drew her attention from the white horizon. Their arms were bare, revealing gray-blue skin, which made Mora smile—Kai was coming along well. Perhaps he was finished. . . .

"Kai," she called out. "Come here for a moment." Kai broke from the others and tried to jog toward her but stumbled in the thick snow. Mora laughed, which made Kai grin as he hauled himself to his feet.

"Yes?" he said when he finally reached her.

"Do you remember a girl named Ginny?" she asked, running a finger along her collarbone.

Kai hesitated, then nodded. "She's a girl I used to know. I can't remember what she looks like."

Mora frowned—she'd hoped he would have forgotten her entirely by now, given how fast he was changing initially. She couldn't be down a guard on the off chance Ginny or the Fenris made it across the lake. Mora reached down, letting her fingers dance along the inside of Kai's wrist. "Edward and Larson are inside. They're going to play a little concert for me. Join them?"

"Of course," Kai said, then followed Mora into the house. The door remained open, casting snowflakes across the gray wood floors. Larson was clearing his throat, standing by a piano that Edward was polishing gently. Most of her current guard were pianists or strings players. There'd been a period where she'd mostly wanted woodwinds, and another where she collected folksy guitar players—most of them poor, dangerous-looking boys with a swagger she enjoyed.

Mora went to the opposite side of the room and sat down on a stiff-cushioned couch while Kai ran to fetch his violin. She drew circles with her fingernails on the couch arm, smiling at the way her rings sparkled like blocks of ice on her fingers. Eventually, her eyes wandered to the bookshelf at the far end of the room.

In the center of one shelf was a ship in a bottle, one she'd found in an antiques store ages ago and bought with a smile and a kiss. It was beautiful, intricate, with giant white sails and CITY OF GLASGOW written on the side in gold. She bought it because it reminded her of a ship in the ocean, one she and the other ocean girls lived near. It was the only thing that anchored them to a single spot in the vast, unforgiving sea. The bottled ship was polished and sleek, but the one underwater had anemone-covered staircases, shelves covered in starfish, and still-corked bottles of wine, things she eventually saw as part of her home, the way humans might see a bedroom set or a front door.

She'd tried once, ages ago, to help her ocean sisters leave the Fenris. She tried to find the boys they loved, so they could be kissed and freed. She never found a single boy—never even worked out where to start looking. How do you find a boy who loved a human girl, when the human girl is fading fast, turning darker by the day? It was impossible. Mora decided it was better to accept the fact that she was a fluke, an accident, and embrace her new life.

A life she wouldn't give up now, not over some stupid girl unable to leave well enough alone. Kai returned, violin in hand; she smiled at him and folded her hands in her lap. He spent a few moments tuning the instrument, then raised his bow, looking nervous.

"Go on," Mora whispered, and Kai obeyed. He drew the bow across the strings; a low, solid note filled the room, swimming through the walls and floorboards. Edward joined him with high notes on the piano. Larson began to sing in Italian, voice booming like the loudest instrument of all. Mora sighed and sat back. *Such talent shouldn't be left in a mortal body to age and rot*, she thought, pleased with her selections.

When they finished, she let her eyes dance across them, her gaze remaining on Kai the longest. Finally she rose and walked over to Larson.

"Larson," she said, leaning in to drag her lips along his collarbone. "You'd never leave me, right?"

"Of course not," he said immediately. Mora smiled, kissed him deeply and bit at his lip. She stepped away and left him looking starved and wanting. She moved to Edward, who turned around on the piano bench to face her.

"What about you?" she asked him. She wrapped her arms around his neck and allowed him to pull her into his lap. Mora always liked the way Edward held her—he cradled her, as if she was something precious. "Do you want to go back to your old life?" she whispered in his ear, pressing a palm against his cold chest. It felt like rock, smooth and solid.

"I don't remember it," Edward said, shrugging. "How could I leave *you* for something I didn't even bother to remember?"

Mora tilted her head, relieved she hadn't gotten rid of Edward after all. She stroked his cheek, then rose and walked toward Kai. She inhaled slowly, keeping her eyes locked on his. A gust of snow swept through the house, up and around their bodies, drawing them closer. Kai sighed as Mora slid a hand up his chest and wound her fingers through his black hair; it looked like spilled ink on her pale skin. Kai set the violin down on the piano as Mora teased at the bow that remained in his right hand. She ran her fingers up the boy, up his arms, and finally curled both hands behind his neck.

"Kai," she whispered, arching her back so her chest met his. "Do you love me?"

"Of course. More than anything," he answered, and brought his lips down to kiss her. She shook her head and pulled back; Kai shrank beneath her hands.

"I mean it," Mora whispered, voice now barely audible over the wind that whipped ever louder outside. "Do you love me? Promise you'll never leave me? You'll protect me?"

"Yes." This time, his voice was breathy and serious; his eyes on hers. Now she locked her hands behind his head, pulled him to her mouth, and kissed him so hard she felt him flinch with pain. It was only a moment, though, and then he gave in to her and wrapped his arms around her tightly, lifting her off the ground. When Mora finally released him, Kai's eyes were beautifully dark, the color of tree bark in the winter.

"Am I like the others now?" he asked as he set her feet back on the floor.

"Darling," Mora said, running her fingers across his lips, "you're perfect."

CHAPTER TWENTY-NINE

꩜

I blink, unsure when, exactly, it got bright enough for me to see. It's gray outside, misty and monochrome. Wind rattles the naked branches of the tree outside the hotel room window, sending wafts of snow across the balcony.

Lucas is still asleep—*did I sleep at all?* I'm not sure. I rise, grimacing as my joints crack, and pull the blanket off my bed. Tightening it around my body, I open the sliding glass door a crack, pausing to see if Lucas stirs. . . . He doesn't. I step outside onto the balcony, the wood so cold it burns the soles of my feet. The air is still and mean, biting at any exposed skin, making it difficult to keep my eyes open.

Our hotel is at the top of a small hill dotted by trees with fat trunks. Ice is perfectly balanced along the tops of branches, like an outline. Every now and then I hear a cracking sound that reminds me of a gunshot, a rumbling, and then see a quick burst of movement—branches giving way to the added weight of the ice and snow.

I blink a few times, then stare across the lake. Is that the island? It's far, a gray shadow on the horizon, and it takes me a long time to decide if it's a cloud or land—it isn't until the wind blows some of the mist away that I'm certain it's Isle Royale. I wonder if Mora knows I'm still following her, or if she thinks I gave up after Nashville.

I wonder if Kai knows that I haven't given up yet. Surely. He knows me, better than anyone. I close my eyes and think for a moment about the way he'd pull me close when I said something funny. The way he'd laugh and kiss my forehead and tell me without saying a word that he loved me. I want that right now, so badly—not only to be reminded Kai loves me, but to laugh with him again. Just one more time.

I start to lean on the balcony railing, but it's caked in ice so clear it looks as if it's wrapped in cellophane. The wind gusts again, blowing snow like dust down the embankment leading to the lake, across the lake's surface—it's frozen over. I look at it curiously; I've never seen something like that outside of movies. Leaves and brush are blowing across the surface, disappearing into the fog.

Something stirs in the brush in the woods. Something alive and warm-looking, picking its way through the trees. I lean forward, squinting—a deer. It picks its legs up high, taking giant, exaggerated steps to move through the snow. I wonder how Flannery's deer is doing, now that it's free.

The deer pauses; its ears prick forward—listening, waiting,

watching. It moves again, to the ice, and takes several steps out on it. After a few cautious licks at the ground, the deer lifts its head and begins to slowly, surely, walk out toward the center of the lake. Toward the island.

So that's how Mora gets there.

It must be. It's her ice, it's her world—of course it's thick enough to hold her.

I inch the sliding glass door open again, overwhelmed when the heated air hits me. I silently put on a pair of jeans, thick socks, shoes, gloves, and long sleeves. I pull Flannery's knife from its sheath, inspect the blade, and tuck it into my coat pocket.

Just see if the ice will hold you. Get an idea of things. I lie to myself over and over, ignoring the real reason I'm sneaking out: I'm afraid Kai has already changed, afraid Lucas is right. Afraid I'll have to kill him.

And I'm not sure I can do that in front of everyone. Like he told me once, in the end, it's just us. Even if it means I'm outnumbered. Even if it means he kills me first.

I grab a room key and let myself out, hurrying downstairs to the shop. It's empty, though the cases are already packed with pastries and bagels.

"Morning," the clerk says. "Looking for breakfast?"

"No, thanks," I say, walking over to the counter. "I just need some sort of flashlight."

I stumble down the embankment with decidedly less grace than the deer, following her footprints, destroying them as I go. The hotel windows watch me—I keep looking back, certain I'll see Lucas's panicked face at ours. It doesn't happen. The world is silent and peaceful. I pause at the edge of the lake, looking at the yellow glow behind the clouds, the sun's desperate attempt to break through. It's no match for Mora's power.

I put a foot out onto the lake, cringing, waiting to hear it crack.

Nothing.

I pull my other foot across, so that my weight is on the ice entirely. Still nothing. A step, another, another. I shine the flashlight down, hoping I'll be able to tell if the ice is solid or thin, but it doesn't help much. I can feel my heart shaking, begging me to turn around and go back to shore. No, not now. Another step, another. I turn and look at the hotel—still no signs of life. No one will be here to save me if it gives. The air is so cold already—the water must be like knives. It would kill me quickly, perhaps more kindly than whatever awaits me on the island, but I at least want a chance to fight....

Another nervous step, but I begin to grow more confident. I move faster, always pausing as I bring my foot down. I move farther and farther onto the lake, toward the sun, the island. When I turn around to look at the hotel again, it's in the distance, a football field or two away.

There's no point in looking back again.

She's not really a queen. She's a girl, a lonely girl. She's lost everything, and she's just trying to make up for it now. I keep my flashlight trained on the ground in front of me even as the sky lightens. I think I can see the island now, a dark mass ahead. It's huge, so big it almost looks as if I've crossed the lake entirely and am on a new shore. It's getting colder; my eyes are watering, and my ears feel as if they'd break off my body if someone hit them too hard.

I hear a clattering sound; I grab Flannery's knife from its sheath and clench my fingers around it even though it's so cold I can't feel them. Something is running at me, coming from ahead. Something moving faster, faster, faster. I try to remember everything Flannery told me about knife fighting. Wait for your moment, don't try to create it—

The creature behind the noise finally breaks through the fog. I see its eyes first, the frenzied, panicked look in them, wide and trembling—

It's the deer. I duck down as she bolts toward me, skids on the ice, and nearly slams into me. Her legs are like sticks being thrown around, falling all the wrong ways as she rushes back the way we came. I turn and watch her go, then stare into the mist, waiting for whatever scared her to come charging through.

If Kai is a wolf, will I recognize him?

I imagine a monster with his eyes, fur the color of his hair. *That's what I'll see next. That's what will come at me.* The fog is thick, a curtain that's taking a moment too long to reveal its secrets. The sound of the deer running away fades, and the world is silent again, still.

I'm shaking, but I take another step forward. Keep

moving. The deer may be running from Mora, but Mora is running from me. I think about what Flannery told me, about fighting—before you start, know who is going to win. *I know it will be me. I know it will be me.*

I'm lying. I don't know anything. But it keeps me moving.

I push through the fog—I can hear the sounds of branches on the island ahead breaking now. The ice beneath me grows uneven, the snow thicker. I'm several yards in before I realize I'm not walking on the lake anymore; I'm walking on the shore.

I'm on Isle Royale.

CHAPTER THIRTY

ख०

"You know I'm in love with you, right, Ginny?" Kai said, looking at my knuckles, running his thumb across them. His eyes flickered to mine. It was the first time he'd said it aloud, or at least, aloud and meant it like *that*. "I've always been in love with you."

"I know," I whispered, and he smiled, leaned forward, and kissed me. I lifted out of my chair and moved to him; he pulled me down into his lap and wrapped his arms around me. My fingertips curled at the nape of his neck, and when we broke away he found my eyes and was silent for a long time. He exhaled, reached up, and tucked my hair behind my ears, letting his palm linger by my cheek.

I smiled and said, "I'll always—"

I didn't get the chance to finish the phrase that feels so much more real now, so much more proven. *I'll always love you, too, Kai.*

I'll always love you, no matter what I have to do.

I trudge inward, tucking the flashlight inside my coat but keeping the knife out and ready. Every time I hear a snap or a rustle, I freeze, waiting for the wood to spring to life. But then nothing happens, and I have to take a breath and move on. I wonder if this was what Grandma Dalia's life was like, after the red-haired boy was taken, after she learned that the world was full of hungry mouths. Waiting for the bottom to fall out, for them to come back for her.

They did, in the end.

Something cracks over to my right—something louder than the other noises I've heard, something that sounds like a foot coming down on a branch. I pause and turn toward it, but see nothing. I try to remember the map of the island on the brochure. How big is it? What if I'm stuck here overnight before I find Mora and Kai? I'll never survive the cold. I lift my fingers to my mouth and try to warm them with my breath, but it's barely warmer. I wish I could cross my arms, but I want to have the knife ready.

A rustle to the left—again, something that sounds living. I hold my breath, listening, but the trees fall silent again. I keep going, another rustle—

A growl, stifled and so low I almost miss it.

They're watching me.

My body wants to cry, to drop to a ball and pretend it isn't happening—all my resolve from the hotel room, from the ice, is gone. I didn't want to be running again, didn't want to be the prey. How many of them are there, watching me? Is Mora with them? Is Kai?

I can't be still too long; they'll realize I've figured it out. *Wait for your moment*, Flannery's voice reminds me. Let them lead; wait till you know where they are. How many of them there are. I fold my arms now, but only so I can swap the knife between hands every few moments, keeping them in the dark as to which hand it's in.

It's hard to keep my pace—something alive and screaming in my chest begs me to run, but I keep moving steadily. The haze of sunlight that made it through the clouds earlier is being swallowed by the gray. I'm just over mourning its absence when it starts to snow. Lightly, compared with yesterday, but flakes are falling, spiraling down to my lashes, forcing me to blink them away, my heart stopping for the flicker of a moment that I can't see.

My feet hurt, my lungs hurt, and my fingers hurt. I feel that I might shatter like glass if I were to fall down. The noises in the trees grow louder, more frequent. Every now and then I can't stop myself from whirling around, certain I'll see glowing eyes, but they stay hidden as I start uphill, toward the center of the island.

By the time the ground flattens out I feel beaten, exhausted—the high from my fear is wearing off, and raw emotion is brewing in my chest. I haven't heard them in a little while; I stop, turn around, and listen carefully. Where are they? It's snowing harder now, thick enough that I'm wary of the branches waving back and forth above me. I hug my arms to my chest, shiver, and spin around—

And there they are.

Five boys—men? Boys—standing in front of me. Their eyes and chins are sharp, and they're wearing T-shirts but look comfortable in the cold.

And they're smiling.

"Are you lost?" one asks. His voice is low, as if it's coming from the back of his throat and rarely used. Over his right shoulder is a house, cottage-like and made of stone. I can't tell if it looks abandoned or not—there's nothing broken about it, but there are no lights. There's no movement, either, and the flower boxes that line the windows are empty.

"Miss," another says, and the way he hisses the *s* makes my skin crawl. This one has blond hair, so blond it's nearly white, and I realize I recognize him—the opera singer, Larson. If not for the hair, I wouldn't know him. In the photo I saw, he looked happy. Here he looks hungry, eyes low, cheekbones jutting out as if they were carved.

"I'm looking for someone," I manage.

"Here?" say the first boy, the one with dark hair. "There's no one here."

"A boy," I say. "I need to see him."

This seems to throw them a little—their eyes flicker to one another. They say something I don't understand in the glance.

"Why do you think he's here?" another one asks. This

one is older than the others, but still handsome; the silver in his hair matches the sky.

"He came here with a woman," I say. Swallow. "He came here with the Snow Queen."

"The Snow Queen?" Larson says, sounding amused. "She'll like that title, won't she, boys?" They rumble in agreement. "We can take you to her."

"Yes," I say immediately.

"But she'll kill you."

They expect this to shock me, and when it doesn't, they look at one another again, thrown. They wanted me afraid. I remember the beasts from the car with Lucas, how they licked their lips when I screamed.

"Why is she here?" a new voice asks.

I stop. My knees feel weak; my lungs are melting in my chest.

He walks around the side of the cottage, hands slung in his pockets, and joins the other five. His skin is pale, his eyes black, and he moves with the same still, easy confidence that they do. I should keep my eye on the other four, but I can't help it. I stare, unsure if the tangle of emotion in my chest is relief or horror.

"Kai," I finally say, the word slipping out as a whisper.

He meets my eyes and narrows his own. "And who are you?"

CHAPTER THIRTY-ONE

෫ଠ

I was prepared for him to be a monster; I wasn't prepared for him to look at me with such icy indifference. His expression is like the other five's—he doesn't know me, not the smallest bit. Somewhere, deep in my mind, I expected—no, not expected, *wanted*—him to see me and remember.

But he's gone. There's nothing of my Kai in his eyes, no spark of recognition, much less love.

Can he change into a wolf now? I need to know for sure; I have to know for sure. I need to see him change into a monster.

One of the others is looking from me to Kai, seemingly bored with the entire exchange. That one takes a step closer to me; when I instinctively take one backward, he smiles again.

"So, you'll be coming with us to see *her*?" he asks, in a way that tells me the answer he's hoping for is no. The answer he's hoping for is pleading, is begging, is fear.

If you don't have the upper hand, create it.

I take another step back. Their eyebrows lift ever so slightly, a way they don't think I notice. Another step, and they lean forward, excited. Another, another—

I turn and run.

I hear them shouting, whooping behind me in excitement as I tear down the hill, following the path I came on. Faster, faster, keep moving—are they chasing me yet? I try to listen to know for sure. Yes, yes, they're crashing along behind me. I can't outrun them—they know that, and when I glance back, I see they're hardly even trying. Still human, barely jogging, grinning in a way that makes Flannery's smile look sweet.

They don't know, however, that I'm not *trying* to outrun them.

I wait until I go over the hill, down the slope—just barely out of sight, where the trees are slightly smaller. I hold my breath and slam my body weight into a tree. The cold combined with the impact shoots pain through my bones, but I keep going—I hit another, another. Each time, snow crashes down; the shaking branches incite other branches to fall; powdery snow rises up like dust behind me. I can't hear the boys anymore over crashing snow and tree limbs—but they can't see me anymore, either.

I just need one, one good one—yes. I leap for a low-hanging branch. It stirs the tree and sends snow falling to the ground like all the others, but this time I hold on tight, pulling myself up and off the trail. I release and slam forward, falling down a short ravine; I'm bleeding, I think, and my head is foggy, but I grimace and lie still, quiet.

281

Snow is still falling, but it's hard to hear the difference between the ruckus I created and six pairs of feet running after me. They're moving faster now—they realize they've lost me. I squeeze my eyes shut as they near my hiding place; if just one looks to the left, he'll see my red shirt, I'm sure of it.

But no. It works. They pass by the ravine without a second glance, following my old trail—the raccoon trick Lucas told me about. I raise up just in time to see the backs of their heads disappearing. Human heads—they didn't change. Does that mean Kai can't yet?

I rise, find my own trail, and follow along behind them, crouching down low in the snow. When we're back by the frozen lake, they stop and stare out over the ice. They've lost my trail; they don't know what to do. They mill around, something of the wolf in the way they pace back and forth at the lake's edge.

They spread out along the shore, eyes on the rocky ground, scouring it for any sign of me—I could be circling back around to the shore. The older one in the center, at the mouth of my trail. Larson goes to his left, and Kai to his far left. I step into a thicket of snow, cringing when it comes all the way to my knees. When I look down, I see spots of blood in the white—my knee is bleeding from where I hit the ravine.

I cut along sideways through the woods, slowly, slowly so I don't make a sound. I finally make it over to the stretch of shore Kai is exploring, his shoulders hunched forward and his breathing slow and methodical. He stares out over the lake, as if he thinks he sees something. Larson, on his right, a few dozen yards back now, is walking a few feet out onto the ice.

I grab a handful of snow and lob it as hard as I can in Kai's direction. He pauses and turns; I see his eyes flicker to an area ahead of me. Kai takes a step forward. Yes, yes... though if he signals to the others, it's over. *I should have waited till they were more spread out, till he couldn't reach them—*

Kai starts up the bank toward me. Larson is preoccupied with something on the lake and doesn't see him going. I exhale in relief, tuck myself against a thick tree trunk, and rub my fingers gently, readying them to hold the knife, reminding myself that he might not be Kai anymore. That it might be too late, and this is what Kai—*my Kai*—would want. I stare at the knife blade as Kai's footsteps quicken. He runs forward, runs past me—

"Kai." I say his name, refusing to let my voice shake.

He whirls around and finds me. He smiles; the slow, heinous expression doesn't fit his face.

"How do you know my name?" he asks in a playful voice. He doesn't blink; his eyes are wide and crazed-looking, void of any warmth.

"I know you," I say. "Do you remember?"

He shakes his head, as if this delights him. It feels as if my heart is crumbling, becoming ash in my chest.

"Are you sure?" I ask, and my voice finally breaks. I won't let tears fall—I can't, I can't risk not being able to see—but the sob in my throat won't be stopped.

Kai takes a step closer to me, extends his fingers, and then balls his hands into tight fists. "You got away from us," he says smoothly. "That was clever. You're clever. What are you doing here?"

I exhale, forcing my shoulders back. Grip the knife. *Say it, just say it, even if your voice cracks.* The words jumble in my head before finding their way past my lips.

"I'm here to kill you."

Kai smiles wider. And then he lunges for me.

I leap backward and spin around the tree trunk. He doubles back the other way, but I expected it; I lash out with the knife, catch his shirt, and slice at it, barely nicking the skin. Just as Flannery promised, he glances down at the wound; I fling myself at him, catching him off balance, and we tumble down together. He punches me in the stomach, hard, and I can't find my breath, but don't stop, don't stop. *This might be your only chance.* I bring the knife down, dig my knee into his chest, and position the blade over his heart. He goes to swipe it away, and I press down, drawing the tiniest bit of blood.

Kai's arms fall back; his eyes find mine, cold and hard and hateful. He twists underneath me; I press the knife down again, grimace as I feel it pop through a layer of skin. Kai tries to swallow a groan, but I hear it anyway. His chest trembles in pain.

"They'll kill you," he whispers at me. "They'll tear you apart. As soon as she realizes you're here, she'll come; my brothers will come. They'll eat you, one bite at a time, from the inside out."

The boy I loved is gone. I don't need to see him change to know it's true.

I want to close my eyes, but I can't—he'd use the moment to get away. I brace myself and slam one hand down over his eyes so I don't have to look at them. Do it. Make it fast; make it quick. I shift my weight forward so I'll be able to use my whole body to drive the knife in. The skin on his forehead and cheeks feels so cold underneath my hand.

One. Two. My eyes wander across his face, trying to memorize the details—*I won't see him again. Ever again.* I'm shaking. I have to do this now before he moves, before he sees that he has the upper hand.

I bring my lips down to Kai's; they're so cold they burn mine. Yet behind the fire, they're familiar. Lips I've kissed before. Lips I thought I would spend a lifetime kissing. I want him to wrap him arms around me, holding me tight as if it's the first time all over again, but of course he doesn't. So I pretend. Pretend it's like before, pretend Kai loves me and I love Kai and no matter what either of us becomes or does, where either of us goes, the fact that we love each other will never change. I focus on the fantasy, on Kai's lips against mine as I inhale, preparing to drive the knife in on the exhale—

Kai shoves me, hard, sending me flying backward. The knife flies from my hands, and I crash to the ground. *Find your footing, get up, quick, find the knife.* Kai fumbles away from me, and I frantically search the snow. His back hits a tree; he stops, pulls his hands out of the snow, and stares at them, red and aching from the cold. Finally, his eyes find mine, and when he speaks, his voice is a shaky whisper. "Ginny?"

CHAPTER THIRTY-TWO

ℭℬ

I stare. Is it a trick?

"What does three flashes mean? With the flashlight?" I ask hurriedly.

"I..." Kai shakes his head, squinting. "It means come over."

"What did Grandma Dalia call me?"

"The neighbor child."

I inhale, nod. Tears are rising in my eyes, but I blink them back furiously. "What were you playing with, the day we first met?"

"A Frisbee. Ginny," he says again as he begins to shiver. I walk over to him, staring—his lips are pink again, but they're dimming, slowly turning blue once more. His eyes are hardening, his skin paling—

I grab his hand.

He jolts upward, the warmth returns. His eyes are shaky

and his breath is uneven when he speaks. "What happened to me?"

"Kai," I say, exhaling, and wrap my arms around him. He feels bony and wrong and broken, but he buries his head against my neck the way he's always done. His hands find my waist pull me closer, quivering like a sick person.

"What happened to me?" he asks against my skin.

"It's . . . complicated," I say. "What do you remember?"

"I remember Mora," he says. "I remember . . . I remember everything, but it feels like a dream. I think it was a dream."

"I wish," I say. I pull off my coat and shove the flashlight into my hoodie pocket, but in the few seconds it takes me to put the coat on him—during which I have to release his palm—I see him start to darken again. I can't let go, or he'll go back to . . .

Her.

"Kai," I say. I rise. "We have to find Mora."

"Mora," he says, blinking hard. "She's real. It was all real."

"Yes. We have to find her because she still has power over you. When I let go—"

"I know," Kai says, his voice clearing a little. "When you let go I become hers. It's like she's running my body, and I'm falling farther and farther away from it." He squeezes my hand tightly, steps closer to me, and kisses me on the forehead. He's still so cold that it makes me shiver. He inhales, finds my eyes. "Are you going to kill her?"

I look down. "Not unless I have to."

"Like you were going to kill me. If you had to." It's half a question—*would you really have done it, Ginny?* Kai looks as if he doesn't understand how what he's asking can line up with the girl he knows.

"If I had to," I answer in a whisper. "I'd have done it if I had to." Kai nods and seems to accept this as truth. "Come on. The house I saw earlier—is she in it right now?"

"Maybe. She probably went to see what we were chasing—" Kai winces and puts his hand to his temple. He blinks hard, groans.

"What's happening?" I ask.

"I just . . . I feel like two people. I just . . ." He looks up at me. "Come on."

I find Flannery's knife in the snow and let Kai lead—though he can't walk well. It's almost as if he's walking on broken feet, each step rocky and numb. It's still snowing, but I'm grateful for it—it hides our tracks a little.

"How many are there? Like you, I mean. How many boys?" I whisper as we walk.

"Six," he says. "That was all of us." Kai stops suddenly, and I almost crash into him. I glare at him accusingly only to see him lifting a finger, pointing. I look in that direction and through the trees. Mora's cottage. We've come up along the back side, and for the first time I notice there's no snow on the roof, as if the flakes avoid the shingles.

"She's in there right now?" I ask Kai. It's small, smaller than it looked earlier, and it doesn't seem like the sort of place someone like Mora would live.

"I don't know," he answers. "It's not really her house."

"I don't understand what that means," I say, growing frustrated.

"I can't explain it," he says. "You have to see."

I exhale, look at the house, hold Kai's hand tight. "All right, then. Don't let go."

"I won't," Kai says, turning to look at me. The gold in his eyes both soothes and terrifies me—I don't want it to leave again.

Together, we slink through the snow along the edge of the cottage, ducking under windowsills. We reach the front door, and suddenly the knife in my hand feels stupid and small against whatever Mora is.

Kai is the one who reaches forward first, letting his hand run across the doorknob. I hold my breath as he turns it and pushes the door open. The house sighs, as if it needed the air from the outside to blow in. I brace myself for Mora's eyes, for a wolf, for the cold.

But there is nothing. The house is dark and perfect, not like it's abandoned, but like no one has *ever* lived here. It reminds me of those staged homes, where they bring in furniture that's flawless and stiff. The door opens to a foyer that splits into two rooms, one with a dining room table with eight place settings, the forks and knives lined up on either side of white plates. The other, a living room with a camel-back couch and bookcases with one or two items on each shelf—odd things, like unlit candles, empty jars, and an elaborate ship in a bottle. Ahead, I can see a bedroom. The bed is crisply made with silk linens and fancy pillows, and there's a notepad sitting beside it, the pen laid carefully across the top.

I twist around and pull the flashlight out of my hoodie pocket, flick it on, then step inside, balancing the knife and the light in one hand so I don't have to release Kai. The floorboards creak in protest under my feet, and I cringe, waiting for something to happen.... Silence. Another step, another. We pass a table with picture frames on it, and I notice there's no dust—anywhere. Everything is perfectly polished and glossy. I pause, shine the light on each of the photos, and realize they're all of Mora.

But not the Mora I know. They're of Mora in a wedding dress. Of Mora on a boat in a bikini. Of Mora in front of a backdrop that looks like it belongs at a movie premiere.

They're not really of Mora. There's something wrong about them, and when I lean over to see what, I realize that it's Mora's head, but not her body. They're fakes, all of them—Mora's face cut out and pasted on top of other girls' bodies. Pictures of the life Mora thought she would have, not the life she's living.

"Look at these," I say to Kai, forgetting to whisper.

"That's what I meant," Kai answers. "It's not really her house."

I angle the flashlight on one of the largest photos—a black-and-white shot of Mora wearing a long, silver dress with a fancy headpiece, something reminds me of the 1920s. I narrow my eyes—it's real. It's her, Mora the way she really is. I inhale, shake my head, and turn back to Kai—

"She came to kill you," he says.

"What—" I begin, but then I realize he isn't talking to me.

Kai's eyes are dark again. Skin a strange bluish gray. And his hand is now heavy in mine, like an ice carving instead of an appendage. A flutter of movement, and Mora steps out from behind him, her slender hand carved around Kai's other arm.

"I know," she says, and smiles at me.

CHAPTER THIRTY-THREE

Kai pulls his hand from mine; the air that swoops to my skin is warmer than his fingers were. I lower the flashlight's beam to the floor and stare at Mora.

"Come to kill me?" Mora asks simply.

"I want him back," I answer, because as much as I want to stop her, to end what she does to boys and the girls who love them, what I really want is Kai.

"I know the feeling," she answers, almost sympathetically, and steps between Kai and me, dangerously close. She emanates cold, so much that I take a step back to escape it. Mora leans against Kai, who swoops one arm around her and kisses the top of her head tenderly. She takes his hand and walks into the sitting room, as if I'm merely a houseguest to whom she's giving the grand tour.

I inhale, turn, and follow. Mora sits down on the couch, Kai beside her; he hardly ever looks away, as if he adores her too much to warrant looking at anything else. *Lucas warned me. He warned me Kai would trick me*, I think, feeling sick. Mora smiles again and motions toward a swan-arm rocker opposite her, indicating I should sit.

"I'll stand," I say stiffly.

"You'll sit," Mora answers. "My home. My rules. Drop the knife, by the way."

I pause and let the knife clatter to the floor, but I keep my grip on the flashlight. This seems to satisfy her; she motions to the chair, and I reluctantly sit down on its edge—not because I'm playing by her rules, but because I haven't worked out a plan yet and any time is borrowed time. She looks pleased and runs her fingers up and down Kai's pant leg. I shiver, fiddling with the flashlight switch when my body can't handle the nerves.

"I liked you, Ginny. You're the kind of girl I would have been friends with, once."

"I can't say the same," I answer curtly. I notice magazines on the coffee table—fashion ones, though they're strangely dated. Some from the sixties, some from the eighties, some more recent. She catches me looking at them and sharpens her tone, as if she's embarrassed.

"Why are you really here?" She takes Kai's hand again; I look away, though I wish I could meet his eyes for a moment.

"I'm taking Kai back. You can't just take people because you want them, Mora."

"That's what happened to me—"

"I don't care," I snap—it's so quiet in here, like a vacuum

except for our voices. "I get it. The Fenris stole you; they stole your life. But that doesn't mean you can do the same thing to others."

"So you know about them," Mora says quickly, and something akin to fear flashes in her eyes. "Did they follow you?"

"I don't know," I admit.

She frowns and then leans her head against Kai's shoulder; he puts an arm around her. "They stole me from my life—took everything from me. But I gained so much more in return. Power you could never understand—power that means I can, in fact, do what I want." Mora grins.

"He remembered when I touched him. He'll never really be yours. None of them are," I say, whispering. I can see my breath now—it's getting colder in here, though Kai and Mora don't seem to notice. I shiver without meaning to and squeeze the flashlight in my left hand, causing the beam to flick on and off.

"No one is ever really ours," Mora says, tilting her head as if considering her words. "But he's more mine than he ever was yours. You're a silly little girl, Ginny. I admit I underestimated you—I didn't think you'd keep coming for him. But that doesn't change the fact that you don't deserve him—you don't appreciate what he is." It's getting colder, colder, colder. Mora stands up, pushes her shoulders back, and walks toward me slowly. My hands are a strange purplish blue, and it hurts to keep my eyes open. I struggle to breathe and realize I've stopped shivering. *No. No. Don't give in.* I look down at the knife on the floor, reach for it—

Mora grabs my wrist, her skin so cold it burns like fire. I cry out, but Mora holds on, laughing so loud the sound echoes throughout the house. "Come on, Ginny. Really?"

I crumble, hating myself—but the pain is too much. It rushes through me like lightning that freezes my bones, my blood. The room is growing even colder, and Mora's fingers feel stuck to my wrist. I shake, I can't stop; it's a cold and a hurt I haven't known before, one that seems impossible and heavy on me. I squeeze the flashlight in my free hand, or at least, I try to—but my fingers feel as if they're shattering, and for a moment I'm not even sure I'm holding it anymore.

And suddenly, it begins to get warmer. I exhale in relief— it's a strange sort of warmth, after all that cold, one that seems to start somewhere near my chest and build out until it burns around my neck and wrists. I glance down at my hand and see I'm still blinking the flashlight nervously, automatically. The skin is blue, the movement sharp and robotic. Mora steps closer to me, lightens her grip on my wrist— though she's still holding tight enough for me to know I can't escape.

"It's a lie," Mora says delicately, right by my ear. Am I sweating? I shake my hair to the side, trying to cool my neck. "Right before you die from the cold, your body lies to you. Tells you you're warm. Has mercy on you." Kai shifts behind her. I flash the light again as my lungs tighten, refusing to allow another breath. One flash, two, three. One, two three.

One. Two. Three.

Come over.

"No one will take everything from me," Mora whispers. "Not you. Not the Fenris. Not anyone. Not ever again. I'm the one with the power now."

The flashlight catches Kai's eyes. Black—but there's gold. Gold flickering among the darkness.

My response is a whisper, the air hard and sharp in my throat. "But I'm going to win."

Come over.

Kai dives forward.

When Kai slams into me, it feels as if I'm breaking into a million pieces. I fall to the floor, knocking over the rocker and a small table. He shoves Mora to the side, grabs my wrist; his touch feels like fire. Mora screams something. I can't focus, but I see her on the floor, see Kai yanking something off the bookshelf—the model ship—and bringing it down hard on her head. But then I'm falling asleep into the warm world, but we're moving, and I can feel Kai's skin on mine, still hear Mora screaming at me as I drift down into—

I'm awake. My eyes spring open, and I realize Kai is carrying me, sprinting, panting as we run. Suddenly it's warm—not warm, really, but not the dead cold from inside the house. I grab Kai's neck, pull myself up to see behind him. Mora's house is disappearing in the distance, but there's movement on the trail—something's behind us, and Kai can't run fast enough while he carries me. I twist and struggle until Kai lets my feet down. They feel like cinder blocks, heavy and dead, but I force them along.

A tree whips at my face, drawing blood. *How far is the*

lake, how far is the lake? I trip and slide down an embank-ment, but Kai grabs my hand and yanks me up. I can see the smooth, pearly glow of the lake ahead, the path out of her world—

Something growls behind us, and I dare to glance back. Wolves, five of them, with sharp teeth and angry eyes. They dart in and out of the trees, well practiced on the terrain. So close, so close—I heard a crunch as one leaps over a snow-drift and lands near me, but it doesn't have me; they haven't caught us yet.

Kai and I hit the lake, sliding forward but keeping our footing. The other side is too far away to see through the fog, but we fly toward it. I can tell they're gaining on us by how close the sound of nails on ice is, clattering faster and faster. They'll catch us. We can't outrun them on a straightaway like this. Kai and I lock eyes for a harried instant, and I know he realizes it, too.

We keep running.

Hot breath at my heels, I hear jaws snap. I can't go any faster; this is all I have. Kai's hand hits my back. He pushes me, urging me to keep moving, but it's no good. My chest aches; the wolves are growling, I try to take large steps—

I hit a slippery patch of ice and flail forward. My chin hits the surface first, then my chest, my hands. I try to bound back up, but it's no use. My joints don't work; my body doesn't work. I flip over, draw my legs up as a dark gray wolf leaps forward—

The wolf cries out, falls out of the air. He hits the ice on his side, twitches, and I see drops of blood spattered across the lake surface. I turn around, scramble backward, torn between looking at the still-encroaching wolves and whatever stopped the gray one.

I see her smile first, the wicked one.

"Who is that?" Kai asks, breathless as we scramble to our feet. Flannery answers before I can.

"I'm the future Queen of Kentucky," she says, "and I'm here to save your ass."

CHAPTER THIRTY-FOUR

❧

Flannery isn't alone. Figures appear beside her—Lucas, who runs to my side, and then two others who walk up slowly, methodically.

Callum, with a rifle held up, eyes locked on his target. He fires a single shot, and the wolves slow. Beside him, Ella, hair streaming behind her in a high ponytail and a pink handgun held out in front of her. She glances at Flannery as she runs past me to yank the knife out of the gray wolf's side; as she does so he transforms, becomes Larson again. Flannery grimaces at the sight, but rises—

"Come on, come on," Lucas says, and I realize he's been shouting at us. We start to run again. Kai's skin is warm now, his arms tight around me. I can see the shore ahead.

"Kai!" Mora shouts; I whirl around. She's walking up behind her wolves, looking at Kai with eyes so blue that the world around her looks colorless. There is something in them, though: the tiniest bit of hesitation. Of worry. Fear. The confidence is gone, the certainty, and it reminds me that through this, through all of this, she was really the one running.

Kai looks back at her, grits his teeth, and continues to run for the shore. Mora says his name again, screams it; he ducks his head down, presses his free hand to his ear to block the noise. I hear a cry again as another bullet finds its target, wonder which wolf they hit—

A new sound, one that I think is a gunshot at first, but it goes on too long. A low sound that I feel through my legs, shaking up to my chest. Lucas suddenly skids to a stop, sliding a few additional feet and nearly pulling me and Kai down.

"Don't stop," Kai yells at him as he tries to pull me farther.

"Look." Lucas nods ahead, panting, while the long, low sound rings out again. Now that we're stopped, I can tell it's definitely no gunshot. I look to where Lucas is nodding and see a crack in the ice, thick and spreading like lightning across the space ahead. We turn around, see Mora walking forward, her fingers extended toward the ground—she's doing this, breaking the ice apart.

Callum and Ella are preoccupied, firing at the remaining wolves that pace back and forth in front of Mora, threatening to attack us should the bullets pause. Flannery, however, realizes what's happening to the ice—she sees her chance and runs forward, flinging a knife at Mora. It goes spinning by her head, but it gets her attention. Mora whirls around, glares at Flannery, who ducks down to avoid one of the guards. He leaps over her; a shot rings out and he falls and turns back into a boy, bleeding and naked. One guard left; I see Ella adjust, aiming at the remaining wolf, while Callum frantically reloads. *Shoot her, shoot her!* Flannery runs for her knife, black hair screaming out behind her.

The last guard hits Flannery so hard, so fast, that I'm not sure where he came from. They fall away, I hear Flannery scream, the wolf growling. I scream at Ella to shoot the animal, but she can't. She's aiming, waiting for a shot, but she'll hit Flannery—

And then I'm twisting away from Kai and Lucas. I'm running for Mora. I have to stop her; I have to end this. Lucas is shouting at me, Kai too, everyone is yelling, the roar of the gunshots and the wolf and Flannery's screams as it tears at her.

And then a sound louder than the rest. Deep, something that reverberates through me and hurts my ears as I run at Mora. She's still, tense, watching me, holding my eyes to hers—

Keeping me from looking at the ground. From seeing the crack in the ice that I trip over. I fall forward again, bracing for the pain when I strike the ground, but this time it isn't there. There is no ground—there's water.

I slide down so quickly that I'm not sure what's happening until a thousand swords are digging into me all at once. I try to flail, try to swim, but I can't feel anything except shooting pain in my head—because I can't breathe, I realize. My lungs are still, won't even struggle for air. There's bright light above me in the sea of dark, and I want to swim toward it, but the darkness of the water is spilling over into my vision. I finally inhale, but my lungs fill with ice. My chest screams a final time before fading—

Something sharp tears into my shoulder, brighter than the pain of the freezing water. The world swirls around me, and suddenly air is sharp and hard on my body, the world is loud again. I'm pulled backward, away from the water, the ice hard and angry against my body. Everything feels heavy, and I want to close my eyes—is it getting warmer? I can't tell. I force myself to look over to whoever is dragging me out of the water.

My lips part. I try to scream but there's no sound—it's not a hand digging into the soft spot of my shoulder. Teeth, sharp and white, black lips pulled back over a pale brown muzzle. It's a wolf; a low, steady growl vibrates from his throat into my body. I finally find the strength to struggle, to twist away—it's not as hard as I expect it to be. I crawl backward across the ice, slipping when my hands are too cold to find traction, unable to look away from the wolf as it follows me, one slow step at a time. It lifts its eyes, looks at me—

They're golden. A gold I know, a gold I've seen a thousand times before.

"Kai?"

The wolf stares and drops his head low. I lift a shaking hand toward him. I need to touch him, need to feel that this is real—

A clicking noise from behind Kai—I look around him and see Ella, gun out in front of her.

"No," I say, voice breaking and weak. "No, no, it's him. Don't." Kai stays perfectly still. He doesn't move as I scramble forward, wrap my arms around his neck, and let my fingers dig into his fur. Ella's eyes are steeled; she's breathing heavy, staring. Behind her, I see Callum helping Flannery. Blood is streaming down her arm from bite marks across her shoulder and chest.

"Move," Ella says.

"Please, Ella, don't shoot him—"

"Not *him*, Ginny. *Move*," Ella hisses at me. I turn, look behind me, and suddenly I realize what she's really aiming at. Mora, standing perfectly still but breathing hard, furiously. Her eyes go from me, to Kai, to Ella, back again. I can see the body of one of her guards behind her, a pool of blood spreading out on the ice and freezing, turning dark purple. There's a cracking sound.

"Stop," Ella says to Mora, voice steady. "Break this ice one more time and I'll shoot."

"You've only got one shot," Mora snarls. "Better not miss."

"I didn't miss back in Nashville," Ella reminds her, and Mora's face contorts with anger. "Ginny, Kai, *move*. Get to shore."

I rise, steadying myself against Kai. My legs don't work right—they don't bend—and my clothes weigh a million pounds. Yet we slowly, carefully pick our way away from Mora, away from Ella. Lucas is waiting for me where the ice is thicker, casting Kai a wary look before picking me up and carrying me the rest of the way to the shore. There's a body in the grass nearby—one of the guards, I realize with relief.

"We're all alive, then?" I ask, just to be sure.

"So far. But there's one bullet left, and it's the one in Ella's gun," Lucas answers grimly, setting me down beside Flannery on the embankment. She's pressing hard on her shoulder, trying to stop the bleeding. Callum is beside her, searching through bags frantically, gun in his hand—looking for more ammunition. I look over, realize Kai has stopped at the edge of the ice. He looks at me, turns back to see Ella. Neither she nor Mora have moved an inch. Lucas is pale, his fingers shaking.

Kai finds my eyes with his—still his, even in the wolf's body. I swallow, and he turns and bolts back toward Mora and Ella. He stops in front Ella, then paces back and forth between her and Mora, head low, looking more and more like an animal with each step.

"Just let Mora go," Lucas says under his breath, standing at the edge of the ice. "Everyone back away, just go. Ella, baby. Come on."

Something snaps behind us, farther up the embankment. I can't bring myself to care at first, but the sound grows louder, becoming more frequent. Becoming footsteps, dozens of footsteps. Flannery looks first; her eyes widen, I see something like a scream forming on her lips, but it never escapes. I finally look away from Kai, turn my head to see—

Wolves. No, not wolves. Fenris. Running at us.

CHAPTER THIRTY-FIVE

೧൬

A strangled sound emerges from Lucas's throat. I see him close his eyes, bracing for the teeth, the claws. I exhale. After all that, this is how we're going to die?

The first Fenris leaps over us. Then another, another. They avoid us entirely, instead heading for the ice, faces and jaws elongated, their teeth yellowed and bloody. They look so different from Kai, from the guards we killed. I can't believe I ever thought Mora's wolves were Dalia's beasts.

The sight breaks through Ella's calm exterior. I can see her panic; one shot left, a dozen wolves, Mora...there might as well be zero shots. Kai lowers his head and growls so loudly I can hear the sound from here, but they don't stop; they pass him, finally stopping between Ella and Mora. The Fenris at the front of the pack pauses, and then twists, contorting. His snout sucks into his face; there's a cracking sound as his spine changes, as his haunches become hip bones. He becomes a man with a wild, angry grin.

"Mora," he says in a singsong voice. "Darling."

Mora doesn't answer. Her confidence fades; her shoulders slacken. She doesn't move, doesn't look at them—if it weren't for the slow, even rise and fall of her chest, I'd say she wasn't breathing. As strong as she's always looked to me, she now resembles a ragdoll, something to be tossed around. Behind the Fenris, Ella softens her grip on her gun and takes a step away.

"Time to stop all this and come home," the man—the Fenris—says, extending a hand to her. Behind him, the others pace, scratching at the ice and snarling to one another. They look at Mora hungrily, angrily. She reaches up, her hair behind her ears, and seamlessly, as if she's sliding into a dress, changes.

When the Fenris change, it's violent—cracking, popping, skin to fur and nails to claws. When Mora's guards change, it's faster, simpler, but it still looks painful. Mora, however, looks beautiful as she slips away from her human form and becomes a solid white wolf with clear blue eyes.

So that's why they want her, I realize, watching. *She's theirs.*

"You did well," the Fenris says. "We thought we'd never find you, for a while. Who'd have thought it would be a mortal girl to lead us straight to your door?" His eyes flash toward me, vulgar and leering. He smiles again.

Mora stands perfectly still. A gust of wind ruffles her fur;

306

Kai and Ella continue to slowly, carefully retreat, wary of drawing the pack's attention.

"Are you sure there's no more ammunition?" Lucas mutters to Callum.

"Not a single round."

"Then someone here better figure out what we'll do when they come back this way. They're slower in this weather, but they're faster than *us*," Lucas says gravely. Flannery looks over at me, reaches down, and presses a knife handle into my hand. My fingers are too cold to close around it.

The pack leader walks over to Mora, running his hand across her head as if she's a dog. "There we go," he says. I can see her shaking, not from fear, I don't think, but from rage, the kind that has to be bottled up but threatens to shake you from the inside out.

I rise, unsteady, using a tree and Flannery's shoulder for support. The others look at me as I clear my throat, trying to find enough warmth in my chest to make my words reach across the lake.

"Mora!" I shout.

The Fenris and Mora turn to me; I jolt at a dozen yellow, horrible eyes setting on me at once. *Ignore them, ignore them.* I find Mora's eyes instead—they're still ice blue, even in the wolf's body. One chance.

"No one will take everything from you. Never again," I call across the ice.

The pack leader raises an eyebrow at me, as if I'm some sort of lunatic. For a moment, I think I might be; Mora just

307

stares. There's so much hate in her eyes, so much fury. She blinks, ducks her head down, and then seamlessly turns back into a human, the act pushing the pack leader's hand off her head. He looks at her incredulously, raising an arm to strike her—

The ice cracks.

I look to Kai; he understands. He dashes forward, brushing by Ella as they run for the shore. The Fenris look around, confused, as the ice reverberates beneath them. It grows louder, louder, louder, until it sounds like a train in the distance coming ever closer. The pack leader looks down, watching as the ice beneath his feet begins to crumble—

"Get off the ice!" he shouts to the pack.

It's too late.

They crash through the ice with a screeching, screaming sound. Jaws and teeth slide into the water as the ice gives way. Mora is the last to fall; she doesn't flail, doesn't try to catch herself. It's over in an instant, blonde hair sliding out of sight.

My eyes move to Kai and Ella; they're almost here, but the ice is being swallowed up behind them. Ella is slower on two feet than Kai is on four; Kai glances over his shoulder and realizes this. He turns back, grabs hold of Ella's coat, and charges forward. The ice is moving faster; the whole lake is caving in on itself; they just need to make it to the shallows and we can get them. Water licks at Kai's heels—

He leaps away from the deep water, into the shallows just as the water catches him. They slide onto the remaining solid ice—Lucas runs down and pulls Ella out. Kai bounds to the shore, shaking, looking less like a thing to fear and more like a thing to pity. He collapses onto the ground; I crawl over to him, not caring about the added cold when water from his fur soaks against my chest.

Beneath me, Kai shifts. I let go, watching as he curls first into a ball and then begins to change. His limbs elongate; the fur fades away and becomes skin; there's a cracking sound, and he groans as his spine straightens. As he becomes the boy instead of the wolf. I reach forward and grab hold of his hand as the claws draw in, becoming fingernails. His skin is still cold, his face still pale blue, and he's naked, trembling.

I grab hold of his shoulders, bring my lips to his; he reaches up in response, tangles his fingers in my wet hair, pulls me closer. I finally pull away from his lips, but not his face, leaving my eyes on his, my cheeks close enough that I can feel him breathing.

"You know I love you, right?" he says hoarsely, and I nod against him.

"So that's him?" Flannery asks. I turn my head, see her propped up on her good shoulder. "I dunno, Ginny," she says, surveying Kai. "For all the trouble, I expected him to be taller."

CHAPTER THIRTY-SIX

ↄ୦ⱺ

They assure me the water in the bathtub is barely warm, but it feels scalding for the first few moments after I get in, clothes and all. Kai sits beside me on the tile floor, staring at his hands, while the others sit in the main room, bundled up in blankets and towels, Ella cradled against Lucas's chest. The Travellers refuse to go to the hospital, despite the fact that both Flannery and Callum probably need stitches.

"They'll give me a number," Callum says, folding his arms. "I don't want to be a number."

"That's not how it works," Lucas says. "You'll just get checked out and stitched up. I'll pay."

"You think we need your charity?" Flannery says, her unblackened eye widening.

"That's not what he said—" Ella argues.

"Who are they again?" Kai whispers to me, the question

sincere. He's sitting outside the bathtub, as close to me as he can get without being in the water. He's barely met my eyes since returning to the hotel.

"It's complicated. I'll explain some other time," I say, reaching forward to add the smallest bit of hot water. My lungs still ache, and as feeling returns to my limbs, I become more and more aware of just how many cuts and bruises I got. I wince, reach down, and tug my socks off, tossing them over the edge of the bathtub alongside my coat.

"I have a question," I say slowly as I slide deeper into the water. Kai nods but still doesn't look at me. "There was a boy in the back of Grandma Dalia's cookbook. A boy who Mora took from her, the same way she took you. We shot him in Nashville—he died. Do you know what his name was?"

"Red hair?" Kai asks, voice grim but a little louder—he has to be, to overpower the sound of the Travellers and Lucas arguing over health care. I nod. "His name was Michael," Kai says as he pulls one knee to his chest, half hugging it. "He was nice. We were . . . we were brothers. Sort of. When I changed for the first time I was so happy. I was finally perfect; I was one of her guards. I wanted to be with her. I wanted to be everything for her . . . I loved her," he says, shaking his head as if he doesn't understand. His eyes find mine and I see him freeze, as if he realizes what he's said aloud.

I look at him for a moment, inhaling slowly. "It's all right," I say, and it surprises me to realize *how* all right it genuinely is. I reach across the edge of the bathtub and open my palm; he puts his hand in mine.

"It's not all right for me," he says numbly, and I can't think of a response. Perhaps because I know it'll take more than kind words to stop that spinning feeling of wrongness, of hurt.

I watch him for a moment, then rise, creating waves in the bathtub. The others look over from the main room; Flannery reaches into her bag and pulls out a hotel robe I assume she was stealing, tossing it to me. I duck behind the shower curtain, drop my soaked clothes on the floor, and tie the robe tight.

"Can you feel everything?" Ella asks, looking at me doubtfully. I sit at the top of the bed, tuck my feet into the blankets.

"I'll be fine," I say, reaching over and squeezing her hand. "Thanks for coming."

"Don't think we aren't going to fight about you sneaking out on the drive back," she jokes.

"You're going back with them?" Flannery asks, alarmed.

"What? I don't...I don't know. Can't I figure that out when I don't have hypothermia?"

"Yeah, sure, if that's what you want," Flannery says quickly. "It's just, whatever you're driving—and no offense to you, Ella—it isn't as great as Wallace."

"It's a private plane," Ella says, confused about what "Wallace" is.

"My point exactly," Flannery answers. Callum laughs under his breath, though, and the sound seems to divert the scowl forming on Flannery's face. She grins at him. "Anyway," Flannery continues, looking to Kai, "you're awfully quiet for the man of the hour."

Kai has hardly moved. He's sitting in the bathroom doorway, as if he doesn't want to really be in the same room as the rest of us. "Sorry. I just don't..." he begins, then stops, as if he planned to say more but can't work out what. He exhales, rises, and walks out of the hotel room, head slung low. Flannery raises her eyebrows toward me; I hurry from the bed and go after him, letting the room door slam accidentally.

"Kai," I call out softly, expecting him to be halfway down the hall. I'm surprised when I realize he's just beside the door, sitting with his back against the wall. The wallpaper is covered in a pattern featuring elk and plants, and the hallway smells like old coffee. I sink down to the floor beside him.

"I don't know what happened," he says quietly, voice broken. "I don't know what to do now."

"Neither do I," I say. "But we'll be fine. All of us. Me, you, them..."

"You almost died," he says. "More than once, because of me. Right? I mean, I'm guessing—I don't even *know* what happened to you. But you've got these...people and stories and you...you're different now, Ginny, and I missed it." He sounds crushed—not guilty, but something closer to scared. His voice sounds the way I felt when I saw him in the garden with Mora, when the possibility of him ending our love, our life together, our future, our dreams, was painful and raw.

"First off, I *didn't* die," I say. "Second, I saved the stories. Every one, so I could tell them to you. Before all this, I didn't know I could survive without you, Kai. And sure, I've changed. Now I know . . . I can make it on my own. But that doesn't mean I want to. It doesn't mean I ever stopped loving you."

Kai exhales, something of a broken, relieved laugh on his lips, and leans his head back against the wall. He stares at the ceiling for a moment, then turns his head toward me. "Am I remembering right—I killed all the roses?"

"They might be fine," I say, shrugging. "They're tough."

He nods, then drops his gaze to where our hands rest on the hotel floor, close to each other but not touching. Kai lifts his fingers, brings them down on mine delicately. "All of them?"

"I think so," I say, nodding, and turn my palm over to meet his. We stare down at our hands for a moment, Kai running his thumb across the scar on my left hand, the one that matches his.

"I wasn't strong enough for you," he says, the words falling from his mouth as if they're the ones he desperately needed to say.

I shake my head at him. "I didn't need you to be."

"When I said before that I loved her, Ginny, I didn't mean that I stopped—"

"I know," I say. I smile. "I mean, I might have doubted it for a minute there in Nashville. And when I got in a knife fight with you. But I know."

"Are you sure?" he asks.

"Remind me."

"I love you," he says, eyes hard on mine. In the end it's always been us, together, but knowing it and hearing it, seeing it, feeling it, are different things. In a single, sweeping motion, I pull Kai toward me and find his lips with mine. I kiss him the way I've wanted to for weeks, the way I want to forever, our arms around one another, breath hot, heads spinning. It's hard to pull away, but when I do, I smile, because I know we'll kiss like that again, and again, and again.

We sit in the hallway in peaceful silence, curled against each other, until I finally rise and offer a hand to Kai. "Come on," I say. "Let's go back inside."

"Do they hate me? I mean, since I almost got them killed, too?" he asks, voice weak. He gives me a worried look, as if he knows how silly this sounds yet can't help but ask.

"Lucas and Ella don't hate anybody," I say. "And the others sort of hate everybody. But not really. Usually."

Kai smiles a little, allows me to help him stand, and we go back into the hotel room. The others look up immediately, as if we've walked in on a conversation. They eye one another as I lead Kai to the edge of the bed, where we both sit down.

"So...we're taking bets." Callum breaks the awkward silence, rolling a coin between his knuckles as he speaks.

"On?" I ask.

"Him," he says, pointing to Kai. "We're betting on whether or not you're going to turn into a wolf again."

"I'm not sure," Kai says slowly, glancing at me. "I think...I could. If I wanted to."

"I think you could, too," Flannery says. "I'm positive. Try it."

"Quiet, you can't *bait* him," Lucas says, throwing a pen at her. "Against the rules."

"I'm just *suggesting*," she hisses back.

The room stares at him, waiting.

"I'm not going to do it *now*," Kai says, rolling his eyes. The Travellers grumble and slowly fish into their pockets, then slap money into Lucas's outstretched hand. He grins, folds the money, and sticks it in his back pocket.

"And to think," Flannery says, folding her arms and glaring at Kai, "I fought a werewolf for you."

"Sorry," Kai says, shrugging. "Maybe I can pay you back for it someday."

Flannery snorts and shakes her head. "Not if I can help it."

EPILOGUE

‿〇‿

There were plenty of reasons to love the winter.

Fireplaces. Stews. But most of all—*at least, this year*, Ginny thought—Christmas.

Most of the neighborhood houses were covered in pretty but simple decor—candles in windows, wreaths on doors, and perhaps some tasteful white lights on a single tree in the front yard. Lucas and Ella's house, however, was covered in lights of every color and size. Some blinking, some not; some white, some rainbow-colored; some trees covered in a strand or two, some trees covered in so many that it looked like the entire thing might catch fire. The lights looked out of place on the mansion, but no more so than the VW bus parked in the driveway.

Ginny pulled the station wagon up beside the van and jumped out, cringing at the temperature. It had been over a year, but there was still always something frightening about the first moment she stepped out into the cold. It passed quickly, of course—this cold was simple, easy. Something that could be ignored or beaten by a decent coat. Ginny inhaled deeply, let the air warm in her lungs, and then walked toward the front door. The house was glowing, and even though Ginny had only been here a handful of times in the past year, it looked—and felt—like home. She lifted a fist and rapped on the door, though there wasn't much need—someone was already racing from upstairs to open it.

Flannery's long dark hair was no longer a tangled, frizzy mess; it was curled neatly into long spirals. Her clothes were new—still mismatched and layered—but her eyes were bright and her grin as wicked as before. Flannery jumped down the last few steps, the impact rattling the framed pictures on the foyer walls. She flung the door open and yanked Ginny inside, hugging her hard.

"Your hair!" Ginny said when she pulled away.

Flannery snorted and motioned to her head. "I know, I know. It made Ella really happy to do it, so . . . whatever," she says.

"It did make Ella really happy. But Flannery also *asked* her to do it," Callum said, walking down the stairs behind Flannery, grinning. Flannery turned around and punched him in the chest hard enough to make Callum cough. "Ginny," he greeted her, wheezing a recovery.

"It looks beautiful, Flannery," Ginny said. "Don't you like it, Callum?" she added pointedly.

Callum looked at the two of them as if they were crazy. "Flannery," he said, shaking his head, "is always beautiful."

"Well played," Flannery admitted, and leaned forward to kiss him quickly. She then turned back to Ginny. "He's not here yet," she said, answering the unasked question. "His flight got delayed."

"How long?" Ginny asked, and Flannery shrugged.

"It can't be more than an hour," Lucas said, walking out from the living room. "Come on. Ella bought cake and is going to pretend she made it. Play along."

"Seriously," Callum says, nodding. "Play along. There was an incident earlier today. Though I don't think you can smell the smoke anymore, can you? Or am I just used to it?"

They walked into the living room; Ginny caught a glimpse at the kitchen, where Ella was hurriedly throwing away a bakery store box. Upon seeing Ginny, she rushed into the living room, hugging her so hard they toppled against a leather armchair and dissolved into laughter. They finally settled, Ella and Ginny on the chair and ottoman while Lucas, Flannery, and Callum took up the couch.

"Tell me something!" Ella said. "Something new."

"I talk to you every week," Ginny reminded her. "There's nothing new to share."

"Come on, there has to be something. Have you thought any more about what you're going to declare your major as?" Ella asked, tucking her feet underneath her.

"Still not sure," Ginny said. "But I took a philosophy

class last semester. Maybe that? I might try a few more weird classes, just in case something sticks."

"I'm telling you," Lucas said. "You. Me. Private investigation firm."

"She can't major in 'private investigator,'" Ella argued.

"I didn't say she should major in that," Lucas said. "It's a postcollege business venture. I'm just saying that between Ginny and me, we could find anyone. We tracked down a mythological creature, remember?"

"*Ginny* tracked her down, mostly, if I recall," Ella said, but when Lucas looked offended she poked him with her toes playfully, and he smiled.

"What about you?" Ginny asked Flannery. "You said this was temporary. Actually, no—if I remember, you said you'd rather be back in jail than spend a week in a buffer house."

Even as Lucas and Ella snickered, Flannery blushed, hard, something that looked foreign on her face. "Actually, we're going back," Flannery says, glancing over at Callum. "Not because of the house. This house is fantastic. Have you seen how deep the bathtub is?"

"I seem to remember it," Ginny said. "When are you going?"

"A month or so," she said. "We talked with Ardan and Declan the other day. They say my mother's crown isn't exactly secure, since I left. People wonder if she can run a camp, if she can't run her own daughter. I'm not letting that happen, obviously, so I figure we'll go back and remind them exactly why the Sherlocks are queens. They might turn us away; they might not. I'm not sure."

"Are you going to tell them the truth about Grohkta-Nap?" Ginny asked.

Callum laughed a little. "Baby steps, Ginny. They'll come around—they're good people, smart people. But we've got to make them accept an unmarried princess, first." Despite this, Ginny noticed that he was still wearing his wedding ring, and that Flannery's was still on a chain around her neck.

Ginny was about to comment on the rings when someone knocked on the front door. She sat up straight, looking from Ella to Lucas. Flannery arched her back over the couch to spy down the foyer; a grin spread across her face, confirming who had arrived.

"Go on," Lucas said. "We'll be in the kitchen eating cake."

"We haven't eaten dinner!" Ella said.

"We're adults. We're allowed to have cake for dinner," Lucas answered, rising. They filed into the kitchen while Ginny licked her lips and hurried to the foyer.

Through the door's decorative glass, he looked like a collection of features. Dark hair. Gold eyes. Olive skin and an angular, willowy stature, as if he was animated rather than born. He was wearing a coat, though Ginny knew he didn't need it—Kai didn't feel the cold now; he hadn't ever since Mora. Ginny's face spread into a grin, and she rushed forward and opened the door.

321

The cold didn't have a chance to touch her—Kai moved in first, wrapped his arms around her, and enveloped her, pulling her head to his shoulder, burying his face against her neck. He smelled like cinnamon and soap, and she pushed her full weight into him, until he lifted her from the ground, kissing her temple as he did so.

"You're late," she whispered as he put her down, smiling.

"Delayed due to ice," he said, raising his eyebrows at the irony. "But I'm here now." Ginny rested her head against his chest for a moment, listening to his heart beat as he held her.

"Maybe I should ditch New York after all. Go back to Portland with you," he murmured against her hair.

"You say that every time we're together, you know. But if you're expecting me to argue, you're going to be disappointed," she said, smiling as she lifted to her toes and drew his lips to hers. Her head flooded with heat as they kissed, and he held her tightly, as if he couldn't be close enough.

"You're missing the cake!" Flannery yelled from the kitchen. They broke away, laughing at the sound of the others shushing Flannery. Kai kissed Ginny's forehead quickly, and they walked to the kitchen holding hands. The others were sitting at the table around a deck of cards that Callum and Flannery were using to teach the other two Widow's Lover. They greeted Kai enthusiastically; Callum moved over a chair so he and Ginny could sit beside each other while Ella cut him a ridiculously large slice of cake.

They played for hours—Ella won frequently, since she worked out how to count the cards—and then drifted away one at a time toward bedrooms on the upper floors. Flannery was the last to leave, giving Ginny a wry smile as she flicked the kitchen lights off on her way out of the room. The Christmas lights outside glowed, a sea of color and illumination that shone bright enough to light the way as Ginny and Kai rose and walked to the window to look out over the yard. Kai stood behind Ginny, put his arms around her, and rested his chin on her head.

Ginny looked down at Kai's hands and ran her fingers across his knuckles. "You know I'm in love with you, right?" she asked.

"I know," he answered. "I've always known. Since we were little kids." He opened his mouth as if he was going to say more, but then he stopped and lifted a hand to point. "Look. It's snowing."

Fat snowflakes, gentle and scattered, barely enough to dust the ground. Ginny could feel Kai tense behind her; she knew what memories were running through his head. She turned and ran her hand along his cheek. He sighed, relaxed, and kissed her palm.

"Ginny?" he said. "Let's go to sleep." She smiled, turned, and took his hand. Together they retreated upstairs, leaving the snow to fall.

There were plenty of reasons to love the winter, and this moment was one of them.

ACKNOWLEDGMENTS

I confess that, at this point, I feel a little almost like I'm always thanking the same people—and yet, they absolutely need to be thanked again, and again, and again forever. This said, many thanks are (as always) owed to:

My agent, Jim McCarthy, and editors, Bethany Strout and Julie Scheina, for believing in fairy tales. Kristina Aven, publicist extraordinaire, who was not bothered when I sent her receipts for a million late-night Diet Cokes and pizzas when I was on deadline in Portland. School and library geniuses Zoe Luderitz and Victoria Stapleton, who know everything there is to know about getting people to read my books, and also where to get the best drinks. Joe Davich at the Georgia Center for the Book, whose expression when I said I was considering writing a Snow Queen story turned this book from possibility to plan.

Maggie Stiefvater, my late-night-deadline companion, for always offering a shoulder to angst on, listening to various off-color jokes, and encouraging the consumption of approximately seventy-three thousand lattes. Nelson Dean, who understood why I kept turning the temperature lower and lower, trying to make it feel like winter during a record heat wave.

And, as always, many thanks to my family, for understanding when I say things like "I can't go to Birmingham this weekend. I'm kidnapping a guy and taking him to Michigan."